B L

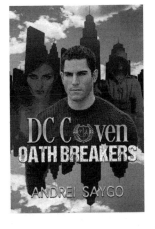

Robert Connor, is a neurodivergent young man living in Washington, DC, leading what looks like a normal life--well, when not battling supernatural creatures unseen by others.

Dea, a gifted witch from a powerful coven, is attacked by a Hashashin in a local night club, and Robert, a skilled martial artist, comes to her aid. An unexplainable connection binds the two and draws them closer. Soon, however, magical abilities manifest in Robert, revealing glimpses into his true nature, raising the question, "Is he a mage or something else?"

An invitation to join Dea's coven leads him on a globe-trotting adventure to retrieve an ancient magical scroll that holds answers to his family lineage and the gruesome slaying of his entire family. Unfortunately, they're not the only ones looking for the document.

Their journey is full of perils from the world city of London to 'Misr' on the Nile. Hunted for a crime he didn't commit, Robert, along with Dea, is battling a host of human and supernatural threats. Barely escaping the clutches of a terrorist group, they return home, where a secretive group inside the CIA recruits him.

Juggling his responsibilities toward the coven and the CIA, and struggling to master the magic flowing through his body, Robert falls hard for Dea. When things begin to settle, the entity responsible for dispatching the Hashashins contacts him, upending everything he thinks he knows about Dea and her coven, himself, and his family.

OATH BREAKERS

DC COVEN BOOK 1

ANDREI SAYGO

G Publishing Partners, LLC

OATH BREAKERS
DC COVEN BOOK 1
COPYRIGHT©2020
ANDREI SAYGO
Cover Design by Wren Taylor

This book is a work of fiction. The names, characters, places, and incidents are the products of the author's imagination or are used fictitiously. Any resemblance to actual events, business establishments, locales, or persons, living or dead, is entirely coincidental.

All rights reserved. No part of this publication may be reproduced, stored in a retrieval system, or transmitted in any form or by any means (electronic, mechanical, photocopying, recording, or otherwise) without the prior written permission of both the copyright owner and the publisher. The only exception is brief quotations in printed reviews.

The scanning, uploading, and distribution of this book via the Internet or any other means without the permission of the publisher is illegal and punishable by law.

Please purchase only authorized electronic editions, and do not participate in or encourage electronic piracy of copyrighted materials. Your support of the author's rights is appreciated.

Published in the United States of America by:

DLG Publishing Partners
San Antonio, TX 78217
www.DLGPublishingPartners.com

The publisher does not have any control over and does not assume any responsibility for author or third-party websites or their content.

This book is dedicated to my family.

A big thank you to everyone who helped me bring this story to life, including my editors (Mary-Theresa Hussey, Courtney Andersson, Dan Larsen, Elizabeth Thurmond, and Jessica Clymer).

CONTENTS

A WEEK EARLIER, Washington, DC . . .

It had been three months and four days since my last encounter with one of them. Since moving to DC, I'd been running into more; however, the past few months had been about work, work, and . . . oh, yeah, work.

Steven signaled the blonde waitress to bring another three bottles.

I hadn't finished half of my first Corona, and Steven and Mark were already on their third. It wasn't my first time going out for drinks with my colleagues, but I was always surprised by how well they held their alcohol.

"Hey, let's go talk to those girls over at the bar," said Steven, eyeing a group of women who were chatting. "We have to celebrate. It's Friday, and we finished the code."

Mark nodded and winked at the waitress, coming with the three drinks. He stood and reached for the chair to support himself. His movements were a tad sluggish. Taking a bottle of beer from her, he gave her a crooked smile.

She kept a straight face, ignoring his poor attempt at a

flirt, probably used to seeing dozens of men trying the same thing every night. "Is there anything else you need, guys?"

"Your phone number," Steven and Mark chorused together. They glanced at each other and burst out laughing, then high-fived.

The waitress rolled her eyes and gave me an expectant look, waiting for a similar comment.

"I haven't finished my first." I raised my bottle for another sip.

She gave me a nod, probably glad I didn't try a pickup line, then she dashed off, muttering, "Idiots."

The waitress was cute in a girl-next-door sort of way. She wore a black top with a floral print that matched her wide-leg pants. All the employees at the club, Yuugen, wore floral prints of various colors, which was a bit unusual for a place like this—or at least, it was something I hadn't seen before.

She swayed between the people and tables like a ballerina, and I had to admire how graceful she was. It was as if the entire place was a dance floor for her.

"Hey, aren't you coming?" Steven's words snapped me out of my trance.

"Not right now, maybe later. You guys go ahead and do some testing." I motioned with a fake grin.

They shrugged, grabbed their bottles, and made a beeline toward the women at the bar.

Working so many hours with them for the past few weeks had taken a toll. I knew all the jokes, all the stories. I wanted some time for myself, to clear my head and focus on something else. But I had a hard time relaxing, feeling like something nagged at me. I turned my chair to gleam a better view of the dance floor and took another sip while reviewing the past week. I'd been skipping the gym, and my body didn't like it—I had too much energy built up.

"Hey, I see your friends have moved to the bar. Should I close the tab, or is there anything else you want tonight?" A silky voice, whispering words close to my ear, brought me back to reality.

It was the waitress, but her tone was different—more enticing.

A quick glance confirmed Steven and Mark were now involved in a conversation with a couple of girls. They were laughing and having fun, and I couldn't blame them.

"No, nothing else, thank you. You may close out the tab." I turned, handing her my credit card.

She tucked a strand of hair behind her ear and licked her red lips. "Sure, sweetie. I'll be right back."

For a second, I thought she was flirting with me, but it must have been my imagination. It wasn't like this chapter of my life was full of stories.

Au contraire. When it came to girlfriends, they were few and far between, and for a good reason. It was challenging to make a real connection with someone and even more challenging to talk about *them.*

One, they wouldn't have believed me and would have thought I was looney, and two, if they did, believe me, they would run away in fear, screaming.

Sighing, I forced myself to shift away from this train of thought because I'd been on this path before.

I checked my phone out of habit, but there were no new emails in the last ten minutes. In a way, I felt like an addict.

It's already 10:30 p.m., so I'll leave in ten minutes, maybe less.

I was getting bored and lonely, even though the club was full of people and my friends were down at the bar.

Out of curiosity, I Googled the club's name and was surprised to find out one of the Japanese's translations meant something like "the beauty within." *What an appealing name, it suits the place well.*

On the outside, it didn't seem like much. It was just another red brick building that had stood the test of time. However, the inside was completely different, with two floors, a balcony, and VIP booths along the walls where dark green couches with tufted backs exuded a vintage-inspired style.

The green sparkle-infused dance floor had a gaudy feel, and the ground floor also hosted a charming wine bar space with exposed brick, where one could pick out a bottle of wine if desired.

All in all, it wasn't a bad place to be, and the noise level was lower than I had expected. At least you could have a conversation without getting into a shouting match.

Steven had found this club earlier today while searching for a place to have a couple of beers after work, even though I suspected he and Mark had a few even before coming here. He said it had opened about six months ago, which I wouldn't have guessed judging by the packed crowd.

"Here you go."

I turned, startled by the purr in my ear.

Damn, she's fast. I took the card from the waitress's hand, carefully ignoring her generous cleavage.

"Let me know if you change your mind. My name's Lydia," she said with an amused expression on her face.

"Sure." A wide smile spread my lips. I was flattered by her interest in me, but I knew how quickly my relationships ended, and I didn't want to do the same thing again.

Most of them ended quickly, with harsh words, basically telling me I was a jackass. One actually ended in cries of fear when she saw me fighting one of *them*. That's when she ran and never looked back or called.

My attention switched to the VIP booths, where two bodyguards stepped aside to let two girls pass. Between the dimmed lights, the flashing disco ball lights, and the swarming party people, their faces were hard to assess.

One was a redhead wearing a beautiful, expensive-looking, knee-length blue dress, and the other one was raven-haired, wearing a gorgeous, long, thigh-split green dress.

A powerful feeling hit me when I laid eyes on the girl in green—a strong sense she was in danger, combined with an even stronger desire to protect her. It was the feeling you had to defend someone weaker, who couldn't protect themselves from someone who wanted to hurt, brutalize, and kill.

My adrenaline levels surged, anger boiling inside me, forcing me to move, to stop what was about to happen. I'd never felt anything like this, and it took a moment to get myself under control.

I stood, and my eyes darted from one side of the club to the other, scanning the crowd.

Every time I had a feeling like this, the hashashins triggered it—at least, that's what I called them, and for some reason, I was the only one who could see them.

It wasn't long before I spotted it, fixing the VIP booth with its eyes devoid of any emotion. It started its fluid movement, how a snake stalked its prey, then went straight for the girls.

I didn't bother to find a path through the crowd. I just locked my eyes on the hashashin and sprinted toward it.

You might think trying to run through a crowded club is impossible, but for some reason, whenever I had a lock on an hashashin, people moved out of my way like waves split by a racing boat.

The hashashin wasn't running, but I had a lot of distance to cover, and I wasn't sure I'd be able to intercept it before it reached the two women.

I put all my energy into a dead sprint, jumping over tables, knocking down a few beer bottles in the lap of startled patrons.

Risking another glimpse at the girls, I assessed if I had made any progress.

The redhead stopped to talk with someone—an older-looking guy—whereas the black-haired one entered a hallway leading to the VIP restrooms. The hashashin followed her through the door, and I wanted to shout, but I knew it was useless because the club was noisy enough to drown the words. And even if it wasn't, I was sure no one would have paid any attention to me.

I crashed through the door and straight into the hashashin, pushing it against the far wall.

Every time I'd encountered one, it had been faster and stronger than I was, a formidable combination to fight— especially when the opponent was invisible to everyone else.

It recovered quickly, and I barely had time to realize it was holding a knife before it lunged at me, his movements a blur.

In anticipation of his attack, I sidestepped the thrust and blocked with my right palm, then tried to grab the weapon. And at the same time, I used my left hand to pop its elbow.

Unfortunately, it understood what I was trying to do and pulled back, slashing my right palm.

A jolt of pain went up my arm, and I felt something hot trickling between my fingers. I adjusted on the fly, taking a step forward, and the heel of my left palm connected with its jaw, followed by a kick, which threw it back a few feet.

Again, it recovered faster than it should have been possible. It stopped, seeming to assess me with its dull, white eyes. Without saying anything or making a sound—they never did —then, it spun around and ran through the opposite door, faster than I could react.

I could sense it leaving the area, and with the danger running away, I turned toward the girl, a feeling of dread gripping me in its clutches. I didn't want to lose someone else to them, even though I didn't even know her.

The hilt of the hashashin's knife stuck out of her hand, pinning her to the wall next to the door. Blood poured from the wound, covering the blade and leaving a long trail down the wall, accumulating in a pool on the floor. She was crying, thrashing, and screaming, trying to get the knife out, but I knew she wouldn't be able to.

I'd seen knives—or more accurately, daggers—like this one many times. They always had a short, curved blade made of something dark, like obsidian, a wooden hilt with inscriptions, and a large red ruby on the end. If anyone but me touched the daggers, they produced a cold burn similar to sticking your hand into liquid nitrogen. I'd been stabbed once with a similar blade, but I knew the pain it caused while inside the body was intense enough to drive one mad.

I quickly approached her. "You'll be okay. I'm here to help." The cut I had sustained during the battle, it didn't bother me much.

Gently but firmly, I pulled the dagger out of the wall with my right hand. I knew from experience it would evaporate quickly once the hashashin was gone.

She wasn't screaming anymore, something I hadn't expected.

Now, she was staring at me with brilliant green eyes and a pained expression on her face, tears rolling down her cheeks.

I took her hand in mine and whispered, "You're safe now, but you need to let me bandage your hand. We need to stop the bleeding."

She made no move to acknowledge she understood what I said.

I took off my shirt and used the blade I just dropped to cut it in two. I had barely finished cutting the material before the knife started melting into some kind of a goo.

I wasn't sure she noticed it. She held her left palm close to her chest and murmured something unintelligible. In her eyes, I saw the moment when she realized what I was trying to do, and she slowly extended her left palm toward me.

With quick movements, I bandaged her hand. A work that any doctor, would have considered sloppy, especially since I had no way to clean the wound. But it was good enough until the EMTs arrived.

"Keep your hand curled in a fist to help stop the—"My gaze met her emerald-green eyes.

Time stood still, and I forgot about everything else. I was spellbound, staring into an abyss. An unstoppable pull tugged at my chest, and something like a low-intensity electrical jolt ran through me.

I had never experienced it before, and though I thought it was a myth, I could have sworn it was love at first sight.

It's a feeling that's hard to describe. Like when you see a shooting star, and in a blink of an eye, it's gone, leaving you with the cold, motionless lights hanging on the celestial ceiling. Except you saw it, you know it happened, and you know your wish will come true. And something inside you radiates this immense emotion of joy and happiness.

That's how it felt for me. My whole being knew I had met the person I was supposed to be with, my soul mate.

A door opened somewhere in the distance, a shriek pierced the air, and a fraction of a second later, I felt a blow sweeping me off my feet and throwing me against the wall.

Luckily, I absorbed most of the impact with my left arm and landed on the balls of my feet in a crouch.

A tall and athletic black guy with a shaved head and angry-looking eyes glared at me. Behind him, an older woman with dark hair pointed in my direction.

The redhead I saw earlier crouched next to the woman in the green dress and checked her wound.

Behind the tall guy was another woman who resembled my waitress, Lydia, except she wasn't smiling anymore—her eyes were angry. She was staring right at me, like everyone else.

I didn't have too much time to study the situation.

The tall bald guy started toward me, fists clenched.

Quickly, I stood and took a combat stance for both

offense and defense, with knees slightly bent. Adrenaline coursed through my veins, and I was ready for another fight.

"Stop," the girl with the green eyes said in an icy tone.

At her words, I saw everyone freeze and turn their heads toward her, stunned. I could swear the temperature dropped suddenly.

"He saved me," she continued, "and no one shall harm him."

My heart swelled. She hadn't screamed, she hadn't run, she hadn't called me a jackass.

Yep. She's the one.

The tall guy took a step to the side. His eyebrows gathered in a frown, studying me carefully.

She approached with graceful steps and stopped right in front of me. I met her gaze, and she pointed to her chest.

"I'm Dea." She had a melodic voice and the way she pronounced her name sounded like Dee-a.

I took a deep breath to steady myself and answered in what I hoped was a calm voice. "Hi, Dea, I'm Robert. Robert Connor."

She smiled the most beautiful smile I had ever seen, and I returned it like we had a mutual understanding which didn't require further words.

"Robert, my name is Candice Mitchell, and I want to thank you for saving my daughter."

The older dark-haired woman brought me back to reality. With some effort, I tore myself away from Dea's striking green eyes and turned toward Candice, who was smiling politely, but the smile didn't reach her eyes.

"If you would be so kind, please tell us what happened. And can someone please clean up this mess?"

"Yes, Mrs. Mitchell," the tall guy said, with a trace of a British accent, and then nodded at Lydia, who floated into the main room of the club.

"Thank you, Henry." Mrs. Mitchell gazed at me again, expectantly. "Please, go on."

"Well . . ." I took a deep breath to buy some time and think about what and how much I should tell them. "Well," I continued, "Dea was attacked by a hashashin, and I—"

"By a what?" Candice's right eyebrow arched.

"Ah, sorry. That's what I call them." I shrugged apologetically. Besides my grandfather, I hadn't told anyone else about them, so people wouldn't think I'm crazy.

Well, I'll try to stick as close to the truth as I can.

"It's kind of a trained assassin." I scanned the room, watching the others clean up the area.

"Trained assassin?" Candice said in an incredulous tone.

"Yes," I replied, a tad annoyed, knowing she didn't believe me. "I've dealt with them in the past. Usually, its objective is to kill a specific target." Even to me, after so many years, it seemed far-fetched when I said it out loud.

"And you stopped it?" Lydia, who had come back unnoticed, joined the conversation.

"No, just delayed it, which isn't a permanent fix. You gotta kill it, or it will continue trying to—"

"Why do you keep calling the assassin an it?" Candice narrowed her eyes.

"Ah, you see, they're kind of, well, not human," I said in a tight voice. "And I believe I'm the only one who can see them."

I was curious about how they would react to my words. Would they dismiss what I said and try to find a rational explanation?

Whenever I'd imagined telling someone other than my grandfather about hashashins, I felt people would start thinking I was crazy—much like this moment.

"What do you mean, they're not human?" Candice asked with a thoughtful look, definitely not what I expected from her.

Everyone stared at me again, including Henry, who had stopped spraying chemicals on the floor that dissolved the evidence.

"Well, it's hard to explain. Once I kill one of them, it melts away. I mean, they kind of look and feel human, but if killed, they disappear, leaving nothing but goo behind."

"He's telling the truth, Mother," Dea said in a clear and powerful voice.

Dea half-turned toward Candice then glanced at the redhead, who nodded at her.

"The thing that attacked me, I didn't hear or feel it coming. I only saw it when it grabbed my hand, pushed me to the wall, and stabbed my palm. Then Robert came through the door and pushed it away from me. I think it also tried to stab him." She focused her gaze on me and lowering it to study my right hand.

"Oh yeah, forgot about that. It's a minor cut." I turned my palm up to examine it.

Well, apparently, it wasn't a minor cut. There was a deep gash on my hand, and blood was dripping on the floor.

Hmm. It usually stings more.

"Should be okay in a few days." I shrugged, not wanting to appear weak. It would probably take a week, maybe more, to return to my usual typing speed, in all honesty.

Henry threw me some wound dressings, which I deftly caught with my left hand. He nodded at me, and I pressed a dressing onto my cut to stop the bleeding. I used the wrapping to try to clean the blood off my hands.

"I think he needs a shirt as well," Lydia said before she disappeared into the club again.

I hadn't noticed my shirt's condition, but when she came back, she was right. I needed one, especially now that the adrenaline was wearing off. I felt cold. Even though it was May here in DC, the temperature was around sixty degrees

11

during the day, and when the night settled in, it was getting closer to fifty.

". . . and then Robert fought it and saved my life," said Dea, and I realized I'd missed part of the conversation.

Just then, Lydia brought in a black T-shirt with the name of the club, Yuugen, on the front and back.

"Here you go! We wouldn't want you to get cold." Lydia handed me the T-shirt. "Even though I really don't mind if you *don't* put it on." A big smile stretched across her face, and I also caught sight of Henry grinning.

"Thank you!" I put it on and noticed it was a tight fit, but was definitely better than nothing.

"Dea, let's go home and get you cleaned up," Candice said with authority. I hadn't observed earlier, but Dea's lovely dress was ruined, with blood trails all over it. Her hand, rebandaged, looked like something done by a professional, presumably by the redhead.

"Mr. Connor, we are grateful you saved my daughter. Please, let us know how we can repay you," Candice said in a cold tone that didn't exactly match her words.

"No need, ma'am. This is what I do."

Actually, I wanted to say I was grateful for the opportunity to save Dea, but before I did, I realized they might conclude something else from my words. Like maybe I was glad the attack had happened, or something. Best to keep it short and simple, so they wouldn't think I was more nuts than they already did.

"Nevertheless, there has to be something you want," Candice said with an annoyed expression on her face—like everyone had a price, and she just wanted a sum to get rid of me forever.

Each time I saved someone from being killed by a hashashin, I did not expect a payment, and I never got one. Most of the time, people didn't even realize I had saved them from certain death.

On a couple of occasions, they'd seen "something," but before they could react, the hashashin had melted away and I was gone, not wanting to wait for the police.

This was the only time I'd had to explain myself and talk about hashashins. Surprisingly, this felt good. Still, I didn't want anything from Candice. In a way, I wanted to prove to her that not everyone has a price.

But a thought kept nagging at me, and a moment later, I realized there was indeed something I wanted, but not from her.

"Well," I said, directing my gaze at Dea, "would it be possible to get your phone number?"

She beamed at me. Her brilliant green eyes sparkled like diamonds. She then glanced toward Lydia, an expectant look on her face.

"Sure. I'll give you her number," Lydia said, smiling. I glanced at Candice, who wasn't smiling anymore, not even a fake one. Her lips pursed into a thin line, and she seemed irritated with me again.

"Alyssa, do you want to go with Dea? I have things to finish at the club," Lydia said.

Maybe it was the tone of her voice or the look she gave to Alyssa, but I had a feeling she meant more—her words taking on a double meaning—things I wasn't privy to.

"Sure," said Alyssa, the redhead I'd seen earlier, and she wrapped an arm around Dea.

"You have to be careful," I said to Dea. "The hashashin may return. I don't think it's going to happen tonight, but if you want, I can stop by tomorrow to make sure you're safe. In the meantime, make sure you're not alone."

"The limo is here," announced Henry.

Henry opened the door and held it for the ladies. He was glancing everywhere, trying to pierce the night's veil in search of threats.

Kind of useless. I was the only one who could see the

hashashins, but even if I tried to explain it to him, he would have checked anyway.

"Don't worry, Mr. Connor. She'll be perfectly safe," said Candice, and she headed toward the door.

Candice exited first, followed by Dea and Alyssa. Before she stepped out, Dea turned her head toward me, and a quiet "thank you" formed on her mouth.

The way her lips moved, it felt like a kiss.

Anytime," I whispered, and to my surprise, I meant it. I would protect her with my life.

A few seconds later, the limo drove away into the starlit night.

"Hey, pretty boy, there are things I have to tell you." Lydia startled me out of my focus on the departing car.

"I hope her phone number is one of them," I said, half-joking and half-hopeful.

"Yes, but first I have to tell you—or actually warn you— she definitely isn't like any other girl you've met. In normal circumstances, I don't think you would have stood a chance. However, since you saved her life, we'll see." She gave a quick laugh, then she added, "Your friends left with the girls at the bar."

"Oh." I tried to clear my head, having forgotten about Steven and Mark. "Good for them. In that case, I guess I'll leave too." I took out my phone to order an Uber. "So, what's her phone number?"

With a grin, she extended her hand, gesturing for me to give her my phone. She typed something and handed it back, and I could see Dea's name on the list, along with what I hoped was her number.

"There it is. Now I have to teach her how to use a phone." She laughed, probably an inside joke I didn't know.

"Thanks," I said, unsure about the joke, and ordered a car to get me home.

The map showed the vehicle was a couple of blocks away,

and I headed toward the door, but after a couple of steps, I felt Lydia's gaze on my back and turned.

"Thanks again for everything. I hope we didn't keep you from work or anything. You'll probably have to explain to your manager what happened."

"I'm sure she already knows," she replied with a light laugh.

I stepped out of the alley, and the sounds of the city collapsed over me, taking me by surprise. All the people shouting, cars honking, and tires screeching to a halt, blared in my ears. My heart rate accelerated, and I felt the need to breathe.

My ride home pulled to the curb, waiting. And without losing another moment, I got in and shut the door behind me.

The driver said something, but my mind was buzzing with the night's events, so I grunted the address, then fixed my gaze out the window, trying to relax.

This evening had been totally different from what I had expected, and for the first time, I had talked about hashashins with someone else other than my grandfather. I was surprised by how good it felt, and even more surprising was no one thought I was barking mad—or at least no one said it. But the thought the hashashin had been so close to killing Dea made my chest constrict and my stomach clench. My breath shortened, and even the idea of anything happening to Dea made me sick.

Before long, the driver pulled up in front of my apartment building on Connecticut Avenue, waking me up from my reverie.

"Thanks." I gave him the highest rating plus a tip, then entered the building. After a brief elevator ride to the second floor, I was in front of my apartment.

I closed the door, but before I had a chance to turn on the lights, something next to me touched my legs, tripping me.

The thing then went away without a sound, and from the darkness in front of me, I heard a meow.

"Hi, Ariel. Miss me already?" I turned on the lights and crouched so that I could pet her.

She was a fourteen-pound "gentle giant" black Maine Coon with a white spot on her chest.

"Let's see if you have any food left." Even though I left her bowls full of food and water, you never knew with Ariel; she could eat like a dog.

Once I was sure she had enough food to last until morning, I took a quick hot shower to relax my sore muscles.

The hand didn't bother me anymore, and I was exhausted, but my mind was racing, and I knew if I continued like this, I wouldn't be able to sleep for several hours and would be a zombie tomorrow.

I had trained myself to wake early in the morning, with the help of an old teacher of mine, a retired Navy SEAL instructor who used to say, "Son, wake up early, get aggressive, and attack the day!"

A warm glass of milk worked wonders, though, and despite my agitated state, I swiftly fell into a dreamless sleep.

2

PUFFY PAWS KNEADED MY SHOULDER, and whiskers tickled my ear, making me scratch. I opened my eyes to total darkness, even though the blinds were open, and when I checked my phone, the display read 4:55 a.m.

I'd probably had around five and a half hours of rest, good enough for a Friday evening or a Saturday morning after a late night out. Even with so little sleep, I felt fully rested. My muscles didn't feel sore, and I was full of energy.

Her mission accomplished, Ariel jumped from the bed, turned her head toward me, nose in the air, meowed once, then left.

"You couldn't have finished all the food."

When I entered the bathroom and checked her litter box, I saw the fresh, steaming reason for her hunger, and I hoped she hadn't left any traces on my T-shirt.

My mind took flight to last night's events. And my brain navigated Daedalus's Labyrinth, but no Ariadne was coming to my aid.

The apartment complex I lived in was fancy enough to have a gym on the ground floor, which, right now, was a must for me.

So, I went downstairs to blow off some steam. I hadn't been to the dojo in several months, and I had to take the edge off somehow. It was a decent size and, most important, had weights and a punching bag. I wasn't a big fan of weightlifting, but I used the dumbbells during shadow boxing sessions.

Punching the bag was a mindless, repetitive task. It helped me put my thoughts in order and go through some doubts I hadn't considered before. What had happened last night felt like a dream, and I was quite sure there were things I had missed. Like why Candice was so cold even though I saved her daughter. Or how I ended up flying straight into a wall without being hit.

Even with my adrenaline at high levels and my attention captured by Dea, a kick like that should have left a big bruise or broken some ribs in the very least. But I was fine, not even a sore muscle this morning. Probably the most incredible part was that Dea seemed to like me, or at least she didn't seem offended when I asked for her phone number.

My concern was, and my stomach was in knots each time I thought about it, she had accepted out of obligation because I saved her. I was afraid to hope she genuinely liked me, and I had somehow misunderstood the whole thing.

Maybe I should code an algorithm to go through each question and calculate the possibilities, maybe use Tremaux's method in the mix. My geeky side surfaced.

Two hours of intense workout helped me tremendously, but my stomach rumbled, demanding immediate attention.

I knew Ariel wouldn't let me eat by myself, so I made her favorite, pan-seared mackerel.

When I checked my phone, messages from both Steven and Mark were waiting on WhatsApp.

The one from Mark yesterday at 10:37 p.m. read: *Dude, don't c u, we're leaving with the girls.*

Steven's message came in at 1:19 a.m.: it was a photo of him next to a sleeping girl, followed by a grinning emoji.

He had addressed that one to both Mark and me. I had an idea, and I searched YouTube for "commercial woman sleeping in plane photo fail."

I checked the results, found the one I wanted, then pasted a link into my reply to Steven's message with the text: *Like this? ;)*

No new emails, except for some automated messages saying the website was up and running.

Phew, that's great!

I wouldn't be up for troubleshooting. We'd been working on this project for several months for one of our clients, and we had pushed the code to production yesterday.

A few years ago, I'd joined the company after I graduated from college, about four months after the company formed. I knew the founder, Brad, and he convinced me to work with him. Basically, we were the entire IT Department for DC-based companies that didn't have one, and we handled everything: infrastructure, development, security, and technical support.

It wasn't my dream job, but the pay was good, and my colleagues were okay. They understood my quirkiness, or at least they didn't seem offended whenever I needed to be away from everyone else and focus on a single task for hours on end.

My dream job was to work for the government and travel the world, partly because I felt the need to help people and use all my skills. But I guess a part of me was curious if hashashins existed beyond the DC area.

Like many college graduates in the city, I had applied for a job with the Central Intelligence Agency, and after a couple of weeks, I got a phone call from them to arrange a phone interview.

I had answered some basic behavioral questions, which I passed, so they called me later that week to arrange an on-site visit. I got there early in the morning and spent the whole day in one-on-one interviews with CIA officers and psychologists.

At the end of the day, I was exhausted but excited. In my opinion, I did well, I had answered all their questions to the best of my abilities, and they seemed satisfied with my answers. And then silence.

I waited patiently for a week, then two, and after a month, I contacted the recruiter, who told me I was in the queue for a background check process, but he couldn't provide any other information.

Around the same time, Brad contacted me about a job at his company, and as I was running low on money, I accepted his offer. The only other people who knew about this were my grandfather and Andrew—my Sensei.

They both told me these things take time, but I think it was more for my benefit. All the things I've read on various forums and websites said it took less than six months to hear something back. Even after almost two years, the sad part was that whenever I received a call from an unknown number, my heart skipped a bit, thinking it was them. But they were only scam calls.

Enough reminiscing about the past, I wonder if I should message Dea.

Hmm, maybe 7:30 a.m. isn't the best time.

But I could use this time to look her up on social media. I also needed to know where she lived, so I could make sure everything was all right.

A "quick" search on Facebook, Twitter, Instagram, LinkedIn, Flickr, and Google revealed absolutely nothing, and a couple of hours later, I decided to take a break.

Just my luck to meet a girl who doesn't exist.

If not for the wound on my hand, which wasn't bothering me, I would have thought it all a dream. I decided to remove the bandage and replace it with a new, clean one, but I barely saw a thin red line across my right palm. The entire wound had healed overnight.

Too bad I hadn't kept the packaging. I would've loved to know the brand of the wound dressing.

I rechecked the time—Nine-thirty in the morning. Still early, but she should be up by now, so I searched through the list of contacts on my phone until I found her name, and my heart skipped a beat.

For a second, my finger hovered on top of her name, afraid of what she'd say when I texted her. Then I opened the entry, and under her phone number, saw her address.

A smile crossed my lips, and I mentally thanked Lydia, then began to write a message.

About ten minutes and twenty versions later, I had this: *Hi, Dea. It is Robert Connor. I wanted to make sure you're okay and see if I can stop by later.*

I didn't like what I wrote. It was too simple, too banal, and didn't convey my feelings. But I had no other ideas, so I sent it. Sometimes I wish I were more of a player, like Steven or even Mark so that I could talk with girls more easily.

Unfortunately, my lifestyle hadn't prepared me for this. I could hack computer systems, fight a human opponent, or one of the hashashins, and I could save people. But I couldn't chat up a girl or even text her properly. I had plenty of experience on all the other fronts, but I was afraid I didn't have the proper words, worried I would say something wrong when it came to women.

My first girlfriend was Olivia, whom I met during high school. I lived with my grandparents in Laytonsville, thirty miles outside DC, but since it was a small community, I had to travel to Gaithersburg, a nearby town, to attend school. Our relationship didn't last long. My training and the seven-mile commute didn't allow us to see each other too often. We both decided it wasn't working out but promised to remain friends, but only a few words had passed between us since.

After coming to DC, I'd been on a few dates, mostly set up by Steven. Almost all had ended up being awkward because I realized we didn't have anything in common. Only one showed promise. Her name was Sandy.

She was a goth and seemed to like my darker side. The one I tried to keep hidden from everyone, that rejoiced when I was in a fight and when I killed a hashashin. Everything was going well until our third date, in the Smithsonian park. We were walking hand in hand watching the moonrise, and I had the familiar feeling one of them was around and saw a hashashin stalking a homeless guy. With a hasty apology, I went after him, but by the time I returned, she was long gone.

Now, I tried calling her several times to apologize and even left a few messages, but she never replied. So yeah, I didn't have much experience with girls.

I decided to get dressed, hoping I'd get a message from Dea when finished. I couldn't put my finger on it, but something told me I should be there. It was that pulling sensation on my sleeve, hurrying me.

It didn't take long to put on a pair of jeans and a T-shirt, and when I checked, my inbox was still empty. So, I searched Dea's address on Google Maps because I wanted to recognize the house when I got there, and my jaw dropped to the floor.

Street View showed an estate, or should I say a mansion, on Falls Road, which I knew was an expensive DC area. Trees partially hid the property, but I could see a two-story red brick house in the middle of a forest with one access road. It looked like a forty-minute drive to get there, so I decided to take my car, less expensive than getting an Uber or a cab.

Forty-five minutes later, I heard the familiar message coming from my dashboard.

"You've arrived at your destination."

I parked across from the access road, which led to the building, and I peeked through the bars of the front gate.

It was an elegant building and seemed well-maintained like it was newly painted or maybe recently renovated. I spent several minutes admiring the house and its surrounding forest and thinking about what I should say. I didn't believe Dea would mind my stopping by. However, I hadn't gotten a good vibe from her mother or the tall black guy, and apart from Dea, only Lydia had been kind to me.

My heart was thumping like it was about to jump out of my chest. A cold sweat trickled down my spine. The thick bars of the front gates loomed in front of me and, together with the shadows cast by the trees, gave me an eerie feeling.

Even the air seemed colder here, and a shiver ran down my spine. On a tree next to the gates, I spotted a security camera watching my every move, or so I assumed. I pressed the call button on the intercom on the left side of the front gate.

A couple of seconds later, static played.

"Good morning, sir," said a man, but it wasn't Henry's voice. "How can I help you?"

My mind went blank. I hadn't considered the possibility of someone else answering the intercom, especially someone who had no idea who I was, and what I did last night.

"Ahem. I'm here to speak with Dea Mitchell," I said a couple of seconds later after I jumpstarted my brain.

"Do you have an appointment, sir?"

"Not exactly. I told her last ni—uh, yesterday, that I'd stop by." I cringed when I realized how lame my words sounded, and I couldn't remember the last time I felt so embarrassed.

"I'm sorry, sir, but she isn't available right now," the voice crackled.

The person probably thought I was a nutter or a stalker—or both.

"Oh, uhm . . ." I replied, unsure what to say next.

"One moment, sir," came through the intercom.

A second later, a buzz sounded, and the gate opened.

"Please come in," the voice said, and the connection closed.

Hoping Dea had realized I was here, I started along the path to the mansion.

Even at a brisk pace, it took me a couple of minutes to get to the house, and I must have considered going back to the car at least five times because, with each step, I was more and more embarrassed. I could even imagine Dea waiting, wondering why I wasn't showing up.

When I arrived in front of the double doors, they opened outward, and Henry came out, along with some other guy who, based on his build and tight haircut, probably had a military background. Considering his ear mic, covert bullet-proof vest—which I could see through his shirt—and sidearm, I would say he was a bodyguard.

He gave me the once-over, probably assessing me as a threat, and then moved past me to scan the area outside the door. After the attack last night, they were on full alert. Probably everyone inside were trying to figure out the best way to protect Dea.

"Hello, Mr. Connor. Lydia mentioned you might come over today," Henry displayed a tight smile without teeth.

The man was a head taller than me, way over six feet, dressed in a dark suit, and was wearing a golden earring in his right ear, which I hadn't noticed last night.

"Please come in." He gestured politely, then took a step back, giving way to allow me to enter.

"Thank you." Inside was way more significant and much quieter than I had expected. In fact, I couldn't hear anything; no murmurs, no voices, nothing.

White marble floors, brass chandeliers, and what looked like a formal dining area sat to my right. A graceful staircase with a curved mahogany handrail to my left made me feel like I'd stepped into the last century. I wouldn't have been surprised to see a ballroom here as well.

Next to the staircase, a black pedestal planter stood holding an expensive-looking porcelain vase with elaborate decorations.

"It's been in the family for centuries." Henry noticed my gawking. "Follow me, please."

I followed him past a fluted white marble column and turned into a library with a high ceiling. Wood crackled in a fireplace, and four plush red chairs surrounded a coffee table in the middle of the room. Floor-to-ceiling shelves housed beautiful leather-bound books, and the diffuse light was just enough to allow reading.

The ceiling was jet-black and dotted with countless star-like lights.

If I were to dream of a perfect library, this would be it.

"Please have a seat." Henry motioned for me to sit on one of the chairs. "Would you like tea or coffee?"

"Tea would be great, thank you."

"My pleasure." With a quick bow, he left the room.

Every time I sit, and for as long as I could remember, *which is only a dab for more than half of my life*, a phrase from *Dune* comes to me.

Don't sit with your back to any doors.

That's why I picked a chair on the left side of the door, next to the fireplace. Unless this library had some hidden doors, at least this way, I'd see anyone coming.

Sometimes a tiny bit of paranoia helps.

Compared to last night, I got a different vibe from Henry. Yesterday, I was either a target or someone amusing him. Now I was a person of interest, possibly someone who could help them.

"I hope you like our little library. It has a good collection of books." He held a wooden serving plate, which he carefully placed on the table in front of me.

The plate contained a dark green ceramic teapot and two empty cups, each on a saucer and the same shade of green. In the middle of the formal display sat a crystal bowl with sugar cubes. And on a cloth napkin by to the bowl, two silver spoons glistened. Next to the teapot was an open wooden box containing what I thought was an assortment of teas.

He sat across from me, and his gaze became intense, assessing me.

"What kind of tea would you like?" He pointed to the box in front of me, which contained many different tea sachets of various colors.

I couldn't read the labels, but they seemed neither Chinese nor Japanese. The writing appeared to consist only of symbols. Each tea sachet had one embossed golden symbol painted on it, and if there was a fine print somewhere, I couldn't see.

I didn't want to look too picky, so I plucked a small green envelope and handed it to him.

"A good choice," he said and started to prepare the tea. He must have done this a hundred or times or more.

His fluid, steady movements radiated confidence. While training in various Japanese martial arts, I'd heard about the tea ceremony and watched a few clips online, but I'd never seen it performed live. If it was anything like this, I had to agree. It really was an art.

He performed the preparation in complete silence, and several minutes later, he handed me the cup, brimming with a steaming liquid, and then took his seat opposite me at the table.

"Thank you." I gave him a nod.

I felt like a student being taught a lesson by a grandmaster.

"Why are you here?" His tone remained calm, friendly even, but those eyes told another story. This was an inquisition.

I took my time answering his question, during which I considered some answers I had prepared while I was waiting in the car, and in the end, I decided to go with the most honest one, though it didn't encompass all my reasons for being there.

"I wanted to make sure everything is all right, and Dea is safe." I gingerly took my first sip.

The taste was like nothing I'd ever experienced. It was smooth, bitter-sweet, with a hint of an earthy undertone. Gradually, the lights dimmed. The sounds became muffled, and I felt like my whole body was being drawn inward into darkness—but not complete obscurity.

There were specks of light coming from all around me. My body, if I still had one, started floating from one pixel of light to another, filling me with energy each time I touched one.

A random quote I must have either heard or read somewhere came to mind: *each cup of tea represents an imaginary voyage.*

In my mind, I was traveling among the stars, seeing the infinite expanse of the universe, the galaxies spinning in a cosmic dance, and then I was speeding faster and faster toward a point in time and space.

The point is here; the time is now.

I opened my eyes—I hadn't remembered when I closed them—and everything was bright, too bright. I blinked a few times, and everything came back into focus.

Henry was still across the table, grinning, watching me like I had won a prize or something. He looked the same, but at the same time, he didn't; he seemed sharper, clearer, like until now, I had only seen him through foggy glasses, and now I could see the real person.

Have I been drugged?

Slowly, I moved my legs, shifting my position to check if I could do it, then noticed my hands were holding the cup, so that was not an issue either. I wondered how much time had passed, then remembered I had left before 10:00 a.m., and the drive took around forty-five minutes, maybe less, so I put the cup on the table.

"Excuse me a second." I took my phone out of my pocket and checked the time. It was 10:47, around what I estimated it should be. So, it appeared whatever it was, neither caused me to lose time nor impeded my movement.

"It's amazing, isn't it?" Henry said, still grinning.

"Sorry? What's amazing?" I asked absently and put the phone back in my pocket.

"The tea. It's a rare plant, originally from Tibet, and the first time some people try it, it can have a powerful effect."

Henry's confession of sorts relaxed me a little, even though it would have been nice if he had told me before so that I could've braced myself.

"Ah, yes. I've never had anything quite like it, and it took me by surprise."

"I'm sorry about that. I forgot how powerful the effect could be," he said with an apologetic smile.

And then it hit me, the same feeling I had experienced last night, but even more potent.

A hashashin is here.

Henry saw the change on my face, and his eyes instantly became alert. His entire posture changed, and he suddenly radiated a dangerous vibe.

"Where?" He was already out of his seat, heading across the room.

"Not sure. Let's get to the front door now." I ran, following Henry.

My blood started pumping vigorously. A wave of energy inundated my arms and legs. My breathing accelerated, and my whole body felt like a coiled spring.

I can't let anything happen to Dea.

We exited the library and headed toward the front doors,

but it was too late. One burst open, throwing the bodyguard next to it into one of the nearby marble columns, where he slumped to the ground, unconscious or worse.

Damn! I hadn't expected the hashashin to attack so soon.

Every time I'd thwarted one of their attacks, they didn't manage to kill the target the first time. It'd taken a couple of days to try again.

Through the door, I could see the familiar shape of the attacker, the same one I had fought yesterday. Like every other time I'd encountered and fought them, the hashashin wore a dark gray, loose-fitting jacket, pants made of some black matte fabric, a dark cloak, and a sash around the waist —three knives tucked in snug against its body.

A cloth mask hid the face, and the eyes were white, showing no emotion. Henry stopped, unsure of what to do, and a glance showed his face was a shade paler than before.

He's scared.

A second hashashin stepped around the first, and it was holding a curved single-edged short sword. It was the first time I ever saw two hashashins simultaneously, and the first time I saw one carrying a sword.

They didn't see me, never did, at least not until I made physical contact or threw something at them.

Running toward the broken door, I picked up the porcelain vase I'd seen earlier and hurled it into the first hashashin to distract it.

"I'll take the one with the sword," I shouted, but I immediately had to jump to the side, barely avoiding a slash aimed at my head.

The hashashin raised its sword to finish me off, but my training kicked in, and I made a forward dive roll to get inside its guard. It tried to evade and cut at me with short jabs, but I was already too close.

My left hand shot up and struck the blade's hilt while my right fist went for the groin.

The hashashin invader turned sideways, pivoting on its right foot, which allowed me to grab its wrist and twist it. I took advantage of the leverage to pivot on my left foot, raising my body until its right elbow was on my right shoulder. Then I pulled down with both hands and heard the cracking of bone.

Without making a sound, the hashashin dropped the sword. But I caught it before it hit the floor, then pivoted on my right foot and slashed its throat.

Dark blood splashed on my face and clothes, unfortunately not for the first time.

It raised its hands to clutch at its throat, but then it fell to the marble floor.

I looked around to see Henry trying to dodge the knife attacks of the remaining hashashin—his expensive black suit already had a few cuts in it.

Henry jumped and raised his left hand, and almost at the same time, the hashashin threw a knife, which buried itself to the hilt in Henry's upraised palm. Screaming, Henry went down on one knee, trying to get the blade out—a massive mistake because he left himself exposed.

The hashashin didn't skip a beat and sprinted up the stairs.

I wanted to run after it, but I had to check on Henry first, and in three strides, I was at Henry's side. With a swift movement, I pulled the blade out. He then dragged a white handkerchief from his pocket to bandage his injured hand.

Not willing to wait for him, I ran up the stairs, desperate to catch the hashashin before it reached Dea.

At the top of the second-floor platform, I saw two hallways.

The hashashin had already gone down the one on the right.

I sprinted after it, then stepped inside the passageway.

At the other end of the hall, two security guards had their weapons raised, firing at the hashashin.

Dodging fired bullets, I dropped to the floor.

Lucky for the others in the mansion, once a hashashin attacked, whatever made it invisible dissipated, leaving it visible to everyone else.

I'd never seen a hashashin being fired at by anyone else other than my grandfather, but I knew the guards had no chance. Either it was much faster than them, or it could accurately predict where the guards were going to fire because it blurred from one side to the other, advancing toward them.

None of the bullets touched it, and then it was too late for the guards—the hashashin was already upon them.

The one on the left received an overwhelming punch to the chest. And the hashashin simultaneously dealt a devastating kick to the other guard's stomach. Both men were thrown into the walls behind them and slumped to the floor, out cold.

I got up and took two steps before the hashashin tried to open the door to the room the guards were protecting. The entire doorframe started glowing with orange light. Then there was a thunderous blast.

The hashashin flew past me and landed next to the stairs.

Unsure of what type of mine could produce such a blast wave, I didn't have time to figure it out. Turning, I focused my attention on the hashashin, which had recovered and was getting up.

I stepped into a *seigan no kamae* stance, with my arms held forward, elbows slightly bent, and the tip of my captured sword pointing at its eyes. I knew I didn't have much time, and the sword would melt, or maybe it wouldn't, because one of them was still alive.

Downstairs, Henry shouted orders to more security

guards. The loud noises and the explosions on the first floor drowned out parts of his speech.

Oddly enough, the hashashin looked at me for a second, probably considering its chances, then turned toward the stairs, preparing to run.

No, you don't. I started after it, but a split second later, its body twisted, and its right arm shot toward me.

It took me a moment to realize it had thrown a knife at me, then I dove to my right, and that was what saved my life, I'm sure of it.

The blade penetrated my left bicep, a few inches away from my heart, with such a force, it spun my body, and I crashed into a wall.

Damn. That hurts.

The pain was agonizing. My entire arm was on fire, and I felt it going numb. The sword was still in my right hand, and I clutched the hilt tighter, not wanting to give up my only weapon. I raised my head, and I could see the hashashin kneeling in front of me, its foot on the blade of the sword.

"You have interfered too often," it said in a hoarse voice. "Never again."

It pulled out a second knife and aimed the next strike at my chest.

There wasn't anything I could do to stop it.

Wriggling away, I let go of the sword and block, using my injured arm even though moving it brought extreme pain, but I was too slow, and the knife was coming far too fast.

Then, for the second time today, the hashashin rose off its feet and flew into the stairwell.

Thunder boomed over and over, and it took a moment to realize it was gunshots.

The noise was deafening. Eyes closed, I focused on my pain to manage it. I'd only been stabbed with such a knife once before. And the blade hadn't gone in this deep.

However, even that had taken a lot out of me. It had burned so much. I wondered if venom had coated those blades.

The pain caused now was unnatural. It would drive me insane if I had to bear it much longer.

I clenched my teeth, willing myself to be strong enough to pull out the knife because I didn't want to find out what would happen when the knife melted away and all the goo entered my bloodstream.

When I opened my eyes, I saw the face of an angel looking down at me with a worried expression.

It took me a few seconds to recognize Dea, and for a moment, all the pain was gone and forgotten.

Her eyes were red and puffy but didn't detract in the slightest from her beauty.

The burning heat of the knife sliding out of my arm grabbed my attention. As the last hashashin died, the blade melted, then vanishing from sight.

She must've used a glove or something to pull the knife out. Otherwise, she would've been screaming in pain.

Dea stroked my face, and I heard her repeating, "Hush, hush, go to sleep, go to sleep." Her voice reached my ear from farther and farther away.

A burning sensation engulfed my wound, but before I had the chance to scream, a black veil enveloped me in blissful silence.

3

Is this heaven?

Birds chirped, or music played—possibly a gospel choir—and muffled voices.

I opened my eyes to a fluttery white curtain. Cold, fresh air blew through the open window, bringing with it the birds' chirping. A second later, I identified the musical source —a television mounted on the opposite wall.

All-white walls and the lack of furniture, except for a nightstand and a chair next to my bed, made me think I was in a hospital.

The door to the room opened quietly, and Dea stepped in, somehow sensing I was awake, or maybe she had great timing. This was the first time I'd had a peaceful moment to admire her beauty and saw that her flowing black curls contrasted with her ivory skin and full red lips. The high cheekbones gave her an air of royal elegance, and the sparkling green eyes added a hint of mystery.

"Hello, Robert," she said in a quiet voice. "How are you feeling?"

"Like I died and went to heaven," I said with a grin, but when

I saw Dea's face turning sad, I quickly added, "Sorry, bad joke. I feel fine. Great, actually." Then I realized I was not in pain anymore, the arm didn't hurt when I moved it, and I felt like I'd slept for days. "In fact, I don't remember the last time I've ever felt this good, as weird as that sounds." It won me a smile from Dea, which made up for all the things I'd been through.

Despite the absence of pain and the pleasure of seeing Dea, I felt dazed. "What happened? I remember I was fighting a hashashin. It was close to killing me, and then"—I paused to take a deep breath—"something pushed it away."

"Well, you were wounded, after you saved me, again, so we brought you here. The doctors examined your wounds. They said you were lucky there was no major damage. Henry said everything would have been much worse without your help."

I remembered the vase I threw at one of the hashashins to expose it to Henry, so he'd see it coming.

"Ahh, I'm sorry about your vase," I said with a grimace.

For a second, her brows furrowed in confusion, then she seemed to remember and arched only one eyebrow.

"Can't believe you did that. It was my favorite," she said, her face stern.

"Oh, if there is anyth—"

"Don't worry about it. I was just joking," she said with a short laugh. "We totally understand why you did it. You saved Henry's life. In hindsight, you probably saved everyone's life. The sp . . . the thing we had on our door should have stopped it. If you hadn't been there, well, I don't know . . . Anyway, I'm glad you're okay. You are okay, right?"

"I'm glad I was able to help." I fidgeted, trying to pat my legs under the blanket without Dea noticing.

Good, I have pants on.

I released a fart, climbing out of bed, but Dea didn't bat an eyelash.

The air felt a bit chilly, and I quickly realized my T-shirt was nowhere in sight.

"Sorry about your shirt. It was stained with blood," Dea said with a wince. "Lydia brought you this." She handed me a new T-shirt from a chair next to the door. It was similar to the one I'd gotten the evening before: black with the name of the club, YUUGEN.

"Of course she did. Please tell her thanks."

"You can tell her yourself. She's just outside."

I thought I detected a trace of annoyance in her tone.

Hmm, might she be jealous?

I started toward the door, not fond of hospitals—been in them too many times—but realized I was missing something. I had started patting my pockets when I figured out I wasn't wearing my jeans, but some Under Armour sweatpants.

"Uhm, do you know what happened with my jeans and what I had in the pockets? And how did I get these on me?" I asked with an embarrassed smile.

She pointed behind me. "Everything should be on the nightstand. The jeans were stained as well. Henry got rid of them. If you don't like the pants, I'm sure you can use one of the hospital's gowns."

Was that comment meant to amuse herself at my expense, or did she offer a bit of sarcasm? Her face betrayed nothing.

I picked up my wallet, keys, and phone, then quickly checked the time and saw it was 12:29. A sudden feeling I'd spent days in the hospital and Ariel was home without food and water swept over me.

"Do you, by any chance, know what day it is?"

"Saturday," she said with a questioning look. "Are you sure you're okay? Maybe I should get a doctor to—"

"I've been here for less than two hours?" I thought my injury was much more severe based on the pain I'd felt when the hashashin stabbed me. The other time one skewered me with such a blade, it took more than a week to recover and a few weeks more for the pain to dissipate.

"Yes, we brought you here as soon as possible."

I had a hunch she wanted to say more but stopped herself.

"Ah, good." I breathed a sigh of relief. "Sorry. For a second, I thought it had been longer and was worried."

"Oh, I didn't even think of that. Is there anyone—"

"Oh, no, I don't have anyone waiting for me but my cat, and I was concerned about her," I said with a smile, and her face lit up.

Her question made me realize I didn't know anything about Dea's love life. Based on Lydia's reaction when she gave me Dea's number, my initial feeling was she didn't have anyone. Now, judging from Dea's response, it seemed I had been right.

"Oh. You have a cat?" She sat on the chair and relaxed an arm on the backrest.

"Yes, her name's Ariel. She's a giant Maine Coon, and she's quite fluffy. Sometimes I think of her as a dog, but better."

"I'm not sure if she'd appreciate that comparison," she said and smiled.

"What she doesn't know can't hurt her, right?" Her smile disappeared in a flash, replaced by a strained expression, so I changed the subject. "I can tell you more about her, but first, let's get out of here."

She nodded happily, and I slid past her to open and hold the door, a gesture I think she appreciated.

She smiled again, then stepped into the hallway, and I followed, closing the door behind me. Together, we took half a dozen steps, then turned left, where I could see a desk with a sign that read 'reception' on top. Lydia and Alyssa were already there, talking with the nurse, but they cut their conversation short when Dea and I arrived.

I was impressed by how friendly and polite everyone was. My usual visits to hospitals, sprinkled with bored staff, were all I had to draw from. In their viewpoint, I was just another young man who got into a fight.

"Hello, Robert," said the women behind the desk.

"Hello, ladies. How are you?" I did my best to contain my facial expression to a polite smile; not every guy leaves the hospital with three beautiful ladies.

"Oh, we're happy to see you in one piece." Lydia grinned.

Dea gave her an annoyed look, but it didn't seem to bother the waitress.

"Here are your discharge papers." Seeing my surprised face, she continued. "It's easy when you own the hospital."

My eyebrows rose even higher because I knew they had money by looking at their house and their security guards, but not that kind of money.

For a moment, I felt a pang of shame about the way I must have appeared to them, like some poor, destitute guy who happened to save a rich girl and was now trying to stay close and see if he could get any scraps. But now wasn't the time to feel bad. After all, I was alive and apparently in good health, and I knew my feelings toward Dea had nothing to do with how much money she had. Actually, I couldn't care less if she had a single dime or millions of dollars, I only knew I liked her a lot, and it puzzled me. I never felt this strong about anyone, especially someone I knew nothing about.

Pushing these thoughts aside, I focused on getting out of there.

"I assume my car is at your place?" I asked Dea.

"Yes, it is. Our car is waiting. We can take you there if you wish," said Alyssa.

"Okay, I'll follow you, then," I replied, glad I could go with them and spend more time with Dea. *Anytime, anywhere.*

Alyssa pulled out a phone and typed something while Lydia headed toward an exit sign. Both Dea and I followed Lydia, with Alyssa trailing behind, still texting.

Once outside the hospital, a limo stopped in front of the

building. The driver got out to hold the door, and Lydia climbed in. Then I invited Dea and Alyssa to get in, and when I entered, I saw both Lydia and Alyssa were on the seats to my right, and the only spot left was next to Dea.

I definitely didn't mind, and once I got situated and closed the door, the limo started moving.

"So, you managed to save our little sister twice, and not even twenty-four hours have passed." Lydia kept a smile on her face, but I detected a hint of worry in her voice. "One might say fate brought you to our doorstep."

I studied Lydia and Alyssa for a moment, then shifted my attention to Dea, noticing something I hadn't observed before.

The three didn't seem to look much alike—not like sisters, anyway—so maybe the comment meant they were just good friends. It would explain why Lydia was serving tables yesterday, and now she was in a limo. Perhaps, she was a friend of the family.

"Oh, I don't know about that, fate, that is. I just wanted to check and see if everything was all right. And I uhm, set out to protect you, and instead, you saved me, and I'm grateful. Thank you."

I'm not used to being saved by anyone, and it gave me a refreshing feeling—or more like two feelings combined. One was fear. For the first time, I had almost died. Even though the hashashins had always been more robust and faster than me, the element of surprise was always on my side because they couldn't see me. And they didn't realize someone saw them until I acted.

Plus, my fighting experience allowed me to predict some of their moves, at least enough to block, sidestep, retreat, or advance when I saw an opportunity. However, a bit of luck was also necessary. Even a small mistake could mean the end of my life, just like today, when I wrongly assumed the hashashin would run.

The second feeling was different and hard to put into words.

For more than a decade, I'd been alone, and in all the fights I'd had, I never had backup to help me in case something went wrong. But this time, someone did back me up.

Someone shot the bastard and stopped it from killing me.

A warm, tingling sensation engulfed me. It was like being outside during a harsh winter, then entering a warm, cozy house filled with the aroma of fresh-baked pies. For the first time, someone had been there for me when I needed them most, and a deep feeling of gratitude settled in my heart.

"By the way, what did you shoot it with? A shotgun?" I asked, remembering how the hashashin flew off me.

"Yeah, something like that," Lydia said before Dea had a chance to answer. "Dea was the one who saved you."

"I'm in your debt, then," I said, not shifting my gaze from Dea, who blushed and looked away. "What happened afterward? How did I get to the hospital? How's Henry. And how are the security guys?" I wanted some clarification about what had happened during the hours I was out.

"Oh, don't worry about it, everyone's fine. Henry has a flesh wound, and the guards have some minor injuries," Dea said in a tone that suggested she was happy to change the subject.

It hadn't seemed that way during the fight, and I distinctly remembered pulling the knife out of Henry's hand, but I decided not to press the matter. I hadn't paid any attention to how serious everyone's wounds were. Even mine, apparently, was less severe than I thought, considering how quickly it healed.

"I'm glad everyone's fine, and I'm sorry I didn't get a chance to finish my tea with Henry. I've never had anything like that. Do you know what kind of tea it was?" I looked at all three of them, one at a time, then gazed at Dea.

"Oh, we have many different types. We get them from all

over the world, so they're usually different from the local brands," Alyssa said.

"Good to know. I have to say, at first, I thought it had some drugs in it. I mean, the experience was fantastic, to say the least." A short burst of nervous laughter escaped my lips.

Everyone laughed, but it sounded forced. Probably, my comment regarding drugs struck a chord or involved something I wasn't supposed to know about. I knew they were rich, and apparently, they could easily buy drugs and pills—they owned a hospital, for God's sake, so maybe someone had a problem with substance abuse and my comment reminded them of that.

"What did you feel? Did you see anything?" Dea turned to face me. Actually, all three focused on me, evidently interested in what I had to say.

"Well," I tried to remember what I felt, "the moment I had my first sip, it was like the universe opened, and I could see the bigger picture. I could understand so much more. I was like a kid who had discovered the beautiful world of books and found an infinite library full of extraordinary stories. It's tough to describe it, and it ended so quickly." Recalling, it brought back an echo of the feeling. "Does this happen every time you drink it?"

"No, it doesn't, only the first time. Very few people have an experience like yours, and everyone's experience is unique," Dea said in a serious tone.

"Have you experienced something similar?" I was hoping to find a connection, something we had in common.

She beamed. "Yes, I did. It was similar to what you described."

Before I had the chance to ask more questions, the car came to a stop, and one of the security guys opened the door on my side.

The man, built like a professional wrestler with a crew

cut, wore Oakley sunglasses. A shoulder holster pegged him as former military.

I exited the car, nodded my gratitude, and turned to help Dea out of the vehicle, letting him know I had this. When Dea's hand met mine, it felt like an electrical discharge with actual sparks. The difference was, it didn't hurt—her hand felt warm and soft, then she smiled and got out of the car.

"Oh, such a gentleman." Lydia appeared from the other side of the vehicle. Alyssa grabbed her arm, and they sauntered out of my field of vision.

I realized I was holding Dea's hand, and she was studying my face as if waiting to see what I would do. My heart wanted to burst out of my chest, so I took a deep breath to steady myself.

"Dea." My throat went dry. "I know a lot of things have happened, but I wanted to ask you if you would be available later today for dinner, or maybe drinks? Unless you have someone."

I held my breath, and seconds passed.

She didn't say anything but still studied me.

My heart was pounding like I'd run ten miles, and I started to have doubts about the whole thing, that somehow I'd misread her.

"Yes and no," she said with a mischievous glint in her eye.

She must have sensed my confusion because she stepped forward and kissed me on the cheek. It was gentle, soft, and if I hadn't been looking, I would have said it was a delicate breeze of warm air. Then she moved toward the door.

Before going in, she turned and said, "Tonight at Yuugen? Around nine?"

"Sounds great." Her words allowed me to breathe again, my whole body happy with her answer. "I'd also like to ask you something. I hope you don't mind."

"Of course, and I have to tell you something as well, but

not now—tonight," she promised, looking into my eyes, her face serious again.

"Tonight it is, then." I took a step toward her, gently cupped her hand in mine, and kissed it. I heard the sounds of "ooooh" and "mmmm" from behind the door, from Lydia and Alyssa, who were waiting, maybe even watching through a peephole I haven't seen yet.

When I looked up, Dea's eyes were shining, and her face was one big smile.

"Okay. Got to go now. Your sisters are waiting for you."

"They can wait a little longer." She leaned in and gave me another peck on the cheek, and I felt my heart skip a beat. "See you soon, Robert," she whispered in my ear, then a moment later, the door closed, and I returned to reality.

Okay, time to go home.

I didn't get home until after 3:30 p.m., mostly because I forgot to program the GPS, and I stopped at a grocery store.

Ariel threw a glance at me, sniffed, and then hurried, tail held high, to the grocery bags. A few seconds later, she must have decided whatever I brought home was beneath her and went to the balcony to enjoy the sun's warmth.

I prepared something to eat, and Ariel came to investigate and kept me company. Lingering, she studied me with her feline eyes. An act she didn't often do. So, it must've been my lucky day, despite it being the day I almost died. I stayed there for a while, stroking Ariel's fur and thinking about how ephemeral life was.

Everything could end in the blink of an eye, but in that blink, someone could save you as well. Your entire life could change at the speed of thought.

Life and death were incredible that way.

Afterward, I washed the dishes. I remembered reading somewhere a writer—I forgot her name—said she didn't like doing the dishes, but doing so helped her create murder scenarios for her stories. For me, it helped order my thoughts.

Two things occurred that had never happened before: I saw two hashashins simultaneously, and I heard one of them speak.

The main question was, *why today? What was so different compared to the other attacks I'd stopped?*

I couldn't get the hashashin's words out of my head: *you have interfered too often. Never again.*

I'd never heard any of them make any sound until then. They were like ghosts, and I had always wondered if they acted alone.

All the legends I'd read about invisible assassins depicted them as lone wolves. Of course, most of them referred to Japanese ninjas who were sent by their clans to fulfill various tasks, mostly assassinations, but they weren't invisible—they just had good disguises and excellent training.

After the first attacks I'd prevented, I had wondered if there was just one reincarnated each time. But even though they usually wore similar clothes and kept their faces obscured, I realized there were differences.

Some were taller and others shorter, and their fighting styles and strategies differed. Apparently, once killed, a hashashin remained dead, and another took its place. I guessed it meant they were individuals.

Should I start thinking of each hashashin as a he instead of an anonymous it? Well, none appeared feminine, so, maybe.

The thought sent a chill down my spine. I hadn't considered myself a killer until now.

What were they? Did they have families, friends, and relatives? Would someone miss them?

A pounding, throbbing pain gripped my head, like something from inside my brain was trying to get out, and my eyes filled with tears.

They say the first kill is the one that makes or breaks a

warrior. Right now, I felt close to the breaking point, even though it wasn't my first kill. I'd killed many other hashashins before, so it wasn't one murder on my conscience, but all of them, and my breathing became heavier, and my vision darkened.

Then I remembered why I had to do it. *To save other people, to save Dea.*

If I hadn't killed the hashashin, he, not it, would have killed her, and I couldn't let it happen. *Never again.*

One by one, the faces of the people I'd saved over the years appeared in front of me, like ghosts coming to say goodbye for the last time. Some of them knew something had happened, but most had no idea how close they had been to their deaths.

I took deep breaths, and slowly my vision returned to normal. My chest felt as if a weight had lifted.

A few hours remained until our date, so I started thinking about the questions I wanted to ask Dea. It was nagging at me, them attacking so soon.

Why were there two instead of one? Plus, why did one of them have a sword instead of just knives?

The only conclusion I could draw, there was something different about Dea, something I was missing, and I was hoping she would answer some of my questions.

But would she want to? She definitely wasn't what I usually expected a woman of her age to be like.

Dea seemed close to me in years, but her manners and behavior differed from those of other girls her age. Maybe she grew up in a different country, but I couldn't detect any foreign accent, or perhaps she went to a private school with a different set of rules. And it wasn't only her, but her entire family was, well, a bit different.

It wasn't a bad thing, I had no problem with it, and I definitely wasn't the one to cast stones—not with my past. I knew I was different, too, and it wasn't just the invisible assassins. I had been in therapy when I was younger. I'd had pills prescribed to me, they didn't do any good, but one thing remained with me. I realized I saw the world differently than other people. I just wasn't sure how different.

I was sure Dea's family had a secret or two to hide. We all have them, but in her case, a hashashin wanted her dead—actually, two.

Hmm. Did the second one want to kill everyone else or me?

For some reason, the thought didn't scare or even bother me. The darker side in me embraced this thought and welcomed it, always happy for a fight and ready to kill.

I wanted to kill all of them out of revenge for what they did to my family, and many times, I wished to go back in time when they attacked my mother and father or my grandmother. Sometimes, I fell asleep imagining the adult me, not the eleven-year-old version, was there to save them. Life would've been so unimaginably different. I would've had parents to love me, protect me, and help me when I needed them the most.

I could feel the cold rage building inside me and had to stop to calm myself. There was a time for it, but the time wasn't now.

Okay, back to Dea and her family.

On the one hand, I expected to see security personnel after the attack on Friday, but then again, who has an explosive device tied to their bedroom door frame? Or at least, that's what I thought it was, considering how powerful the shock wave had been when it detonated.

Dea saved me, took me to a hospital, and stayed with me until I woke up. She genuinely seemed interested in me.

Did it matter what secrets she had? *Did I care?* I was curious, yes, but who wouldn't be? It's human nature to be curious.

Soon, I'd completed a list of twenty questions I wanted to ask her and then realized it would sound like an interrogation if I brought it with me. No matter how much I wanted to know, I did not want to upset Dea.

Tom, my grandpa, once said to me, "With patience, answers will come," and until now, he'd been right.

It was getting late, so I decided to meet her and see how things progressed from there. I put on a dark green sweater and black pants, then went out the door, leaving the list of questions on the table.

4

AT 9:13 p.m. on the dot, I arrived in front of the club and then spent another twenty minutes trying to find a parking spot. I hoped driving would be faster than ordering and waiting for a ride, but I totally forgot about parking, which sometimes could be a nightmare.

When the doorman saw me, he promptly opened the door to let me in. "She's expecting you," he said . "Have a nice evening, sir."

Before I had time to ask where Dea was, Lydia appeared out of nowhere with a scowl.

"You're late. She's been asking about you. Now follow me." Without waiting for any acknowledgment from me, she took my arm and guided me to a cordoned-off area on the second floor.

Dea sat at a booth, seemingly reading the menu, but I suspected she was just as nervous as I was and trying to act normal.

A long-sleeved green chiffon blouse with a plunging neckline, which gave her a magical luster, along with dark blue jeans, fit her well. Black high-heeled boots finished off the outfit. Beautiful didn't even begin to describe her, and my heart skipped a beat.

"Here he is, your knight in shining armor," said Lydia with a smirk. "Or maybe I should say in a Ted Baker jumper?"

I don't know how she knew what brand my sweater was. If someone had asked me, I would have had trouble recalling the name.

She must live and breathe fashion.

Another interesting word fun fact, she used the word *jumper* instead of *a sweater*. I had a couple of friends from Ireland, and I've heard them use the same wording, but of course, I never asked what it was, not wanting to betray my ignorance. The way she pronounced the last few words, I thought I detect the trace of a British accent, something I hadn't noticed before.

"Our colors seem to match." Dea smiled, reviewing my black hair, the dark green sweater, black pants, and black leather shoes.

"Indeed, they do. Sorry for being late. It's difficult to find a spot at this hour." I took the seat across from her.

She just waived a hand, like it was nothing I should be concerned about, and I assumed she never had to worry about such trivial things.

"I'll have someone stop by later to take your order. You guys enjoy your evening," said Lydia before dancing away.

I nodded politely to Lydia's back and turned my gaze to see Dea studying me carefully. She looked like she was considering how to approach a delicate subject.

"So, you said you were going to tell me more about Ariel, but you never did," she said with a playful frown, which quickly turned into a grin.

"When did I say that?" I asked, surprised because I genuinely didn't remember.

"Back at the hospital. You said you have a cat and that you'd tell me more about her."

"Oh yeah, now I remember. Well, Ariel is a Maine Coon,

black and fluffy, with a white spot on her chest, which, in my opinion, is very cute. She's not shy with strangers, and she stays with me or goes around the neighborhood when I'm away."

"How'd you end up with her?"

"I saw her outside a few times when I was coming back from work or other places. I guess she patrols the streets, but I've never seen her chase or get chased by anything."

"So, she's an inside-outside cat?"

"Yeah, something like that. Don't ask me how she gets in or out, though. I've never been able to figure it out, even though I've tried. She's definitely the boss where I live, and sometimes I get the feeling I'm her servant." I let out a laugh. "Her breed is also called the 'gentle giant,' and she fits the description."

Dea considered my words, and I could see a spark of curiosity in her eyes. "Can't wait to see her—that is if you'll allow me." She looked straight into my eyes, which sent a shiver down my spine. I felt like a mouse studied by a cat—the most beautiful cat a mouse had ever seen.

"Of course," I managed to say once my brain started working again.

"Looking forward to it." She lowered her gaze to the menu, signaling this topic of conversation had come to an end.

Seeing her triggered my desire to find out more, to know her, to learn about her family, and why they attacked her. This was the first time I had the chance to talk to someone who had survived an attack and knew it. So, I hoped maybe she had some answers for me.

Okay, it's now or never.

Before I could change my mind or lose my nerve, I said, "If you don't mind, I have a couple of questions."

I'd been working the past few hours coming up with an

entire list of questions. Suddenly they didn't seem significant.

"Only a couple?"

I steadied myself. "You see, the thing is, I've never seen more than one hashashin go after someone, and they've definitely never tried two attacks so close to each other in time. Now, I have a theory about that."

She narrowed her eyes. "And what's your theory?" Her voice sounded cautious.

"I think there's more to you than meets the eye. You're special somehow. I don't yet know how, but you are." *At least to me.*

"Would you like to guess how I might be special?" Her eyes fixed on me, and another shiver ran through me, giving me goosebumps.

"I've thought about it, and I've come up with multiple possibilities. But in the end, it doesn't matter," I said, surprising myself.

Although determined to find out more about her, it all changed when our eyes met.

"Why?" She looked wounded. "You don't want *us* to be friends?"

"Oh, no, no, no. I definitely do," I said quickly, not wanting to give her a false impression.

Oddly, her reaction made me happy. *She might be interested in me.*

"It's just that I always try to stop them whenever they attack anyone, no matter who they're going after."

Now she looked more surprised than sad, then her eyes sparkled, and a smile stretched across her red lips.

"Really? And why is that, Robert?"

"It's a long story, but suffice it to say, I've crossed paths with hashashins before—it never ends well for them."

"So, I see."

"And I surely won't let them hurt a beautiful, charming,

and intelligent woman like you. I also feel we might have some kind of a, uhm, connection." I forced a smile, dreading she might say it was all my imagination.

"Oh, we have more in common than you think," she said enigmatically.

Her choice of words intrigued me, making me want to know more about her.

"But I like your description of me. Is this what you truly think? What if I'm not this person you imagine, or, let me put it another way—not only *that* person?"

"A long time ago, I learned to trust my instincts, and everything in me says I should trust you." My voice left nothing to question.

"Where did you come from?" She looked at her hands, her voice barely a whisper. "I've never met anyone like you. I've tried not to say anything or give you any false hope because I don't want to involve you in this."

She spread her hands out in front of her.

I assumed she wasn't talking about the club because I wasn't too interested in working there, so she was right about that.

Looking straight into my eyes, she added, "But I don't think I can do that anymore. Also, I want to thank you for saving my life."

A torrent of energy inundated me, one of power and lust. An unimaginable pull, like two stars orbiting each other, closer and closer, spiraling inward, locked in a celestial dance with only one possible finale. And then we both leaned forward and closed our eyes, and our lips met.

All sense of time was lost, fell away as if it ceased to exist.

I didn't even know where or when I was anymore. A second or a century could have passed, and I wouldn't have been able to tell.

"Anything to drink, guys?" I heard from somewhere deep inside the dark abyss I was in.

I slowly opened my eyes, and I could tell Dea was feeling exactly how I did, bewildered, or so it seemed. We were holding hands, fingers intertwined, and I didn't remember when it had happened, and judging by the look in her eyes, neither did she.

"Do you guys want anything to drink?" Alyssa asked again, her eyes a bit wider than usual, and her tone pitched higher than normal.

"I think we're okay for the moment, maybe a bit later," I said in a raspy voice, still trying to recover and clear my head.

The sensation was quickly fading away and left me a touch saddened. It felt so incredible. It was like nothing I'd ever experienced, a feeling too difficult to describe. One moment I was connected to the entire universe and could feel its power, and now, I was back on earth, in a club, sitting in my chair. I took a deep breath, and my gaze met Dea's.

"Wow. I have no idea what happened, but it was amazing. Not sure how it was for you, but I've never experienced anything like it."

"Me neither," she said, short of breath. "I didn't expect it would be quite like this—so . . . powerful."

"Yeah, I know what you mean." My mind was still foggy on what she'd expected to happen, but before I had time to delve more into that train of thought, she spoke again.

"Hey, I have an idea. Let's go to your place."

"Uh, sure," I said, surprised by the change of subject.

"I want to see Ariel. I'm curious about her," she said with a laugh.

"Oh, yeah. She's awesome." An embarrassed smile slid across my face.

My brain continued to figure out how we got from a first kiss a moment ago to going to my place now. At least I kept it neat and clean. Mostly.

I got up, opened my wallet, and asked, "Did you order anything?"

"What? No, it's our club, anyway." She got up, a black leather jacket in her hand.

"Your club?" My eyebrows raised in astonishment. "Now it makes sense how you get all the best spots even when the club's full."

Actually, considering she or her family owned a hospital, nothing was surprising about them having a club too.

"If you want, we can take my car," I offered, even though I suspected she would prefer to take the limo. But she seemed to consider my offer for a moment and then nodded.

"Yes, let's do that."

Dea and I had managed to take a couple of steps when Lydia showed up at the top of the stairs.

"Hey, guys. Where are you going so fast?" She looked at me with a puzzled expression.

"Oh, we're just going for a walk," said Dea, saving me from a sudden brain freeze.

I'm pretty sure that anything I said, she'd use against me later. I couldn't imagine what she would think if I had said we were going to my place, mostly since it wasn't my idea.

Huh. What if she does this with every guy she dates or has drinks with?

As I pondered this unpleasant thought, she interlocked her fingers with mine, and we moved away, leaving Lydia with a stunned look on her face.

Yeah, based on that look, I don't think she does this all the time.

5

TOGETHER, we left the club through the same side exit we'd used last evening.

Dea stopped for a second, released my hand, closed her eyes, and took a deep breath.

"That was close," she said, her voice a barely audible whisper.

"What was close?"

"Yesterday, over there." She pointed to the small hallway where the hashashin had attacked her. "Thank you again for saving me."

"I'd do it again in a heartbeat. I'm just glad I had the chance to meet you."

She opened her eyes, looked at me, and said, "Me too."

I spent a moment or two looking at her, and she at me, then, at the same time, we shared a quick laugh.

"The car is this way." I gestured with my left hand.

We started walking, both silent, enjoying the chilly night, and she leaned on my arm, probably for warmth and comfort, but it felt good. This might have been the first time I was glad I wasn't able to park nearby.

"You know, until last night, I was totally uninterested in

this mundane world and its people," she said once in the car.

Driving, I wondered if I should say something in response.

"Probably the best word to describe me would be *arrogant*." A glint of light glistened in her eyes.

"Is this what you said you wanted to tell me at the hospital?" I asked, realizing I'd forgotten to ask her about what she wanted to tell me.

"This is a start, but there are other things as well."

I tried to meet her mesmerizing eyes again, but she looked forward and avoided my gaze. She remained silent, so I decided not to pressure her and focused on driving.

"I'm not sure if you've noticed, but my family and I are different from other people." Her voice was barely audible, but I could detect an ounce of anxiety in her tone.

I smiled. "Well, I already know."

"You do?" she asked in a surprised tone.

"Yes, I mean, until you, I've never seen or fought two hashashins at the same time, and that makes you special."

I didn't mention a few other small things I'd noticed, like her fast healing rate—her palm didn't have even a pink mark on it. They probably had access to some cutting-edge cures, similar to those they gave me the night before.

"And we're here." I pulled into the underground garage.

Dea remained quiet on the walk to the elevator. Not the mood I was hoping for, but at least I was starting to get to know more about her.

"So, do you live alone? I mean, besides you and Ariel?" She asked in a brisk voice.

The elevator came to a stop.

"This is us." I paused for a moment, allowing her to step onto the tiled hallway. "Yes, I have no roommates."

I thought I understood the actual meaning of her question, even though I'd told her back at the hospital I was single —guess she wanted to make sure.

I unlocked the front door and fumbled a bit with the light switch.

Ariel was next to me, her fur standing on end and her tail twitching. "Hey, what's up with you? That's no way to welcome visitors."

"Wow, you didn't tell me you have a Guardian," said Dea. She seemed genuinely surprised, even though I clearly remembered I'd told her I had a cat.

"What? No, she's a Maine Coon."

"That's not what I mean, but anyway . . ." She lowered herself to be close to my cat's face and said, "Hi, Ariel, Robert told me a lot of good things about you, and I promise I won't harm him—not now, not ever."

It was undoubtedly the first time anyone had greeted my cat this way, and if she hadn't been so serious, I would have laughed out loud.

Ariel stared at Dea, and her tail stopped moving. Then, a second later, she turned around, tail held high, and left with a satisfied meow.

"I have no idea what happened, but I think you can come in now," I said with a quick laugh.

"Yes, I can." Dea grinned and stepped inside my apartment.

"Okay, let me give you a quick tour."

For the next minute or so, I showed her around my apartment, which I knew didn't hold a candle to the mansion she lived in, but at least everything was modern.

Once done with the tour, I led her to the living room, where I had a white couch and a couple of chairs. A wooden coffee table sat across from a fifty-inch four-thousand dollar television.

Luckily, I had time to grab the list of questions I had left on the table without her noticing. Next to the living room was a stainless-steel open kitchen, my bedroom, and the hallway.

"So, now, at least, you won't get lost." I tried to make light of how small it must feel in comparison to where she lived.

"That was quick, but I love it. The place is cozy."

"Thanks. May I take your jacket? Do you want anything to drink?"

"Yes, and most definitely, *yes*."

I dropped the jacket over one of the chairs and went to the fridge.

"There's sparkling water, Coke, and orange juice." I looked at the expiration date on the bottle, then amended what I had said. "Hmm, actually, no orange juice."

"What about tea?"

"Sure, any preference?" Dea was on the couch with Ariel on her lap.

She was stroking her fur, and Ariel was purring with her eyes closed like she hadn't a care in the world. Actually, I didn't think she did. After all, she was a cat, and she had a servant for everything she needed.

"How did you manage to convince her to do that? She doesn't even sit in *my* lap."

"She can supervise me better this way," she said with a merry laugh, then her expression turned serious. "About the tea, you pick something for me. I trust you."

"Tea. Earl Grey. Hot." I observed her face attentively.

She didn't seem to react to my Captain Picard impersonation, so I guessed *Star Trek* was something I could introduce her to if we ran out of things to do tonight. At least her mood seemed better than it had been during the ride over.

"Do you want any sugar?" I asked her once I'd heated the water in my kettle and dropped tea bags into the cups.

"Yes, two teaspoons." She continued stroking Ariel.

I added two teaspoons to both cups, then set them on the coffee table in front of the sofa, then took a seat next to her.

"You were saying in the car there are other things you wanted to tell me?"

She looked at me intensely, and after a few seconds, just loud enough so I could hear her, she said, "I am what you would call a witch, Robert."

Have you ever had a moment when someone shared something personal and meaningful with you, and you just couldn't stop thinking it was funny? Out of all the things she could have said, I could picture Dea on a stage, pulling rabbits out of a hat.

My limbs became weaker, my larynx closing, and the muscles in my face contracted, and it took all the self-control I'd gained during my fifteen years or so of training not to burst out laughing.

She must have picked up on that because her body became rigid, and indignation flared in her eyes. Dea's face grew emotionless, and a cold realization swept over me.

She's not used to having anyone not take her seriously.

In an earnest voice, trying to convey my apologies and respect for her, I said, "I'm sorry. What do you mean by that?"

"I *mean*, I can actually transform you into a toad," she said in an icy tone. Ariel yawned and rolled onto her back, belly up with her paws akimbo, looking at Dea.

"I was kidding, but he's so annoying," said Dea in an exasperated tone, seemingly to Ariel.

"Okay, okay, I believe you." I held my palms up in defense. "I guess you're not referring to stage magic. You're saying you can do real magic?"

This wasn't on my list of secrets I'd thought she had.

"Yes, it's real magic, and *yes*, I can show you," she said, anticipating my next question.

Dea murmured something unintelligible, then pointed at my teacup, which started moving away from me by itself.

For a few moments, I couldn't believe my eyes. My whole body froze, and my mouth hung agape. I stared in awe at the teacup, which stopped moving before it reached the edge of the table. Several seconds later, my brain started working again, and I tried to decide if this was a trick or not. I couldn't figure out how she did, and she had no reason to trick me.

Like Lincoln Logs falling into place, the thoughts surfaced: me flying into the wall yesterday at the nightclub. The hashashin flung into the stairwell earlier today and her unusually fast healing.

And I thought she was on drugs.

Her confession left me wondering what other things she and her family were capable of. And some part of me wondered why she so quickly convinced me of this news. But then, if invisible assassins existed, why not witches?

"So, how does it work?"

My mind raced, trying to remember any details about witches or wizards I had encountered during my research on the hashashin's true nature. I did come upon legends involving magic, but I had always dismissed them, even though obviously I shouldn't have.

"Well, it's quite complex, and Henry can probably give you more details, but basically, we contain the ability to manipulate certain things: the elements around us, material obj—"

"Wait a second. Henry is a . . . what's the term? Magician? Wizard?" I found it hard to believe I was having this conversation.

"He's a mage. But mages aren't as powerful as witches, and their main duty is to serve and protect us."

"Protect you? From whom?" I said before giving myself time to think it through.

"Well, from anyone or anything that might be threatening us. Like your hashashins, for example, but there are other things out there. Some of them are what you would call supernatural beings, like other magic users. But some normal humans wish us harm, as well."

"Why would anyone want to hurt you?" I felt a sudden desire to protect her from everyone and everything.

"In the past, humans feared witches and most of the time for a good reason. My kind did equally terrible and great things. But history only recalls the horrific events—and for that, Man drove us to near extinction. And even now, we continue to be hunted, although not as much as before."

I could hear the sadness in her voice. "When you say, we—"

"No. It was before my time. In a way, we're the reason for the Dark Ages, when people revolted against witches because of the things a few of us did. There weren't many of us then, and we are even fewer now. We think that probably somewhere between five and ten thousand witches were found and executed back then. That's out of tens of thousands of mostly innocent people," she said, and I felt the anger in her voice.

"But what triggered this witch-hunt?"

"During the Middle Ages, an all-out war erupted between most of the covens in Europe, and there was a lot of collateral damage. Entire villages were decimated by curses, which took the form of different types of plagues or famine."

"Well, that would do it, I suppose."

"People became enthralled, children kidnapped, blood spilled, and monsters unleashed just so one coven of witches would have more power over another."

"That sounds intense."

"It was. Times were dark then."

She picked up the teacup, took in the fragrant aroma, and then drank from the rim.

"The witch purge that followed, from the fifteenth century until the early eighteenth century, got rid of most of the covens, including ones that didn't take part in the war."

"And normal humans too."

"Yes, tens if not hundreds of thousands of people died."

Her eyes were unfocused, lost somewhere in the distant past, her face contorted in a grimace of pain.

I didn't say anything, trying to process all this information. It was different from what I learned at school and from history books. They had some of the facts right, but not the reason behind them.

"You said a war took place between covens during the Middle Ages. Why?"

"It all started when the high priestess, the most powerful witch of that time, was killed. That's when the power struggle began."

"High priestess? How powerful was she?"

Dea remained quiet for a moment, studying me, and for a second, I was afraid I'd asked something I shouldn't.

"A high priestess is more powerful than all the other witches combined."

"All the witches from a coven?"

"No. All the witches and mages put together. From everywhere."

"But if she was the most powerful witch, how could she have been killed?"

"No one knows. The high priestess's power is orders of magnitude above that of all the other witches. It should have been impossible."

"Wasn't anyone else capable of taking her place?"

"It doesn't work like that. You see, every seven generations, a powerful witch is born, and she's supposed to, if not rule, at least keep all the other witches and mages in line."

"If one is born only every seventh generation, who keeps the peace in between?"

"Our lives can be longer than a couple of centuries. But after two hundred years, our magic begins to fade."

"And the head witch? What about her?"

"We believe the two *high priestesses* who followed met a

similar fate, murdered before they were able to develop most of their powers."

She avoided answering my question but figured she'd get around to it at some point, or so I hoped.

"There is an entire ceremony when the title of 'High Priestess' is transferred to someone else. But it hasn't happened in centuries. Usually, the power starts to manifest after we turn eleven."

"That's young."

"And by the time we reach twenty-one, we begin to gain adequate control over it, but one's powers don't fully develop until our mid-thirties. Of course, it takes a lifetime to master it, as Henry would say." She gave me a quick smile.

I couldn't grasp exactly how powerful a high priestess was. I had no frame of reference, but I trusted Dea. The whole notion of time must be entirely different for someone who can live for centuries.

A few experiments suggested our perception of time was different based on our age. Younger people felt time passes at a slower rate compared to older people. For someone a couple of centuries-old, a year probably felt more like a day.

It's well, mind-boggling.

I could've spent more time considering the implications, but I was also curious about what spells, if it was the correct term, witches could do. I mean, I'd seen Dea doing magic, and even though it may not seem like much, having a cup of tea moving in front of you, by itself, when you know, it shouldn't be able to so, well, it's mind-blowing.

"Do all the other witches have similar powers? What kind of spells can they . . . can you do?"

"Some powers give a witch or mage control over an element: air, water, earth, and fire. Others are a bit different, like time magic, divination, transmutation, and so on."

"Wow. So, your magic is all different?"

"Yes and No. You can find witches and mages who have

similar powers, but let's just say we all have different strengths and flavors. We can also cast various spells. However, compared to our innate powers, they require more energy."

I raised my eyebrows. "Different strengths and flavors?" I've never heard about magic having flavors.

"When we use our powers, we need time to restore them afterward. We have what we call a 'magic well' inside us. That's the power we have at our disposal. Magic is like a living thing. Everyone's magic is different, and the individual's personality shapes it."

She must have read the expression on my face correctly— a blend of extreme curiosity and absolute confusion—as she gave me an apologetic smile and continued.

"Let me give you an example. Let's say you have a witch with a hot temper. If she has an affinity for fire, her power will manifest itself as a white-hot or even blue beam of intense heat. On the other hand, if she's a calm person, the power will manifest itself differently, perhaps as a trickle of cherry-red fire."

It made sense, and I was glad that at least some laws still applied. From what I remembered from my physics class when you talked about a flame, it was about temperature and wavelengths. A flame could progress through different colors like red, yellow, and of course, ultraviolet. Ultraviolet was the one you're not supposed to look at. It would burn your retinas. That was why we shouldn't look at the sun. Or nuclear explosions. I had a frightening thought. *What if a witch could gather so much power, she could create a nuclear explosion?*

I hadn't studied nuclear physics, so I had no idea about the energy requirements, but I was afraid to ask if it was possible.

On further thought, I decided not to. I didn't want to know the answer.

Instead, I wanted to be better than all those people hundreds of years ago who decided to kill instead of learning about it when they were afraid of something.

"So, what powers do you have?" I let my worries dissipate for now.

I didn't want to take any chances because I didn't know if she could read my mind. And it wasn't right to make suppositions without having all the facts.

"Almost all witches have one, maybe two, innate powers, while mages have one. My power is to project kinetic energy outside my body, just like my mother's."

"Your mother is a witch too?" I asked, although, I wasn't entirely surprised.

"Yes. My mother, Lydia, and Alyssa all are."

"Wow, are you guys listed in the phone book under witches, or do you run a magic shop by any chance?" I hoped she'd get the references to two of my favorite fictional heroes.

"What? Don't be stupid." She obviously didn't get it.

I guess she didn't need to read fantasy books involving wizards, vampires, and other supernaturals since magic was part of her life.

"Oh, sorry, it was something I read somewhere, never mind. So, why do mages have only one power?"

"No one knows for sure, but compared to us witches, mages are less powerful. I would say the most powerful mage has half the strength a regular witch does, maybe less. Plus, while a witch may need several hours to a day to regain her powers, a mage usually needs a couple of days or more."

"Wow. That doesn't seem all that fair."

She did a quick eye roll, then continued. "However, magic isn't always about raw power. One's knowledge, imagination, and determination play important roles as well."

I had the feeling she was quoting someone, maybe whoever had taught her magic.

"So, how do witches learn all that? Is there a school you go to?"

"No, there's no Hogwarts," she said with a laugh. "Magic ties into our bloodlines, so we learn in the family or the coven."

"So basically, you learned magic from your mother and sisters?"

"From my mother, yes. Technically, Lydia and Alyssa aren't my sisters; they're just part of the coven. But then, when you join a coven, it's like you've joined a family, and now, for all intents and purposes, they're my big sisters."

"But they don't seem older than you."

"Oh, they are. They've just put on a bit of magical make-up," she said with a grin. "While I was born less than three decades ago, both of them were born in the thirties—the 1930s. During the Second World War, an explosion destroyed their coven's house, and during one of London's first bombings, most of their members died."

"That's harsh."

She nodded. "Alyssa and Lydia were the only survivors. They managed to escape to the states soon after the war had ended and found us, and they've been part of our coven ever since."

"Does it mean they're like eighty or ninety years old?" I asked, unable to wrap my mind around the thought.

"Something like that," she replied, but my face must have betrayed my confusion. "What can I say? It's magic," she continued with a crystalline laugh and reached for her cup of tea.

I stretched out my hand to do the same, though it must have been cold by now. The difference was my cup didn't get into my hand all by itself.

Ariel, who had been purring patiently in Dea's lap, decided we were probably too involved in our discussion to give her much attention, so she left, heading for my bedroom. I took a moment to put my thoughts in order, try to process and filter this torrent of information, and decide what I should ask her next.

"Would you mind a couple more questions?" I asked hesitantly, but she motioned for me to continue, still sipping her tea.

"Okay, the first one is, well, actually, they're kind of related. Why don't I see any kind of injury or scar on your hand? Second, why don't I see any trace of a cut on my palm?"

She set her tea on the table and looked at me. "You see, a side effect of being able to use magic is our bodies can heal much faster from injury or disease. Now, regarding you, Henry has a theory."

She stopped to look at me as if to study my facial reaction.

I was stunned. Not even in my wildest dreams would I have thought I could do magic or even considered magic existed.

If only I would have known sooner, I can do magic!

My face must have betrayed nothing from my internal tumult because it looked as if unsure of what to say next.

"Well, he thinks that yesterday, after you saved me when you bandaged my hands with your injured palm, your blood came into contact with mine. Usually, this wouldn't have any effect on a normal person, unless you're a Sensitive; however, in your case, the effect was much stronger." Her expression was exceptionally grave, and it concerned me.

"What's a *Sensitive*? Am I one?" I asked, curious about this term, which I'd never heard before, but more importantly, intrigued to see what she'd say about me.

"Sensitives are otherwise normal humans who have an affinity for magic, mostly in one particular area. For example, a Sensitive might have good intuition, be charming, or have strong powers of persuasion."

"And you think I'm one of these, a Sensitive?" I asked, disappointed I couldn't do magic as she did.

"No, the effect wouldn't have lasted. This morning your palm completely healed, and I don't see you experiencing any pain when you move your arm."

It took me a second to grasp what she was saying. I had forgotten about the knife wound, which should have kept me in bandages for at least a week, if not longer.

"So, if I'm not a Sensitive, what am I?" My breath caught in my throat.

"We're not sure. It might be the tea you had at my place. Henry said it had a powerful effect on you. You see, the tea you chose is supposed to bring forth a person's power, albeit for a short time."

"And that means what?"

"For normal people, it doesn't have any effect, but for us, it acts like a quick boost, similar to a Red Bull. We checked the CCTV recordings of the fight at the house, and you were moving faster than a normal human."

That was news to me. No one had ever said that before, not even my Grandfather.

"And there's one other thing—"

"Of course, there is."

"Earlier, there was some sort of power transfer between the two of us at the club. I could feel what you were feeling, and I'm sure you could do the same with me. That's not common, not even among witches. So, we're not sure what's going on. Plus, you can see the hashashins when no one else can." Dea studied me carefully.

I hazarded a guess. "Maybe I'm a mage?"

"Maybe." Her voice sounded unsure. "Can you tell me more about yourself?" She focused her full attention on me.

"Sure. What do you want to know?"

"Everything."

6

DEA KICKED OFF HER SHOES, then curled up on the couch. Tea in hand, she waited for me to speak.

"Everything started the day I turned eleven when my parents died."

A calmness came over me that I couldn't explain. Here, now with Dea, I felt I could say or talk about anything. Even about how I forgot my past.

"It was nighttime. We were in a dim-lit parking lot after an evening of bowling with some family friends. And just before we reached the car, I saw movement out of the corner of my eye."

I took a moment to compose my thoughts, and she waited patiently.

"When I turned, there was someone behind my mother, planting a knife in her back, straight into where I knew her heart was. She looked at me with a desperate expression full of love, then crumpled to the ground—the light vanishing from her eyes."

"I'm sorry you had to see that at such a tender age."

The memory unfolded in my mind. "I screamed and went

to her, trying to push the attacker away. But my fingers only brushed the flowing robes he wore."

"One of the . . . the same creatures who attacked us?"

My head nodded in response. "The man pulled another knife and went straight for my dad. Or at least, I thought he was a man back then. My dad managed to grab the attacker's hand, and then they both tumbled to the ground, the man on top of him."

"And no one heard the scuffle?"

"No." I shook my head. "I knew I had to help my dad somehow, but I was shocked and horrified at what had happened to my mother."

"With good reason." The pat of her hand urged me to continue.

"My eyes focused on a knife the attacker had strapped to a belt on his back." For a moment, I pause, reliving the moment. "I jumped for it and managed to grab it with my left hand. But the attacker must have sensed it and turned to face me."

"What happened?"

"That's when I saw my dad with a knife in his chest, his face frozen forever in terror."

A small gasp escaped Dea's lips.

"For an instant, I was paralyzed with fear, not wanting to believe that in a couple of seconds, everything I knew and loved was gone, taken from me in a flash."

"Did it leave?"

A shake of my head gave her my response.

"Then, quick as lightning, the attacker backhanded me across the face."

The memory of the impact, the sting, made my skin prickle.

"The blow was so powerful I spun on the spot. But somehow, the knife I held slashed the attacker's throat. His blood sprayed all over me—my hair, face, mouth, and clothes."

Dea took a sip of tea, her eyes never breaking contact with mine.

"My anger and rage overcame everything else, and my vision blurred."

Clearing my throat, I composed myself again.

"Lids closed, I stabbed and stabbed until I felt the knife melting away in my hand. When I opened my eyes, I saw the attacker melting away too, and when I looked at my hands, a black, oily goo covered them."

A meow sounded from either the bedroom or kitchen. I figured if my feline companion needed something, I'd know soon enough.

"What happened after?"

"I spit violently, having some of his blood splashed into my mouth. It had a weird, sour taste, like a combination between motor oil and vinegar. A second later, a pain like nothing I'd felt before erupted within me."

With my head against the back of the couch, the memory of that night continued to blow through my mind like a cold breeze.

"I don't know how long I spent writhing in agony, but after what felt like an eternity, everything went black, and I must have collapsed to the ground."

A heaviness settled in the middle of my chest, urging me to continue to speak to release it.

"I woke up in a hospital a few hours later. The police asked me all sorts of questions, but I could tell they didn't believe my answers. They thought I'd bumped my head too hard."

"Yes, humans find it hard to step outside of the realm of what they know and understand."

"Well, the doctors diagnosed me with a form of retrograde amnesia because I couldn't remember anything that happened before the attack."

"You recall nothing before that night?"

"No. I have no memory of the first eleven years of my life. I've tried to remember lullabies my mother might have sung to me when I was young or moments when my dad played with me, but I always draw a blank."

"And your Grandfather, did he help you fill in the blanks?"

"Some. We tried searching for pictures, photos—anything that might trigger something—but haven't been able to find a thing. My memories of life begin with the loving look my mother gave me just before she died with a knife in her back."

Dea draws in a deep breath, then exhales, slow and steady.

"Even now, after so many years, when I think about it, I can feel rage coursing through me. Soon after, since the police couldn't find the murder weapon and didn't have any other leads, they classified it and closed it as a cold case."

I stopped and took a closer look at Dea. Her eyes were full of tears, and one even rolled down her cheek. After a few moments of silence, she wiped her eyes and motioned for me to continue, probably not trusting her voice.

Continuing my story, I told her how I moved in with my maternal grandparents.

"It was about that time I started taking martial arts lessons. It was a way of dealing with the anger I felt about not being able to do more to save my parents."

"That would explain your ability to fight."

"I had a lot of rage. The doctors mentioned terms like neurodivergent. I was always getting into fights with my grandma over things that seem trivial now, and I was doing poorly in school. Didn't fit in."

"Sounds like things were hard for you to process, especially not knowing."

"Not long after I moved in with them, my grandfather, Tom, started teaching me warrior discipline, how to strengthen my willpower, and handle knives."

"He taught you to harness your pain."

"Yes. He had a lot of combat experience from his time in the army, but he never went into detail. He showed me how to be aggressive and precise with my slashes and stabs, but at the same time, to protect my vital areas."

"That's very similar to what we learn in battle magic. Please go on."

"I was young and at a disadvantage against an adult attacker. He drilled into me the fastest ways to terminate a fight, which areas I should target to incapacitate the opponent quickly. He also made sure I understood I was never supposed to use what he had taught me unless it was a matter of life and death."

"I like your grandfather, even though I've never met him. Not harming humans is one of our sacred laws." I was happy to hear her people had laws.

"A few years later, when I was sixteen, another attack happened when on my way home from school. When I entered the backyard, I felt the hair on the nape of my neck stand up, and at the same time, a strong sense of danger washed over me, like when you're in the woods at night and hear something in the bushes."

Dea drew in a sharp breath.

"Then I heard my grandma scream, so I started running. A second before I reached the door, I heard a loud thump, and when I burst through the unlocked door, I saw my grandma on the floor in a pool of blood. Her eyes had no life in them."

Dea extended a hand and touched my arm, her eyes full of sympathy.

"Everything slowed down at that point, and I saw a man dressed in a dark shirt, dark baggy pants, and a sleeveless cardigan with a hood over his head, standing at the bottom of the stairs. He held a black blade in his right hand, and my grandpa, on the stairs, stood with a hunting rifle."

"Again, one of them . . ." murmured Dea.

"The gunshot was deafening. But the attacker had swift reflexes. He jumped to one side a fraction of a second before the bullet splintered the floor where he had stood moments earlier. However, it put him with his back toward me, and a few paces from where I was."

"I grabbed a knife from the kitchen counter and, for a heartbeat, was tempted to throw it."

"Did you?"

"No. I didn't trust myself to hit the target—and, of course, kitchen knives aren't accurately balanced for a throw."

"So, what did you do?"

"I jumped on his back, stabbed his right armpit, and yanked on the blade to slash the axillary artery. But somehow, he managed to twist his body and throw me off. That's when my grandpa shot him in the head, splattering blood everywhere."

"And the body?"

"Several moments later, it started melting away, leaving black and greasy goo all over me, the walls, stairs, and floor just like before."

"It was at that moment I swore to myself no one else would die at their hands, not while I was around. Then I started more serious martial arts training."

"With your grandfather?"

"No. I spent time at every dojo in the area, training six days a week in different styles and mastered various weapons. When I wasn't training, I spent my time researching legends and folklore, and that's when I came up with the name 'hashashin,' which is the origin of the word *assassin*."

"The name makes sense now."

"When I moved to DC for college, I started looking for ex-military, special forces instructors. In a dojo, one can only learn so much. Eventually, all they're teaching is a sport."

"And that wasn't enough, was it?"

"No. I needed more—my fights were always to the death, so I searched for people who have been through those types of conflicts and survived. That's how I spent the next four years: college and training."

"And were there other attacks?"

"Yeah. The third encounter happened soon after I moved to DC. On my way home from training, I was near a poorly lit alley next to a bar."

"Seem they like to catch their prey off-guard."

Her response got a nod from me.

"It was a weekday, so the bar was mostly empty, and it was December, so no one was hanging around outside. I could barely make out a guy in the shadows next to a wall in the adjacent alley, apparently using it as a public toilet."

"Well, that's crude."

"I had the same sensation I'd experienced before—maybe even more potent that time. The survival instinct kicked in—my breathing and heart rate accelerated, and I started scanning the area, trying to locate the source of the danger."

"So, you can feel them, then?"

"Always. Further down the alley, a shadow ran straight for a drunken man. Without going into too many details, that's when I ascertained I'm the only one who can see the hashashins. And when I make contact with them, or they're ready for a kill, whatever keeps them hidden dissipates, revealing them to everyone around.

"That explains why Henry couldn't see them back at the mansion." She paused a moment. "Please, continue."

"That was also the night I found Ariel, or maybe I should say, she found me. When I got home—back then, I was living in a studio apartment—she was sitting in front of my door, waiting. The next day, I asked the neighbors if they had lost a cat. They hadn't, so I kept her."

"That was very nice of her to adopt you."

"What do you mean?"

"It's . . . complicated. Tell me more about what you did next."

"Since then, I've had more encounters, so many I've lost count. On a few occasions, I couldn't kill them immediately, so they attacked three days later."

"Then why did they come so soon to the house?"

"I don't know. The first time it happened, I stopped one from attacking an older woman at a train station. But it ran before I had a chance to stop it. I kept tabs on the woman for two days until convinced the hashashin had abandoned whatever mission he had. When I checked on her a week later, the woman was dead, murdered on the stairs leading to her apartment."

"You couldn't have known." I shrugged, not wanting to meet her eyes. Even after so many years, I was still ashamed I couldn't save the woman. I took a deep breath to clear the painful memories and continued.

"The next two times, I remained around their targets, and both times, they attacked the third day. Until today. This is the first time I've seen an attack happen the next day. And like I already said, It's also the first time I've seen two of them attack at the same time."

Drained from my long account, I stared blankly into the cup of tea I was holding in both hands.

Dea, who had been listening intently, said in a somber voice, "We have no idea who or what they are. Mother and Henry are researching some old documents we have, but it may take a while."

"I've done a lot of research over the past decade. And I haven't found a trace of anything that would begin to explain who or what they are. But then, I assume you have other sources of information besides the internet and the public library."

"Yes, we do," she said, without going into greater detail,

apparently still thinking. "I have to go." She began to rise and then said suddenly, "May I see you tomorrow?"

"Uh, yes, sure," I said, a bit surprised at this quick turn of events. "I can drive you home if you want."

"There's no need. The limo is downstairs."

"How do you kno—"

"Let's call it intuition." She shrugged, then stopped next to my bedroom. "I'm leaving."

Ariel approached Dea, meowed, then rubbed against her leg.

"She really likes you, which isn't like her. Not usually, anyway."

In response, Dea kneeled and stroked Ariel for a few moments, then headed to the door. I accompanied her downstairs. And true to her word, a limo was waiting outside.

Inside the limo, through a half-open window, both Lydia and Alyssa sat smiling.

"Would tomorrow afternoon be okay?" Dea turned toward me, looking straight into my eyes.

"S-sh, sure."

"Perfect. Stop by my place around four o'clock." She gave me a warm hug, holding me tightly.

The embrace transcended any words, and the contact woke a surprising, intense need within me and took my breath away. A need to hug and be hugged was more powerful than I could have ever imagined.

No one had hugged me since I could remember, not like that. Not in a giving way, a personal connection, as though she cared about me as a person.

I think a large wound in my soul was slowly starting to heal, and it wasn't magic, or, at least, not the type Dea possessed. It was something we all have, the feeling someone cares about you, that you're not alone.

My eyes instantly welled up, and I may have shed a tear

or two, but I managed to blink enough times to stop the flow.

Sooner than I wanted, our embrace ended, and she got into the vehicle. Before the car took off, the last image I had of her was her smiling face and sparkling green eyes.

That night, it took me a long time to fall asleep. I stayed in bed, Ariel, next to me. I stared at the ceiling, seeing all sorts of images. My imagination was running wild, and I remembered things of myth and legend, stuff I had read about in old and new books.

I had a thousand questions and was exploring a thousand more possibilities.

Did she like me or see me as a friend? Was magic real, or was it an elaborate hoax? Was Dea truly a witch? How did the magic work? What could you do with it? Could you create lightning bolts, fireballs, and torrents of water and ice? Could a magic-user control the elements? Could a person float or fly on a broom? Did a nimbus actually exist?

My racing thoughts continued, playing out different scenarios, and then my attention drifted inward.

What am I? A mage? Could I perform magic?

And then, of course, I had to try. I started with an old technique I'd read on how to gather and feel your inner energy, your "chi," or "qi."

Lying in bed in the dark with my eyes closed, I raised my palms, faced them toward each other, and started taking a few deep breaths to relax and calm my mind. Slowly, I began to move my palms, making small circles, keeping them facing each other.

With every breath, I imagined energy from around me entering my body, then channeling it into my hands. And each time I exhaled, I imagined pushing the chi, the vital force, out through my palms. After what I guessed was a few minutes, I started feeling a tingling in my fingertips and then a slight pressure pushing my palms away from each other.

And then, after what felt like probably an hour, I gave up. My arms were tired, but, at least, my mind was more focused now.

Ariel leaped onto the bed, circled her spot a few times, then plopped down.

I took a deep breath and pointed a hand toward Ariel, trying to move a few strands of her long hair. Finally, after what felt like an eternity, she twitched.

I did it. I really did it.

Feelings of joy, happiness, and pride flooded me, which were all quickly crushed when I realized she was dreaming of chasing something, judging by how she was twitching and moving her paws.

I finally drifted into unconsciousness around the time the roosters start crowing.

7

A PERSISTENT BUZZ intruded into my blissful, dark abyss.

Slowly, I opened my eyes, one at a time. The phone on my nightstand danced toward the edge in a vibrating gig.

Grabbing it, I checked who was calling and asked in a gruff voice, "What?"

"Dude, did you just wake up?" It took me a second to realize it was Steven.

"Not yet. What time is it?" I closed my eyes and wished for quiet and sleep.

"It's noon. What did you do, party all night?"

I could picture his grinning face. "Something like that. What's up?" I was still hazy and could barely think.

"Did you see the email from Brad? Ah, of course not, you've been sleeping. Read the email, and then let's talk on WhatsApp. I've already started a thread with you and Mark."

"Okay, give me a minute, talk to you later."

"Yeah, talk later."

I dropped the phone on the nightstand and sat in bed for another five minutes, trying to blink the sleep away. Soon, reality came crashing down on me.

Holy heck! I'm not in Kansas anymore. Witches, magic . . . what did I get myself into?

Well, it wasn't like I was living a quiet and peaceful life, and if I did something that messed up the hashashins' plans, I was game. The fact it brought me into contact with a beautiful witch was the cherry on top, but I could think more about it, and last night, later.

The wakeup call from Steven piqued my interest, so I reached out and took the phone, which sat quietly now on the nightstand, and opened the message from Brad:

Hello, gents,

I have some excellent news for everyone!

Please be in the office tomorrow at 9 a.m., sharp. I'll bring the champagne.

Regards,

—B

Curious about what my colleagues thought about this, I started reading my messages on WhatsApp.

Steven: *Hey, guys, did you read the mail from Brad? What do you think???*

Mark: *Yes, probably a new client.*

Steven: *But why did Brad say he'll bring champagne?*

Mark: *Maybe because he landed a deal with a big corp?*

Steven: *In that case, we'll need more people. We're stretched as it is.*

Mark: *Let's wait and see.*

Steven: *Hey, Rob, what do you think it is?*

Texting a response, I agreed with Mark and went through my usual morning routine, even though it was way past 1:00 p.m. already. It was hard to focus on anything. My thoughts kept drifting back to last night, to my date with Dea.

I could barely believe it myself, but I'd had a witch, a real witch, in my house, and it was way beyond cool. It gave me goosebumps just thinking about it.

Magic exists. It's real.

This train of thought made me wonder about her abilities. She said something about witches having one or two affinities, and I couldn't help wondering what else she could do besides move stuff around. I'd read so many fantasy books, so many legends, my imagination was running wild. *Levitation, teleportation, firestorms, lightning bolts, ice bolts, earthquakes, anything's possible.*

Maybe even the hashashins might be magical beings too, because how else could they be invisible to everyone but me? Could my power be I was the only one who could see them?

That would be neat.

At one point, I realized I was staring blankly into the bathroom mirror and had left the water running, which was against my policy of conservation for the sake of the planet. I decided the best way to stop this flow of thoughts and regain my focus was to exercise, so I headed to the gym. After more than half an hour of cardio training, hunger displaced all my worries.

It was almost 3:00 p.m., but I was ready, and with nothing else left to do, I decided to take the bull by the horns and drive to meet Dea. Half an hour later, I arrived in front of the mansion's gate, and before I could even press the button on the intercom, it came to life.

"Please come in," a voice said, and then a buzz signaled the gate opening. This time, I hadn't walked from the front gate, so I parked the car in front of the house.

Henry opened the door and stood in the entry with a wide grin on his face.

"So nice to see you again, Robert. Please come in." He moved aside to let me pass, and next to him, there were two different military-type guys with short hair, black suits, and shoulder holsters. They spent a second analyzing me, but once I stepped inside, they moved around me and exited the house, probably to patrol the grounds.

Even though I'd been here before, I still found it intimidating.

Everything looked so expensive and full of secrets. I noticed the white marble floor was spotless, without any trace of blood. The stairs, the walls, and the white marble column were in perfect condition with no bullet holes or cracks. Even the vase was back, with no trace of damage or a break. It was as if it had never happened—exquisite craftsmanship or magic, who knew.

Henry politely guided me to the same library, and I sat in the same chair I had occupied yesterday.

"Would you like some tea?" he asked with a smile.

"Uh, no, I'm good, thanks. I think I've had enough tea for a while." I grinned.

"Suit yourself." He chose the chair on the other side of the fireplace. "I suppose you have questions. Dea should be here shortly, but please ask away." He gestured for me to start and settled in his comfortable chair.

I had a million questions last night, but I couldn't remember any of them right now.

The burning desire I had to know everything was true, that magic was real, was still there, but I was afraid to ask it out loud. It was one thing to ask yourself, but a totally different thing to ask someone else, especially if that person was a bit, well, intimidating.

"You're a, uh . . ."

I hoped he'd answer my unfinished question because no matter how much I tried, the words wouldn't come out.

"Yes, I'm a mage," he said in a gentle tone like you would use with a kid.

"So you can do, uh, magic? Real magic?"

I felt a bit uneasy like I was facing a nice tiger, but still, a tiger who could strike at any moment, and I couldn't do anything to stop it. I'd seen Henry in action, and he moved with the sinuous movements of a Bengal tiger hunting for its prey.

And now, the fact he could do magic made it even more terrifying to have Henry as an opponent, and I was glad it wasn't the case now.

"If by real magic you mean not the stuff you see on television, then yes."

"And Dea, her mother, Lydia, and Alyssa—are they witches?" I was a bit unsure of myself, and I felt it was an unearthly conversation.

Henry nodded. "Yes, they are powerful witches."

"So, how does it work? You snap your fingers, and stuff happens?"

"It's not that easy. It requires a lot of focus, attention to detail, good drawing skills, imagination, and what I call some form of payment. It's something to get the process started, the fuel to start the fire, so to speak."

"What sort of payment?" I was cautious.

Of course, there has to be a catch.

"Usually, a few drops of a mage's or witch's blood. Let me clarify a few things first—you're quite lucky because, in the past decades, we've managed to understand more about our power as science has evolved. But even so, we've barely scratched the surface of how magic works. Our knowledge is evolving almost at the same rate as that of humankind. Anyway, I hope you remember your genetics from school because, you see, magic is found in the X chromosome; that's why women are usually more powerful than men."

"Because women have two X chromosomes?"

"Precisely. The magical ability lies in manipulating what is now called the 'junk DNA,' the DNA which doesn't encode proteins."

My face gave my confusion away again.

"Okay, let me phrase it a bit differently. Have you ever played with LEGOs?"

"Sure, when I was younger," I replied, even though I didn't understand what one had to do with the other.

The vivid memory of Tom, my grandfather, when he bought me my first box of LEGOs for my twelfth birthday, flashed through my thoughts. Immensely happy, I immediately built a house and imagined the LEGO mom and dad were my family.

I envisioned my parents and me living happily together in a LEGO house, and I used to play with them for hours, even slept with them on my pillow for almost a year.

"Well, then you know with one LEGO set, you can build a car or a boat, but if you add more sets, you can create more complex structures, like a plane, a tank, or even a city."

I nodded, recalling all the different variations of things crafted from the sets I had back during my childhood years.

"Well, the genes are the core building blocks," said Henry. "Although, they make up about one percent of an individual's DNA. Imagine, in addition to the genes, you can use non-coding DNA to build other things, effectively gaining access to the unused ninety-nine percent of your DNA. Plus, some of the newly created structures allow you to access different types of particles and forces, effectively giving you a way to manipulate things around you in your environment."

I took a moment to process this information. It was overwhelming to grasp all the implications with my limited knowledge. I was awestruck.

"The things you can do or achieve, all of you . . . I mean, the possibilities are limitless."

"Exactly. Of course, this is the ideal scenario. We have some innate ability to modify any or all of our genes, and we can even develop new ones that don't exist anywhere in nature, in theory. This allows us to do things which appear like magic like," he said with a broad smile. He extended his hands, palms facing up.

"What can you do? Oh, is it okay to ask?"

"Yes, it's fine, especially for you. How familiar are you with the term 'alchemist'?"

"That in theory, they were able to transform stuff into gold," I said with very little confidence.

"Yes, that's partly true, but it's much more than what you've seen on television or read in books."

He seemed willing and eager to share his knowledge; he definitely would have made a phenomenal teacher.

"So, you're an alchemist?"

He nodded, smiling at me, waiting for my next inevitable question.

"And you can transform things into gold?"

"Metals, yes, but an alchemist can do other things as well. We work with the essence of a material or that of an object. We can manipulate the atomic bindings and combine them in different forms to create something new or different."

"So, you can transform this table, for example"—I pointed to the coffee table on my right—"into a couch or an animal?" Even though I saw yesterday what Dea could do, I was a bit skeptical.

"Not exactly. It depends on what you're trying to do. For example, transmuting metal into another metal is not as difficult as, let's say, transmuting metal into wood, which is actually made of multiple elements."

I focused on his words, trying to absorb each one to dissect later.

"Okay. Look at it this way, both of them require energy, but if the elements aren't similar, they require a lot more energy. Now, to get back to your question, I can't transform this entire table. It would require too much energy. I can only transmute small quantities of materials," he said with a shrug.

"Can anyone else do what you do?"

"Yes, most of our abilities aren't unique. Some other witches and mages can do similar things. You see, everyone has something, one or two abilities which make them unique, besides our ability to use our power to cast spells. For example, Alyssa can both read thoughts and communicate directly to your mind, like a telepath. Lydia is fast, well, she actually can modify how time passes around her, kind of like she's in her time bubble, or at least, that's how we understand it. Candice can act upon objects at a distance." He paused a moment. "I think you call it telekinesis?" He raised his eyebrows.

"Just like Dea." I wanted him to know she had told me about herself.

"Oh, Dea can do so much more," he said with a sly smile, but before I had a chance to ask him to clarify, he continued. "But that's another story, and we can talk about it later. Now, feel free to ask any questions you have about the coven."

I was more interested in Dea than the coven, but I didn't want to push on the subject.

"How many people are in the coven? Twelve?" I asked, curious to know if the legends were true and if there were other witches or mages I hadn't met yet.

He grinned. "No, a coven doesn't need to have twelve witches and mages. There's no set number. Besides the people I've enumerated, Dea's father, Wayne, is actually a Sensitive. You know what a Sensitive is, right?"

Seeing me nod, he continued. "For a Sensitive, he's quite powerful. He can be charming, and he can also tell when you lie." At this thought, he grinned again, probably something he remembered. "Then we have Max, my partner"—he winked at me—"who's a Sensitive too, with good intuition, and last but not least, Diana. She's Dea's older sister, her actual biological sister—well, a half-sister by blood."

It took me by surprise. I hadn't known Dea had a sister.

"So, what's her power?" I asked, wondering if her abilities were similar to Dea's.

"She can ensnare the senses and create illusions, making

you see things that aren't there or ignore things which are," he said in a sober tone. "She's a powerful enchantress, and she's very protective of Dea."

I got the warning behind his words, but I only had Dea's best interest in mind. Well, and I was attracted to her. Surely it wasn't a problem, I hoped.

"Are there normal humans who know about you and what you are?" I was curious to know if I was the only one or not.

"Yes, a few. For example, the people protecting us. They've all sworn an oath not to reveal what we are to nonmagical folk."

"And what happens if they break the oath?"

"It's never a good idea to break an oath, especially when you're dealing with mages and witches. We believe your soul becomes vulnerable, and you lose a portion of it in terms of magical power. When they took the oath, it tied them to the coven regarding the people protecting us."

"And that means what?"

"If they break the oath, it severs the tie, and then bad things will happen to them. That's how the binding spell works. They will literally become the unluckiest people on the planet."

I took the time to absorb what he said. It's not like I was unfamiliar with the supernatural because I had fought my first supernatural being when I was eleven, but this was a new world I knew nothing of. I finally decided to see if he had any ideas about what I might be.

"Yesterday, Dea said I might be a, uhm, that I might have some magical powers."

He nodded. "That you do, my boy, that you do. We don't know yet what kind of powers or how powerful you are. But I would hazard a guess and say you're more powerful than an average mage."

Hearing these words, I felt a bit smug.

"Don't think being powerful is everything. Magic is so much more than raw power. Like I've said, focus, imagination, and knowledge are all more important than brute force."

Okay, that took me down a notch or two.

"You don't just wave your hand and make things happen. Most of the spells make use of symbols, incantations, and . . . well, usually, the more complex a symbol, the more powerful a spell is. Though, that's not always the case."

"What kind of symbols?" I asked, interested to see if it was something I'd heard or read before or not.

"You're probably already familiar with a few, for example, the pentagram, the five-pointed star, or the pentacle when it's drawn inside a circle."

I think he saw a slightly worried expression on my face because of the facial expression he made.

"While a lot of people think it's a symbol of evil, that's not true. At its core, the sign means unity. It brings together the elements of earth, water, fire, wind, and let's call it spirit or nothingness, whichever you prefer."

"Are they always the same?"

"No. There are many symbols, and each holds a different meaning. But the idea behind them is you need to focus on your goal, on what you want to achieve. You have to be calm and patient, open your mind, accept the possibilities, and imagine the result. Sometimes imagination is more important than knowledge."

"Hey, old man, what are you guys talking about?" Dea cheerfully entered the room.

She wore a long-sleeved dress of a floral-inspired beauty, which made me think of spring. The good manners drilled into me from childhood took over, and I stood, waiting for her to take a seat.

"I was explaining to our young Robert here how magic works," he said.

"Is that so?" Dea grabbed the chair next to mine and attempted to pull it closer.

"I'll get that." I quickly moved to help her.

She beamed at me and then snuggled into the chair.

"Please continue," said Dea. "You know how much I love your stories." She leaned to rest her head on my shoulder.

For a few seconds, my body tensed because I wasn't used to this kind of display of affection. But after a couple of moments, I relaxed and enjoyed the scent of her freshly shampooed hair and her exotic perfume, which made me think, for some reason, of a night in a desert, both of us on a warm sand bed, bathed in starlight.

". . . and you can imbue the object with one or more spells."

My thoughts must have drifted for a bit, and I'd lost track of what Henry was saying.

"Imbue an object?" I blinked rapidly, trying to focus my thoughts.

"Yes, as I said, you can apply a spell to an object by drawing the symbol on it and then imbuing it with your power. The result will be an imbued item which has its properties altered by the spell you chose."

The man, no, the mage, had a great voice. It made you want to listen to what he said and be eager for more. He either was a teacher or must have been one in a past life because he knew how to explain things and when there was a need to go deeper into details.

"This is so cool," I said, utterly fascinated. "So, I can have shoes that let me fly, or maybe a flaming sword?" I now had a big grin on my face.

Dea groaned, "Men." However, she seemed amused.

"Technically, yes, you can create shoes that allow you to levitate. However, there are other applications, as well. For example, you can create clothes that render you invisible."

Henry's tone was all business now, and he remained silent and fixed me with his gaze.

It took me a moment to realize what he was hinting at, then the hairs on my neck rose.

"The hashashins," I said in a hushed tone, looking straight at him.

My mind was racing furiously, going through new possibilities, explanations, and scenarios. Either they were magical beings, or they had access to some magic that made them invisible and transformed them into goo. If it was the latter, it meant they didn't possess the power themselves, and someone else must be behind the killings—someone who had access to magic.

"Yes, we believe so."

For a second, I thought he'd read my mind, but more likely, he had reached the same conclusion I did or just paved the way for me to reach it myself.

"Do you know who's behind this?" I asked between clenched teeth, my voice full of muted rage.

"No, but Candice and I found references to an old scroll that contains details on how to imbue clothes to make someone invisible."

"Do you know where this scroll is?" I asked in a surprisingly harsh voice.

"We thought it lost with all the others."

"Lost? How?"

"More than two millennia ago, we lost most of the knowledge we had gathered over thousands of years. With the destruction of the Great Library of Alexandria, we thought it lost. It was where most of the witches and mages of that era kept their most prized knowledge."

"About magic?"

"Yes, among other things. That was during a time when we all shared what we knew." For a few seconds, Henry seemed to be looking past me, into a time that no longer existed.

I took a moment to clear my head, and when I gazed at Dea, she appeared lost in thought as well. It was probably the first time she'd heard about what Candice and Henry had found.

I turned to Henry. "Do you think besides this one scroll, there could be others?"

"We've long suspected a few scrolls were rescued or stolen during the siege of Alexandria, but the hypothesis remains unproven," he said with a shrug.

"Until now?"

"We're not sure, but there is a strong possibility someone has the scroll we found references to. If so, they may use it to make the hashashins invisible to us and to everyone else, except you." We both remained quiet, contemplating the implications.

"Enough of this, otherwise you'll both spend the night here talking." Dea got up. "Robert, let me show you the house and introduce you to everyone."

Her face brightened, and she made a gesture to follow her.

My stomach was in a sudden free fall, like riding a roller coaster. Lydia seemed okay, but Alyssa . . .

It was scary if she could read thoughts. I briefly went through all the moments she was around me, and I wanted to face-palm myself.

She probably heard everything I thought about Dea or her family, all my concerns, and all the suppositions I had. And I remembered the stern look Candice had given me on Friday. She definitely didn't want me anywhere near her daughter.

And what about Dea's father?

I hoped he would approve of me. Otherwise, it would be

difficult even to start a relationship with Dea. And what about her sister, Diana?

Henry's warning came back like a torrent of cold water crashing on a heated rock.

"Don't worry. It won't be so bad. You already know them —maybe not officially, but there's no need to worry. Everyone likes you." She smiled, then pulling me by the hand, helped me to my feet.

The touch felt warm and soft and helped me regain some of my confidence. She didn't let go, and we left the library hand in hand, fingers intertwined.

"Have fun, Robert," Henry's amused voice said.

"He's not coming?" A brief moment of panic washed over me, and felt I had lost one of my two allies.

"No, he has a few phone calls to make but will join us later," she assured me.

I didn't pay too much attention to where we were going, but I could see at least we were heading toward the living room.

Suddenly, I didn't trust my legs, and I had to put in a conscious effort to walk straight. My body felt cold and clammy, like I had just walked through an ice-cold mist. Naked. Even though Dea said they liked me, it didn't mean they liked the fact I wanted to date her. Even worse, Alyssa knew what I was thinking, and it didn't help even one bit.

A dazzling, L-shaped white couch sat centered in the room. A floor-to-ceiling painting graced one of the walls, and a golden chandelier—which appeared to be floating—waved in the living room.

The wooden floor's contrasting colors formed an intricate pattern. A couple of pictures hung on the walls depicting lush green forests and a pleasant meadow near a sparkling stream.

On my right, framed between two huge windows, was a brick and stone fireplace. It provided not only warmth but also an antique and classy touch to the room. They had positioned an elegant, wooden table with intricate carvings off to the side. Two French armchairs sat on the side of the table nearest the entrance.

I recognized Candice on the couch facing us. She looked at me with the barest hint of a smile. On her right, on the other side of the sofa, was Alyssa, who gazed at me, her eyes sparkling. Seated next to the crackling fire in the fireplace was Lydia, who was grinning from ear to ear.

For one second, my legs felt made of rubber, but luckily Dea supported me, so I didn't make a total fool of myself.

After a moment of weakness passed, I took a deep breath, then exhaled.

"Hello, witches." An underline shake in my tone made it sound like my voice cracked, similar to a twelve-year-old boy going through puberty.

Lydia was the first to burst out laughing, followed by Alyssa, whose laugh was more reserved. Even Candice had a real smile on her face.

"Please have a seat," Candice said.

The laughter died almost instantly, and she motioned toward one of the chairs in front of me.

Dea chose the chair next to mine, probably to reassure me everything would be fine.

"I wanted to meet you officially and in better circumstances," said Candace. "From what Henry has ascertained, you seem to possess some ability to perform magic. It may not have fully manifested itself yet, but it is there. As to how powerful, well, that remains to be seen."

Sitting in the chair in front of her, I couldn't decide if I felt like an honored guest or a wayward schoolboy in trouble.

"I don't want to influence your decision in any way, but I want to tell you that if you're interested in exploring your abilities, then you will need someone to teach and support you."

Candice paused, her face masked tighter than a grand chess master during a tournament.

"We can help you to learn and control your power. But you will have to become a member of the coven."

She went straight to the point without any preamble, and it matched my first impression of her, cold and calculated.

I started to say something, but Candice held up a hand.

"Please do not give me an answer now. Wait a week to think this through. It's not a decision to take lightly. After one joins a coven, there is no going back. Right now, we can answer any questions you may have, so you can make the best decision possible," she said, then probably waited for my torrent of questions.

I felt this was one of those life-defining moments where your action determines what course your life will have in the future. I could take the blue pill, and the story would probably end here. Dea and I would continue to live in totally different worlds, and it would be impossible to have a real relationship. Or I could take a leap of faith and swallow the red pill.

On the one hand, joining the coven would set me on a path toward fulfilling a much-cherished desire—to avenge my family. If anyone could help me get some answers and find out where the hashashins were coming from, it was the coven. They had access to resources I couldn't even dream of.

But at the same time, I would be thrown into a world I'd had no idea existed until a couple of days ago. A world I didn't know anything about, even though I was supposed to be a part of it.

I had been doing this alone ever since I could remember —ever since the night I watched the people I loved murdered by a hashashin. The only other person who knew about me, my grandfather, couldn't help me. But the coven could. They could teach me how to do magic, and they could give me something no one else could, a sense of belonging.

But, what do I want, deep in my heart? Why am I even considering being part of this world?

The answer came naturally, and it surprised me.

Dea. Not revenge, not answers, not even a desire to have a family.

It was a craving I'd tried for a long time to keep it hidden, even from myself. I wanted Dea, I wished to protect her, and I couldn't leave her. Not now, not ever.

"Thank you for this opportunity," I said, clearly and without the slightest hesitation. "I appreciate your offer and for giving me time to think about it, but I've already made my decision."

At this moment, I felt Dea stop breathing, and when I turned to look at her, she was a shade paler than she was before.

"I have decided to"—I continued making my declaration gazing into Dea's eyes—"accept your offer." I finished with a smile that flourished on my lips.

Dea leaned toward me and punched my arm. I grinned and resisted rubbing my arm.

Damn, that hurt. She's stronger than she looks.

I then turned my head to see everyone smiling, but they didn't show it if they had been surprised by my reaction.

"Is there anything else I need to do?" I asked, unsure of what would happen next.

"Actually, yes, but not now. Once your powers manifest themselves completely, we will go through a binding ceremony, which will bind you to the coven, and the coven to you. Think of it as a partnership. You will have access to the coven's resources. But breaking it will result in undesirable consequences," she said in an ominous tone. "Until the time for that arrives, though, we'll gradually involve you in the coven's affairs."

"Good, conundrum solved, shall we go for breakfast?" Lydia asked. "I'm starving."

"Isn't it too late for breakfast?" I stood, following everyone else.

"We usually stay up late and sleep until noon, but today, we rose later than usual. You see, magic is much easier to control and use at night because when the sun comes up, it's like everything resets, dampening magical abilities."

"I guess there are a lot of things I need to learn," I followed Dea and the others out of the room toward the kitchen. "By the way, are your dad and your sister going to join us?"

"No, my father, Diana, and Max are out of the country on a business trip. They should be home soon, and you can meet them then."

I was impressed with their open-plan kitchen. It was massive, with stainless-steel appliances and contrasting dark brown wooden trim. The marble countertops lent the room an elegant atmosphere, and it felt more like a fancy restaurant than a traditional kitchen. Even though I'd eaten a couple of hours before, I couldn't help trying the delicious almond croissants filled with chocolate.

For the next several hours, the coven subjected me to a constant barrage of information about the coven, magic, and the people who had magical abilities. Most were things Dea had already told me the night before, but with much more detail. After a couple of hours, Candice and Lydia excused themselves and left to go to the office, leaving me with Dea, Alyssa, and Henry.

Henry, I found out, was a treasure trove of information, especially historical facts. He told me things not found in the pages of history books in any library. I learned how ordinary people had once completely disregarded witches. They were seen as inferior beings and often used in experiments. Most of those experiments failed, but some gave birth to the real monsters I had heard about only in folk tales and fantasy books.

Thousands of years ago, there were two separate groups of magic users: one in the heart of Europe, known then as Thrace, and another one in the Middle East, in what was then Sumeria. In the first group were mages and witches who enhanced their abilities so much, they became superhuman. They developed long, sharp canines, were extremely strong and fast, had heightened senses, and healed quickly. To support their new metabolism, they started to consume blood, mostly because it was the best and most potent energy source at the time.

The other group in the Middle East was part of an experiment conducted by a coven of witches. They tried—and succeeded, in a way—to create human chimeras. They decided to add dog, wolf, or bear characteristics to humans to make them stronger, faster, more resilient to damage, and to endow them with sharper senses. They succeeded and were able to alter some humans' DNA, who become something else, something closer to a beast.

As both groups became connected to their new magical abilities at a deeper level, the dampening or cleansing effects the sun had over magic and spells also affected them more— sometimes even fatally.

After I left, close to midnight, my head swam in an ocean of information the entire ride home and for hours afterward while I lay in bed. If all was true—and according to Henry, it was—then I guessed the legends about werewolves and vampires started because of witches and mages trying to gain the upper hand in their search for power.

It's not every day one learns the origins of the things that lead to man's myths and legends.

8

THE PHONE ALARM made annoying noises. It felt like a few seconds had passed since I fell asleep. I was close to throwing the phone against a wall and then remembered Brad had asked everyone to come in early for a 9:00 a.m. meeting.

Not trusting myself to stay in bed, I woke up and got ready for work through a supreme effort of will.

It was a sunny day, so before I left, I opened the blinds for Ariel so that she could enjoy the sunshine. I didn't bother to leave the sliding door to the balcony open anymore.

I never found out how she did it, but with or without the window or door open, Ariel was usually downstairs waiting for me when I got home from work.

Well, she is a cat, and they are mysterious.

I had no concerns about her getting hurt or lost. She always found her way home.

I decided I was too sleepy to drive, so I caught a cab, which gave me some time to think about what had happened over the weekend. Everything felt so surreal like it was part of a dream.

The driver pulled up in front of the office, and when I exited the car, a gust of wind ruffled my hair, blowing away the last few remnants of sleep. Being back in the ordinary world and doing normal things felt great. I felt in control. I knew exactly what I was doing. Everything was purely technical, nothing supernatural, and if someone needed help, they just had to create a support ticket. No one's life depended on me.

Both Steven and Mark were already in the meeting room at 8:51 a.m., so I rushed to make myself some tea and sat in an empty seat next to Mark.

"Hey, man. Do you have a hangover from Friday night? You look like you haven't slept at all," said Steven. He gave me a mildly curious look, but without waiting for my reply, he continued, "By the way, did you guys see the photo I sent you? Oh, man. You should have seen her. She was gorgeous, perky breasts, long legs, wild in bed and . . ."

He was usually like that, jumping from one topic or woman to another.

"Just once, I'd like to wake up and hear, 'Monday has been canceled. Go back to sleep.'" I yawned.

"Word." Mark seemed just as sleepy as me.

The only difference was he hadn't fought two hashashins, got stabbed in the process, rescued by a beautiful witch, or joined a coven—or at least, I didn't think he did. Compared to Steven, Mark didn't share much information about his love life, but from what I'd seen, I was pretty sure he wasn't sleepy from playing video games into the early hours of the morning.

"And miss the big news?" Brad said in a cheerful tone.

His deep voice could easily be mistaken for a subwoofer, or maybe the room had excellent acoustics. He was dressed for a client visit, meaning he was wearing his dark business suit, white shirt, and red tie, and had a massive grin on his face.

"You guys know how much we've worked the last couple of years to get closer and closer to our first million in revenue. Well, without further ado, today is the day. Even more than that, today is the day we'll beat our target."

He paused and looked at us, and we glanced at each other.

No one was sleepy anymore, and I was alert and hanging on his every word. After all, we had equal shares in the company.

"I was contacted on Sunday evening by a venture capital firm and spent an hour talking to them on the phone. They're offering seven million to take ownership and have full control over the company, and they're coming today at eleven to sign the papers."

He sucked in a breath of air as if needing to fill his lungs for the next batch of information.

"We will all have to sign a contract, to the effect that we'll remain with the company for at least one year and support not only our existing clients but also any new ones we acquire during this time. This also means that each of you will get almost one point five million in your bank accounts based on everyone's shares."

The room fell silent, and all eyes were on Brad.

"So, what do you guys say?" Brad had a huge grin stretched across his face.

"Hell yeah," shouted Steven.

"Oh, yeah, I'm all in." Mark fist-pumped the air.

"Hell, yes." I was overjoyed to hear the good news. We spent another hour or so going through our list of clients and projects. Once done, and Brad was satisfied he had everything for the meeting, all of us headed over to our cubicles.

"Showtime. Look busy, boys," Brad cracked a grin.

"Whatcha gonna do with your share?" Mark sat, then adjusted the height of his roller chair.

Mark and Steven continued to chat about what they would do with their share of the money and powered up their systems.

At my desk, I did a bit of work, checked emails, and tweaked dashboards to ensure things were running smoothly. There were no glitches, but I could tell no one was able to focus properly on work.

None of us could stop thinking and fantasizing about our plans. Both Steven and Mark wanted to travel and visit places they'd never seen before. Steven dreamed of going to Europe and visiting Amsterdam, and Mark's lifelong wish was to tour Asia.

If someone had asked a week before what my plans were, I would have said a trip around the world. Now, things had changed, and I wanted something to bring me closer to Dea. With this kind of money in my pocket, maybe I wouldn't feel so bad she was wealthier, by a few orders of magnitude, than I was.

It wasn't like I envied her. I didn't care much about money, and I was happy with what I was making. But I didn't want her or anyone else to think I liked her only for her money.

The meeting with the lawyers finished up a few minutes after one o'clock, and everyone was smiling and shaking hands, so it seemed the deal went through.

Once the lawyers left, Brad made a beeline straight to the cubicles, a grin smeared across his face.

"Hey, guys, we're all millionaires right now, or we'll soon be. It shouldn't take more than a week, hopefully by this Friday, to finalize everything and have the money transferred. I'm proud of what we've achieved and wanted you guys to know we couldn't have done it without your dedication and support. Thank you."

I saw tears in his eyes. And I knew how much time and effort he had put into this company—his baby. He was a wonderful boss, and I was immensely happy for him.

A few pats on the shoulder and a handshake later, Brad continued, "Let's celebrate. I'm buying."

A loud cheer erupted because he always avoided incurring trivial expenses like this to keep the company profitable. We headed toward the door, but Brad stopped me with a hand on my shoulder.

"Part of today's deal is they need someone to work at their HQ for a month or so, and they specifically asked for you. I hope that's not a problem," he said, a concerned look on his face.

He knew I wasn't a sociable person, not like Steven or Mark. Even when I went to our customers, I spent most of the time alone in their computer labs or data centers, where I kept to myself—but at the same time, he knew I was good at what I was doing.

"For that much money, it's not a problem," I assured him.

"Good, good. Uhm, they need you there today by 3:30 p.m.," he said sheepishly.

I shrugged, letting him know it was fine by me.

"Perfect. I'll send you the address, but we can talk about it later. For now, let's celebrate."

After a steak and a beer, I left the restaurant and hailed a cab. A few minutes before 3:30 p.m., I was in front of an office building on K Street near Washington Circle. I gave my name to the man at the information desk, and he told me to take the elevator to the top floor.

There was only one office with a wooden door, and in large engraved white letters, a sign said Mitchell & Assoc. Ventures.

Hmm, interesting name. Could this have any connection to Dea's family?

I knocked, waited a couple of seconds, then opened the door and stepped inside.

Three desks equally spread across the room housed male receptionists. All screamed military or professional security consultants dressed better than I was.

They sat in silence in their black suits and white shirts,

while I had jeans and a T-shirt with the inscription '*There Is No Place Like 127.0.0.1*' over my chest.

"Hello, sir. May I help you?" said the man at the desk in front of me.

"Hi, I think I have an appointment. My name's Robert Connor."

"Yes, sir, please follow me." The man stood and headed toward a small corridor.

I followed him, and he stopped in front of a door, knocked twice, opened it, and then motioned for me to go in. The door closed behind me, leaving me in a small hallway, and through a window, I saw a conference room with a giant screen mounted on the left wall. On the far side, through a glass wall, the city looked like a postcard—quiet, distant, and majestic.

"Hi, Robert." I immediately recognized the voice.

The door opened, and I came face to face with Lydia.

"Hello. What are you doing here?" I asked suspiciously, already guessing the answer.

"Oh, this is one of our companies." She motioned for me to come over.

Of course, it is—silly me.

When they had invited me to be a part of the coven, I had no inkling they'd buy the company that employed me. It meant the money I was supposed to receive was actually coming from them.

I wondered if Alyssa told them about my doubts at the hospital.

My embarrassment level shot up through the roof, and I wanted to dig a hole and hide in it right now.

But what's done is done. So, I drew in a deep breath and stepped into the conference room.

To no surprise, seated at a large table were Dea, Candice, Alyssa, and Henry, all watching me with various degrees of amusement.

"Surprise. Nice to see you again." Henry approached to shake my hand. I was speechless, not expecting to see everyone here, but things were starting to fall into place.

"If you own this company, does it mean you also bought the start-up?" I asked, looking at Candice.

"Yes. Your company shows a lot of potential, and we also need a way to explain your upcoming trip," she explained.

"What trip?" I asked, a little irritated because no one had said anything about a trip yesterday.

I'd never been outside the country, and I very much wanted to go, but I also hadn't made any preparations for Ariel.

"Please take a seat," Dea said with a soft smile and pleading eyes. She pointed to a chair next to her. "Henry will explain."

"Since the attack on Friday, we've been looking for more information about what you call hashashins. I told you yesterday, Candice, and I found references to an old scroll with instructions on how to imbue clothes to render the wearer invisible."

"Yeah, and what does that have to do with me and traveling?"

"Last night, I got in touch with an old friend of mine who may have a lead," said Henry. "He lives in London, so Dea and I booked tickets for a flight tomorrow morning. We hope you'll join us for this quick trip."

"Oh, yes, sure, but I need to make sure Ariel has someone to take care of her," I said with a sigh, unsure if I could find someone to take care of my cat on such short notice.

"Don't worry about that. I'll be more than happy to babysit your Guardian," said Lydia with a laugh.

"Thanks. Actually, why do you call her a Guardian? Dea said the same thing the other day. Is that a name you give to all the cats?" My gaze alternated between Dea and Lydia. "Or just mine?"

"This is quite an interesting and complex subject," said Henry, and I could feel his excitement. "But the main idea . . . cats are one of the few magical creatures in existence. Their nature allows them to channel magic easily."

"Cats, magical." I shook my head, wondering if I heard him correctly.

"There are a handful who possess some latent magical abilities—for example, being able to pierce through various magical veils, do some healing, or perform chance magic," said Henry.

"And they're called Guardians," replied Lydia.

Henry cleared his throat. "They usually bond with someone and bestow upon that individual and his or her home, some of these enchantments."

The news that Ariel was more than a cat blew my mind.

"In your case, from what Dea sensed," Henry continued, "it appears your apartment is well protected against hostile magic. Anyway, I can probably talk about this for hours on end, but to make a long story short, you'll have to introduce Lydia to Ariel, and she'll take care of her. So, what do you say? Will you join us?"

"Sure, why not." I shot a glance in Dea's direction. The flight would give me the perfect opportunity to get to know her better in a contained area. "What time do we leave?"

"At 6:27 tomorrow morning, Dea and I will meet you at Washington Dulles Airport. We'll fly together to London Heathrow."

And so the journey into my new life begins.

9

I'D NEVER TRAVELED first class before. And I had no idea what to expect from this trip, but at least it started well and with plenty of legroom.

Of course, besides the spacious area, the flatbed, hot towels, and excellent food, with real knives and forks, there was a downside as well. They kept on asking if I wanted or needed anything else when all I wanted was to be left alone with my thoughts.

But even so, they didn't manage to wipe the grin off my face for the entire seven and a half hours it took for us to get to London.

Dea slept the whole way, and I even had to tickle her awake when we landed. Fortunately, she didn't seem to mind it.

After the plane landed, I breezed through passport control and headed toward the exit with Henry and Dea. We didn't have anything other than cabin luggage. There was no need to wait for anything else.

I usually packed light anyway, and most of the things I needed for such a quick trip fit in my backpack.

Each of my travel companions had only a small rolling

carry-on bag big enough to fit no more than a couple of shirts and other small items. I assumed we would be back the next day, even though they hadn't bought any return tickets.

At close to 8:00 p.m. local time, we exited the airport. Once outside, a chauffeur welcomed us, then escorted the lot of us to a fully armored Audi A8.

Henry took the front passenger seat and started chatting with the driver. I closed my eyes for a second. Dea's hand gently touched mine, and then, as if it was the most natural thing in the world, our fingers intertwined.

If I were to choose the best moment in my life so far, this would be it, in London, in the backseat of an armored Audi A8 with my beautiful witch, holding hands.

Dea and I must have stayed like that for the whole journey to the hotel.

"We're here," boomed Henry's voice.

Brown's Hotel was splendid, with Victorian-era elements fused with a contemporary feel. It gave the hotel a glimpse into the past and a look into the future.

The reception desk clerk handed Henry three separate keycards, which made me feel relieved but mildly disappointed at the same time. I guess I was secretly hoping to share a cozy single room with Dea.

"Shall we meet in twenty minutes by the lobby, then have dinner?" Henry asked after we exited the elevator.

"Sure," Dea and I said in unison, then we looked at each other and smiled.

My hotel room had an entirely different look from the classic décor I was expecting. It felt comfortable and elegant simultaneously, with a few modern accents, like the flat screen and the office desk and chair. Both looked and felt better than what I had at home or in my office at work. Artworks lent a touch of personality, and a sumptuous king-size bed invited me to sleep, but I was too excited to even think about it.

There wasn't much to unpack, so I took a quick shower and changed into another pair of jeans and a black merino wool T-shirt.

I was in the hotel lobby in less than fifteen minutes, where Henry was waiting at the bar. He was wearing a suit, as always, but it wasn't the one he'd had on during the flight.

"This hotel is incredible." I took a seat next to him, trying but failing to contain my excitement.

"Yes, it's nice," he agreed, not fully sharing my enthusiasm. His thoughts seemed somewhere else. "And it's close to the Golden Lion Pub, where we'll meet my friend, Akil Razak, in an hour or so."

"And you think he has some useful information?"

"He told me yesterday he had heard of an old scroll we thought was lost in Alexandria. He's quite secretive, so he didn't give me too many details, but hopefully, it's what we're looking for. Or at least it might put us on the right track."

"Is Akil a mage too? Is he part of a coven? Does he have a day job?" I didn't hide my excitement this time.

Henry leaned closer and whispered, "Yes, yes, and yes, he's a mage and a good friend of mine. But please lower your voice. Right now, he's working as an art appraiser at an auction house, mainly because he's passionate about art history. And over the years, he's established a lot of connections in the field. If I had to guess, I'd say that's how he found out about the scroll."

"Hey, sorry for changing the subject, but I have a quick question. Why did we use an armored car? Do you expect any attacks?" Concern crept into my tone.

"No, but it's never a bad thing to be prepared for one," said Henry with a twinkle in his eye. "We trust you when you say the hashashins won't bother us for a while at least, and we can protect ourselves from magical attacks, but hired guns offer up a whole other scenario, so it's best to prepare."

Dea appeared next to me, and I decided not to continue

with my line of questioning, not wanting to dampen her mood. She was wearing a pair of skinny black jeans, a white blouse, and a beige blazer. She looked fresh and gorgeous, no wonder, after sleeping the entire flight.

"I love your jacket," I said and stood.

"Thank you, Robert. You're a true gentleman." A coy smile fluttered on her lips.

"Shall we get something to eat?" Henry headed toward the hotel restaurant.

The food was outstanding, and even though I went with the traditional fish and chips, it was delicious. When the server asked if I wanted dessert, it took me a whole two seconds to decide what I wanted, and I didn't regret my choice—the banoffee pie was exquisite.

We arrived in front of the Golden Lion Pub after a ten-minute walk from the hotel.

The fresh air did wonders for my thoughts, which started to show signs of sleepiness after such a copious meal. It looked like a cramped and unassuming little bar, but then, everything in London seemed to be on the small side. This was especially true of the streets, compared to what DC had back in the state, but on the other hand, everything here was rich in history.

Henry seemed to know the place, so I tagged along, trying to stay alert and enjoying the view. The bar wasn't crowded. I saw only one older gentleman with silver hair at a table in the far corner—it was Tuesday, after all—though there was chatter coming from upstairs.

Dea and I followed Henry up the steps, and at the top, he stopped for a moment to scan the crowd, then smiled and headed toward a table where an older man with gray hair, glasses, and a mustache with white streaks was drinking a beer.

"*As-salamu Alaykum*, my old friend," said Henry with a smile and his arms stretched out.

"*Alaykum salaam*, brother," the older man responded with a slight Arabic accent, smiling broadly.

They hugged like old friends who hadn't seen each other in quite some time.

"Long time no see, brother, how have you been? Who are your friends?" The man gestured for everyone to sit down.

"A long time, indeed. This is Dea and Robert from the DC coven." Henry turned to look at us. "And this is Akil Razak, an old friend of mine."

All of us took a seat at the table. Henry sat next to Akil, and I sat next to Dea.

"Thank you again for agreeing to meet us," said Henry.

"Always a pleasure, you know that." Akil grabbed Henry's shoulder, then, in a lower, more secretive tone, he continued, "I don't know if Henry told you, but we were in the same coven many years ago."

"But I thought you could only join a coven once." I betrayed my naïveté.

"Normally, yes. Unfortunately, our coven was decimated, and we had to flee," Akil said in a somber tone. "Anyway, this was many years ago, and we've since moved on. So, let's get to business. You say you want some information regarding an old magical scroll kept in the Great Library of Alexandria."

"That's right," said Henry. "What do you know about it?"

"Not much. A friend of mine from Egypt has got wind of a scroll recovered from the Serapeum of Alexandria. A few scrolls were kept there instead of in the Great Library; hence, they might have survived the conflagration."

"Good news, indeed." Henry palmed a glass of water and took a sip.

"I can give you his contact details, but you have to get in touch with him soon. The scroll is a hot commodity right now, and I've heard there are other parties involved who want to acquire it." He then pushed a crumpled piece of paper toward Henry. "When you talk to him, tell him I sent you."

"We will. Thank you, old friend, I owe you one."

"I owe you for saving my life," said Akil, brightening up. "Okay, now get the drinks, and we'll talk about the past." He turned toward Dea and me. "I have many interesting stories about Henry that you wouldn't believe," he said with a wink. "However, excuse me for a moment, I need to go to the loo, but don't order another drink for me. One shandy is enough. And don't trust a thing he tells you about me." He pointed at Henry, then, stumbling a bit, made his way across the bar to where I assumed the restrooms were.

"I'll go get us some drinks. What do you want?" I asked.

"I'll have a shandy Heineken," said Henry with a sly smile.

"Just some sparkling water, please," replied Dea.

"Sure, be right back. Henry, did you say you wanted a Heineken?" I didn't catch exactly what he'd said.

"A shandy Heineken."

Oblivious to what a shandy was, I nodded, then headed toward the bar to order the drinks. There weren't many customers in the queue, most were at their tables, and it only took me a minute to return with their glasses and my Corona, which had a lime wedge stuck into the top of the bottle.

Apparently, a shandy was beer mixed with something like Sprite or 7UP. The aroma was intriguing, and I wanted to taste it, but it would have been impolite—plus, they could have seen me.

"Cheers," said Henry, and we all took a sip from our drinks.

"So, you were in another coven?" I asked Henry.

"Yes, Akil and I were both in Egypt and part of the Cairo coven. But in 1919, during the revolution, our coven was attacked and wiped out. By chance, Akil and I weren't there. We were participating in a demonstration against the

British occupation, and when we arrived home, we found everything destroyed and the house consumed by flames." Henry's voice became muffled, and the lines on his face deepened.

"Why were you at a demonstration against the British when you're British?" I asked, confused.

"But I'm not, don't let the accent fool you," replied Henry. "My original name is Henri, the French version of Henry. My dad and I were living in Cairo when my powers manifested, and luckily, we stumbled upon Akil, who introduced me to the local coven and helped me understand what was happening to me."

"So," I said, "you've known him a long time then."

"Yes. He was only a year older than me. And over the next few decades, he became my best friend. When we saw the house burning, we got scared, left, and then traveled for a while. The war had just ended, and the world was recovering from the Spanish flu, so we visited the countries that required help."

"You weren't worried about getting sick?" I nursed my drink.

"No, not since we had developed powers. We used them wherever we could, to help the sick or aid in reconstruction. It would have been easy to get rich again, but we were afraid of being caught. So, we tried not to attract too much attention and didn't stay in one place for too long."

"That must've been difficult."

"It was, but finally, after a few years, we moved to London, and that's where I met Candice. She was preparing to move to the states with her coven, so I decided to join her. But Akil was tired of moving, so he remained here."

"This is fascinating," I said, wholly amazed by Henry's story.

I knew witches and mages lived for a long time, but it hadn't sunk in until now. It was surreal to talk to someone who'd lived for more than a century, to hear about historical events from a person who'd actually lived through them.

We spent a short while in silence, lost in our thoughts.

A scream pierced the veil of stillness, and we jumped out of our seats.

It came from a lady standing in front of an open door with the word 'restroom' written above it.

Henry, Dea, and I stood and rushed over to see what had prompted the scream.

A body was lying on the restroom floor, face turned on the side, at an odd angle, and a pool of blood slowly spreading out to the bar. I focused on a bloody shoe print slowly overwhelmed by the creeping blood.

"Akil," murmured Henry then covered his mouth with his palm.

I looked closer, and Akil's eyes were still wide open, staring blankly at me, with a surprised look on his face. A cold shiver ran down my spine, and I pivoted, trying to see if anyone was leaving the area.

But it was impossible to see anything through the sea of people gathered around us. Everyone tried to catch a glimpse of the morbid scene, curiosity, not fear, etched in their eyes.

"Everyone, back off," shouted the bartender, who was making his way through the crowd.

"Let's go." I touched Henry's shoulder. "There's nothing we can do here." He spun in place with a violent look in his eyes. However, the look quickly subsided and was replaced by one of extreme grief.

"Robert is right," said Dea in a gentle tone. "The police will want to question people, and time is of the essence right now. I know how much Akil meant to you, but maybe if we go to Misr, we'll find out more."

The three of us wiggled our way out of the pub just as two police cars approached. So, as a small group of tourists, we tried our best to walk as casually as possible.

Henry, lost in thought with tears in his eyes, walked on auto-pilot. Dea placed an arm around his shoulder, whispering comforting words into his ear.

I was trying to lead the way back to the hotel, and was looking everywhere to spot something familiar.

Tired after a long flight and after witnessing the aftermath of a crime, I found it hard to concentrate. I tried to pay attention to our surroundings, but there were many people around us.

A van with its lights off quickly accelerated from a nearby street, trying to pin us to the wall.

"Look out," I shouted and grabbed Dea to push her aside.

A few bystanders jumped out of the way, but they shouldn't have bothered. The van was dead set to crash into the three of us.

Instead of fear, a cold fury gripped my heart and thoughts. Ice ran through my veins. After all these years of helping people, fighting and surviving deadly assassins, and after saving and meeting Dea, it just wasn't fair. I only thought of one thing.

Not her. Not her. Not. Her.

I caught a glimpse of a raised female hand, and at the same time, I felt a surge of electricity course through me, then the van slammed into an invisible wall, not three feet from us.

The wall even pushed the car back a few feet, with a horrible screeching sound of metal. The hood smashed and crumpled inward, and the windshield shattered. Behind the wheel, the driver, probably either unconscious or dead, hugged an airbag.

A sudden bone-deep exhaustion engulfed me, and I literally felt my energy dissipating into the ground, the air, everywhere, leaving only my tired, limp body behind. I stumbled forward, my knees buckled, and I could see the cold street approaching fast. Luckily, a hand stopped my body from colliding with the sidewalk.

"We need to go now." It was a familiar voice, and with a supreme effort, I forced my legs to start moving, one step at a time.

Henry held me up straight, more or less, and I was grateful. Without him supporting me, I would've collapsed right there. All I wanted to do was go to sleep.

With my eyes closed, I took one step and then another, and with each forward motion, I took a deep breath. Everything I ate was trying to get out, but the cold night air felt good. It acted as a bandage over a wound, keeping everything in where it was supposed to be.

I lost track of time on the trip to the hotel, and I mostly remembered lights and voices and Dea's hand clasping mine.

At some point, Henry said, "He just had too much to drink," or something like that.

The next thing I knew, my body fell. My face hit a soft surface, and the lights went out.

THE LIGHT of the morning sun tugged at my eyelids, but I kept them closed. It was too bright. Last night's events started unfolding in my mind.

The body lying in a pool of blood came to mind, and a cold shudder rolled down my spine. Even though I'd witnessed my parents' murder when I was younger, and my grandmother's a few years later, not to mention all the hashashins I'd killed, I had never gotten used to it. Then, as if that wasn't bad enough, the van swirled into my thoughts along with how close we were to being killed, and I groaned.

This trip isn't off to a good start. How did we manage to survive?

The van's driver was dead set on squishing us into a paste and was moving way too fast for avoidance.

I guessed Dea or Henry must've done something to stop it. But I was unaware of what they did or how, nor did I comprehend what had happened to me. I'd never felt this tired in my whole life.

A faint snore made me open my eyes, afraid I was in Henry's bed.

To my relief, Dea was sleeping next to me with a peaceful

expression on her face. I was still wearing the same clothes I had on last night, and so was she, which made me wonder if Dea had left or if she stayed with me the whole time I'd been asleep. It wasn't what I had imagined for our first night together in the same bed, but I didn't mind.

For a dozen seconds, I pondered whether I should remain in bed and wait until she woke, but then I remembered she usually slept until noon.

So, carefully, without making too much noise, I grabbed a new set of clothes, took a shower, and then went downstairs to get breakfast.

It was a few minutes after ten, but the all-you-can-eat buffet was still open, and boy, was I glad. I was famished. I didn't pay too much attention to what I piled on my plate, even though I got some curious looks.

Sometime after my second or third run to the buffet, while I was sitting in front of a plate of scrambled eggs, hash browns, and bacon, someone pulled out the chair across the table from me.

Henry, who looked downhearted, met my gaze. I'd been there before when most of my family was murdered, and I wouldn't wish it on my worst enemy, let alone someone whom I considered a friend.

"Good morning, Robert. How are you feeling?"

It took me a second to chew and swallow the food in my mouth.

"I'm feeling better now." My voice was hoarse. "Thanks for your help yesterday. And I'm really sorry—"

"We need to talk about what happened, but not now and not here," said Henry. "Dea spoke to Lydia last night and arranged for a private flight to Egypt today at 1:00 p.m. because we don't have time to wait for commercial flights. This way, we'll be free to talk more on the plane."

Even though he sounded sure of himself, I saw the pain behind his eyes. No doubt, Akil's death fresh in his mind.

I couldn't remember precisely how I felt when my parents died, but after my grandmother's murder, the first stage was denial. I couldn't believe someone I knew was no longer alive. The next stage was rage and self-blame because I didn't do anything to stop it, and last but not least, was acceptance. Only after I'd accepted what had happened was I able to move on and let time throw a veil over my wound.

Someone once said, "Time heals all wounds," but they were incorrect.

Time applies a swathe over it, but even years after, if I sneak a peek under it and think about her, the pain is still there and will remain until the end.

Studying Henry, I perceived it wasn't the time to discuss or remind him about what had happened yesterday, so I continued to eat in silence, respecting his wish.

Not long after, Dea, with a sweet, sleepy face, joined the table, carrying a plate full of food. She was wearing a new set of clothes, denim jeans, a dark, long-sleeved knit top, and ankle boots. She sat next to me.

"Good morning." As soon as the words were out of her mouth, she wolfed down the food.

Henry and I engaged in a typically British conversation about the weather, waiting for Dea to finish.

"I spoke to Lydia before coming down, and Ariel is doing great. By the way, I think Lydia has a new feline best friend. She said we have a Gulfstream waiting for us at a private hangar at Heathrow, and we should arrive in Cairo this evening."

Dea took a bite of a buttery croissant, then washed it down with a black tea.

"We also have rooms booked at the Marriott, which is close to where you said our contact works." She looked at Henry, who nodded slightly.

"On the paper Akil gave us," Henry said in a tight voice,

"we have the contact details for Tarek Khalil, the person we are supposed to meet."

"Nice," she said, then took another bite.

"I gave him a call earlier to let him know we'll be in town, and we have a meeting set up for 9:30 p.m. at a café right across the street from our hotel."

This news made me suspect Henry and Dea were in communication before coming down for breakfast.

"We'll pose as representatives looking to acquire the item for a private collection. No one knows what we are, so let's keep it that way." He gave me a meaningful glance.

Message received. *Whoever we're going to meet had no idea about the magic world.*

A little while later, we all left Brown's Hotel in two separate cars, which I assumed were both armored. Henry said it was for security reasons, which I completely understood.

Everything went smoothly, and in no time, we were aboard the Gulfstream G550 private jet. I'd thought the first-class seats we had the day before were great, but it was slumming it by comparison. It had everything you could want and more: a desk, a television, couches, a table, comfortable chairs, fruits, and a bar stocked with all kinds of drinks.

In less than ten minutes, we were flying above the London clouds on a direct heading toward the country best known for the Great Pyramid of Giza and the Great Sphinx.

I finally got some free time to check my phone. I only had a couple of messages on WhatsApp from Mark and Steven.

Steven's message:
- *Hey, dude, how's work at the new HQ?*
- *Any cool babes around there? :)*

Mark's message:
- *Yeah, how's their network?*
- *What about their servers? :D*

I spent a bit of time thinking about what I should tell

them, but in the end, I figured it best not to mention where I was.

My reply read:

• *They're keeping me busy.*

• *Systems aren't adequately patched.*

• *Their Linux servers need some updates, so long hours doing boring stuff.*

• *Hopefully, I'll be back soon!*

Next, I searched the news for any mention of Akil's murder and the van that had almost run us down. I found several results about a forty-seven-year-old man stabbed in a pub in London.

One article reported: *"The yet unnamed victim was stabbed in the neck in the restroom of the Golden Lion pub in King Street on Tuesday night, police said."*

The article continued with an analysis of public safety in London. Toward the end, there was a line saying the police asked anyone who might have seen something to contact them in bold letters.

That, I thought, was potentially problematic because there weren't many people at the pub. Someone might have seen us talking with Akil, and at the very least, we would be persons of interest to the police. I should have checked to see if there were any cameras in the pub before we left—even though I couldn't have done much about them, but maybe Dea or Henry could have.

The only good thing, there was no mention of the van on any of the major news websites. After more advanced searches, I found a video uploaded on YouTube with the title "Van Attack in London" posted around the same time we were there. The image was shaky, probably filmed with a phone, and it showed a white van hitting something hard, based on how the front end deformed and the steam came out from under the hood. Fortunately, it didn't capture us. It wouldn't have mattered much anyway. The image was so grainy and dark. It was impossible to identify anyone in it. I couldn't even see the driver inside the car.

I spent more time on the phone, trying to find other videos until Dea sat next to me. When I looked up, Henry was snoozing in his seat.

"We need to talk," said Dea.

Usually, when a woman said these words, it meant trouble, but I had a suspicion she wanted to talk about last night. So, I put the phone away and nodded for her to continue.

"It seems you're making a habit of saving me," she said with a smile. "Don't get me wrong, I'm grateful. I wish it weren't necessary."

"So do I." A sad smile lingered on my lips.

People or supernatural things attack and try to kill me all time, but I'm unaccustomed to having someone I cared about being attacked.

It had been a long time since I'd lost people I cared for, and it wasn't a feeling I ever wished to experience again. Thinking back on what had happened, I realized even though I raised the alarm, so to speak, it wasn't me who stopped the van. It was Dea.

"However, I have a hunch that yesterday you did most of the saving." My lips went tight.

"It's what I want to talk to you about. In a way, we both did the saving. You cast your first spell yesterday. That's why you were so tired.

I was speechless and befuddled. *Wouldn't I know if I had cast a spell?*

"Usually, the first time someone does it, they, uh, kind of faint. Their bodies aren't used to energy expenditure, and they don't know how to control it or quickly replenish their power. But don't worry, I'll teach you—if you want to learn, of course," she added with a hopeful look.

I put everything she said about magic, energy, and spells on hold and focused on her last words: *if you want to learn.*

Of course, I wanted her to teach me. I would prefer her to be my teacher instead of Henry or, perish the thought, Candice.

If I was honest with myself, another part of me wanted to spend more time with her, especially doing something she liked. But I wondered if there was some other meaning behind her words. I was attracted to her, and based on our interactions over the past few days, I presumed she liked me too, but doubts still plagued me. We'd never discussed our relationship, and she not have felt the same way I did.

Does she like me, or is she grateful I saved her?

As we were going to land in Egypt in a few hours, and who knew what would happen there, I decided to lay my cards on the table.

"Dea, I hope you know I like you," I said, starting in a steady voice but ending a bit above a whisper. "I've liked you since I first saw you at the club, and I think you like me too. I'm not crazy, am I? There's something here, right?" I tried to keep my voice low and calm, but I could feel my heart thumping like it wanted to jump out of my chest. I didn't think I'd ever been more nervous in my whole life.

She looked at me in silence for what felt like forever but couldn't have been more than a few seconds.

"You're not crazy." She moved a strand of hair behind her ear.

"Was that a yes?" I asked, hopefully.

"Yes."

"Oh, good. Otherwise, this would have been an embarrassing moment." I breathed out with relief.

"However," she added in a quiet voice.

I froze, waiting for the other shoe to drop. I could feel the energy, the heat, leaving my body, and a cold sweat covered my forehead and palms.

"Please understand, I have no experience with this. Until I met you, my whole purpose was my family and my studies."

Unable to breathe, let alone speak, I listened to each word she said, trying to digest each one.

"But in the past few days, you've shown me life means more than that. I'm quite embarrassed to say it, but I have no idea what to do. Until now, I wasn't sure you truly liked me."

"Well, you know now."

A small smile played on her lips. "I even asked Lydia and Alyssa about it, and I got completely different answers. It's like a relationship doesn't have any clear path to follow, and for the first time since I can remember, I feel lost and afraid."

"Afraid? Why?"

"Yes. I'm afraid I like you, and I don't want to lose you. I don't want to lose how you make me feel. I know it's a selfish reason, but that's how I am, if you haven't realized it by now. I'm a selfish person."

I felt she had more to get off her chest, and I wanted to know everything, well, everything she was willing to reveal.

"For the past few days, I've been hoping what I feel about you would go away because I don't think I'm the best person for you. But it hasn't gone away—if anything, it became stronger, and I don't know what to do. I'm sorry to lay all of this on you." She looked at her hands, which were on her lap and balled into fists.

I could see tears forming on her eyelashes, about to drop and leave wet traces on her alabaster skin. Oddly enough, I felt both happy and sad. Delighted she liked me, but at the same time, I felt sorry she thought she wasn't right for me. I was also angry at myself because I didn't know what to do, didn't know what to say to make her believe she was perfect for me.

Something my grandfather used to say came to mind: *Always tell a woman she's right. Then start from there.*

Cupping her chin in my palm, I raised it, so our eyes could meet.

"You're right." I saw a questioning look in her eyes. "Relationships are complicated at best. And there's no sure way to navigate through them. And honestly, I like that I get butterflies in my stomach every time I see your face. See? I'm selfish too." I smiled, and I was happy to see she smiled back.

I slowly caressed her face with my fingers and wiped the tears rolling down her cheeks. Simultaneously, we leaned against each other until our foreheads touched.

The heat radiating from her flushed face matched that of mine. And I sipped on the smell of her exotic perfume and longed to taste the hint of strawberry coming from her lips.

Her hot breath caressed my face, and I wanted to kiss her. I'd never wanted anything so badly in my whole life. But something told me now wasn't the time.

A while later, we both regained our breath. The heat receded, and reluctantly Dea and I moved away from each other, still holding hands. A sense of joy filled me.

"Thank you." She paused a moment. "There's something I have to tell you," she continued in a grave tone.

"What's that?"

"Egypt isn't the friendliest place for us. From what I know, witches have been hunted there for a long time. If things go well, we won't stay long enough to attract attention. But I wanted to tell you, just in case."

"Do you expect any trouble?"

"No, but we should be prepared. I wanted to give you this." She took a dark red leather bracelet out of her pocket, with some strange symbols engraved into it.

"Thank you very much. It's beautiful. What is it?" I took the bracelet and studied it but had a feeling it wasn't an ordinary ornamental band.

There were similar symbols on the inside and the outside, with no clue on what they meant. There were only two different symbols, one repeated three times on the inside and another three times on the outside.

The sign on the outside was a square with a circle of

intertwined knots inside it. And on the inside, it had an inverted triangle with a crossbar. The symbols seemed vaguely familiar, but I didn't remember when or where I had seen them before.

"This will help you control your energy and stop you from using too much at once. It will also act as a small charger whenever you're close to organic matter, which is all the time, given the number of microbes around us. It will collect and store energy for you."

"Oh, now I hope I won't faint next time I cast a spell, thank you," I said, followed by a small laugh. My whole body vibrated with anticipation, and I felt a slight pressure building after I put it on, then my ears popped. "Do you have one too?"

"I don't need one." The corner of her mouth raised in a smirk.

The rest of the flight, I spent talking to Dea about the things I'd found on the internet and discussed several possibilities. From what she had said, the coven didn't have much influence outside the United States. But in the end, she told me not to worry. Every problem has a solution, even if sometimes it's a magical one.

11

THE PRIVATE JET terminal staff was friendly and polite, and the customs check went smoother than expected, even compared to Heathrow. They treated us like VIPs, which, in a way, we were, considering we had our own private jet—I just wasn't used to being one.

Outside the airport, a white Chevrolet Suburban was waiting for us, probably armored as well, especially after what had happened in London the previous day.

The driver, slender, tall, dark-eyed, dark-haired, with a slight beard, spoke in English, but Henry replied in Arabic. I couldn't follow what they said next. I didn't know any Arabic. Even if I did, they spoke too fast for me to follow. It was like a friendly shouting match.

In less than an hour, the driver pulled in front of a lush garden lined with palm trees. Past the trees, the silhouette of a majestic building loomed over us. A couple of minutes later, we opened the doors of a beautiful palace, which reminded me of times long gone, when lavish decorations adorned the walls and giant chandeliers illuminated white marble staircases.

The hotel depicted a perfect mix of modern and last-century oriental design.

On the thirteenth floor, my room had a spectacular view of the Nile River, and I wished I had more time to enjoy it properly. Lights from boats anchored along the shoreline glistened on the water. A world of mystery and wonder swayed beneath my eyes.

A shower and a change of clothes later—I was down to my last pair of jeans—I went downstairs to meet Henry and Dea, both waiting for me. Henry wore a cream-colored suit with a brown tie, not his usual dark suit, and Dea was wearing a plain white long-sleeved shirt and belted denim jeans.

We crossed the street and arrived at Beano's Café, the place where we were supposed to meet Henry's contact. It was a couple of minutes before 9:30 p.m., and we decided to go in and wait for Tarek at a table, less conspicuous that way.

From the outside, it looked like a small coffee shop, but once I stepped inside, it resembled a chic modern restaurant. The crowd was also completely different from what I expected. It felt like a Starbucks—similar design, similar people.

Youngsters worked on their laptops, and businesspeople enjoyed their food or coffee and talked, but not too loudly. I felt right at home.

Henry asked about a reservation for Tarek Khalil, and the server showed us to a round table where a man, probably in his late thirties with short black hair, dark skin, and bushy eyebrows, was texting on his phone.

Dea, Henry, and I shook hands with the man, then everyone took a seat, and we told the server our orders, a tea for me, and hot coffee for Dea and Henry.

Once the server left, Tarek asked Henry in English with a thick Arabic accent, "Sorry for asking, but how do you know Akil?"

"He was an old friend of mine."

I detected a hint of sadness in Henry's voice, but only because I knew what had happened yesterday. In his place, I don't think I would have been so detached.

"I understand." Tarek's gaze darted between Henry and me. "Can you elaborate on what you're looking for?"

His eyes narrowed, and I wondered if he had any other items to sell, or maybe he just wanted to make sure we were who we claimed to be.

"We heard about an artifact recovered from the old Serapeum of Alexandria and are hoping you can point us in the right direction."

"Ah, yes, I know the person who has it, and I think he's interested in selling it, but it might be quite expensive."

"I'm sure we can reach an agreement. Would it be possible to see this person tonight?"

"I'll see what I can do. Let me make a few phone calls." Tarek stood. He left the restaurant but stopped outside to make a call from his cell phone. And the whole time, he kept an eye on us.

"What do you think?" Dea asked, her gaze focused on Henry.

"I think he'll ask us to go with him and meet the seller. If it's a trick and they want to rob us, I cannot say."

Tarek came back a few minutes later. "You're in luck, he is available tonight, but it has to be right now." He rubbed his face.

"Okay, give us ten or fifteen minutes to get our car." Henry put down the coffee cup and stood, and Dea and I did the same.

"We can't wait that long." The muscles on Tarek's face tightened. "He's only available for a short time and will be leaving soon. We can take my car and be there in less than ten minutes."

"I'm sorry, but—" I started, but Henry interjected.

"Okay, not a problem, we'll come with you."

We followed Tarek out of the restaurant to the parking lot, which was full. Based on his reaction when we told him we needed time to get our car, he could either potentially lose a lot of money if he didn't get us there in time or lead us into a trap. Considering how our trip had started, I was betting on the latter, and a glance at Dea and Henry's tense postures told me they expected one too.

We got to Tarek's car without incident, and I relaxed a bit.

The vehicle, parked in a well-lit spot, was an old blue Nissan, with a few red and gray patches.

Henry got in front with Tarek, and Dea and I climbed into the backseat.

He drove past honking car horns, yelling street sellers, and old buildings. The weight of history overwhelmed me and made me forget for a few moments about our mission.

I decided to tune out the conversation between Henry and Tarek and focus on where we were going. To no avail—it was too dark, and most of the streets poorly lit. And the ones with lights didn't have names. Surreptitiously, I glanced behind us a few times but couldn't see anything out of the ordinary.

After what couldn't have been more than fifteen minutes, we arrived in front of a large two-story house with a palm tree on either side.

Tarek pulled to a stop in front of a dark wooden door, which had a huge arched window with a balcony on either side.

Through the window, I saw lights behind closed curtains.

I got out of the car, offered Dea a hand, then turned to Henry, who stood next to Tarek.

"This way." Tarek took the lead and knocked on the door three times. Soon, a huge man appeared in the doorway and exchanged a few words with Tarek. He was a few inches shorter than Henry, but his chest was broader than mine.

The man wore a white shirt with rolled-up sleeves, and I could swear his arms were as thick as tree trunks. He quickly but thoroughly patted down Henry and me, searching for hidden weapons, and he was more thorough than the airport security checks we'd had in the past couple of days.

With Dea, he was a bit less rigorous. She didn't have much room to hide anything. However, there were times when I wanted to punch him. His hands lingered on her longer than I thought necessary.

Once finished, he waved me and the others through without saying a word, then closed the door behind us.

In front of me sat a staircase leading to the second floor. Next to it, a hallway, which probably led to the back of the house. There were rooms on each side of the stairwell. And from the one on our left, people talked, and glasses clanked, or something similar, couldn't tell for sure. The door was closed.

From the room on our right, a voice said, "Please come in."

Inside, a man was sitting on a couch wearing an ankle-length white robe, which I remembered Henry telling me was called a thobe. Behind him, two mean-looking guys, wearing dark suits in tone with their beards, were studying us. They looked like they did the heavy lifting regularly.

"Hello, and welcome to my house. My name is Zaid." He had dark wavy hair, a beard, and a mustache with a few silver streaks. His English was excellent, with only a trace of an Arabic accent. "I'm sorry we had to rush this meeting, but I have to be at the airport soon. Please tell me what I can do for you."

"Very nice to meet you, Zaid, my name's Henry. We hear you have some information about an artifact found in Alexandria, where they located the old Serapeum."

"Yes, I may have heard something about it. However, you

know such artifacts are rare. One could say they're unique. Plus, there are people already interested in it."

"I'm sure we can reach an understanding."

"I'm pleased to hear that. How do you say it, oh, yes, do you have a ballpark figure in mind?" Zaid asked in a soft tone, his gaze a steady, unrelenting stare.

Even though I was no expert on negotiations, I could tell Zaid was. He'd smoothly manipulated the conversation to force Henry to reveal the maximum we would be willing to pay, and if we made an offer, it would be either below what he already had in mind or above it. Either way, it was a win-win situation for him.

"We should be able to add ten percent to any other offer you already have," Henry replied, a confident smile on his face, and I realized Henry might have done this once or twice in his long life.

"Very well. I already have an offer of ten million US dollars. The deal is happening tonight."

For a couple of seconds, Henry appeared to consider the price Zaid had mentioned. For me, it was an enormous amount of money, more than the offer for Brad's entire company.

"Okay, then, we are ready to offer eleven million US dollars if we can have the item now."

Zaid remained quiet for a few moments, and his gaze swept over us, lingering moreover on me. He had the stare of a predator, a shark who smelled blood in the water.

"Then we have a deal." He extended his right hand, and Henry shook it, both of them smiling politely. "As it happens, one of my contacts brought it to me today." He glanced at Tarek, who was leaning against a wall next to the entrance to the room. Tarek then shouted something in Arabic, and I heard someone climbing up the stairs. "Now, while we wait, would you like anything to drink? Tea? Coffee?"

"Tea would be fine, thank you," Henry said with a short bow.

On the plane, Dea had stressed that a flat-out refusal or the decline of an offer to drink tea insulted the host. And one always accepted the drink with the right hand.

A woman wearing a gray tunic and a light blue hijab appeared with a tray of three cups and a teapot. She filled each cup.

"Thank you," said Dea.

Everyone took a cup using their right hand, and we slowly began to drink. The tea was hot but had a sweet taste, and I detected a chamomile and mint hint.

A minute later, two people showed up from one of the adjacent rooms. Both were young, maybe not even twenty years old. One was holding a stainless-steel tube, which I assumed was the scroll Henry had bought for eleven million dollars.

Zaid motioned to him to give the container to Henry, who put the cup down and took it gingerly.

Henry slowly removed the cap and gently handed the cylinder to Dea, who took the tube, closed her eyes, and put her right thumb inside. A few moments later, she opened her eyes and handed the cylinder to Henry with a nod.

"Everything seems in order." Henry took his phone out from the inside pocket of his jacket. "Please let me know where we should transfer the money."

With an amused expression, Zaid handed Henry a piece of paper with some numbers written on it, presumably a bank account.

I took another sip of the delicious tea, and I could feel a warm sensation spreading throughout my body, inviting me to sleep.

Less than a minute later, Henry asked Zaid to confirm the transfer of money. Zaid slowly picked up his phone from the table, and a couple of minutes later, he nodded to Henry. Transfer completed, it was time to leave.

"A pleasure doing business with you. I have one last question. I'm curious how you found out about this relic?"

"An old friend of mine, Akil Razak, told us about it." Henry sipped from his tea.

"Ah, I know Akil. How's he doing?" Zaid asked in a conversational tone, but his face remained locked in a mask.

There was something off in Zaid's expression, or maybe it was the way he was looking behind all of us, but I got the impression this question was essential to him—perhaps some sort of test.

I started running through possibilities in my head, but my brain was slow, undoubtedly from all the time zone differences and jet lag. Still, I thought if Henry said Akil was dead, questions might arise, mostly if Zaid wasn't already aware of it. On the other hand, if he knew of Akil's murder and Henry said he was okay, Zaid might think we had something to do with his death.

"The last time I talked to him on the phone, he sounded fine," said Henry, and technically, it was true. He must have followed the same train of thought I did and avoided falling into the trap laid by Zaid.

"I see." Zaid nodded to someone behind us.

I wanted to turn around, but everything was moving in slow motion. Then something slammed into the back of my head, and the coffee table approached at an alarming speed. Everything went black.

12

MY SENSES RETURNED SLOWLY, and my head pounded. The pain was sharp and intense, and I made an effort to remember what had happened. But a fog spread over my mind.

Lying on my left side with my arm pinned under me, I opened my eyes to a granite wall, illuminated by a soft light glistening from above. My hands, bound behind me, felt stiff, but my legs were free.

A mighty shove with my right knee, and I managed to roll onto my stomach, then turned my head toward the center of the room.

There was one lightbulb casting a pale glow, illuminating a table with a chair next to it. Behind the chair was a closed door. And on the far side of the room, I saw Dea and Henry.

For a second, I was afraid they were dead. Then I noticed they were still breathing—slowly, but breathing.

Dea was facing me, Henry the wall, and they both had their hands tied behind their backs with rope.

Faint, muffled voices came through the closed door, making it impossible to understand anything. I laid there, taking deep, steady breaths until my head cleared, and I was able to think properly again.

"Psst, psst, hey," I whispered, trying to see if either of them was awake, but no luck.

Zaid drugged us all. Probably with something in the tea.

The door opened suddenly, and I shut my eyes, pretending I was still out. Steps approached, then stopped close to me.

A rush of air blew across my face, and then—*bam*—a kick in my ribs made me groan in pain.

"Awake yet?" The voice had a strong Arabic accent, and then I heard steps heading toward the door. I gasped for breath, winded by the vicious kick, and worried I might have a broken rib.

Several minutes later, Tarek entered the room, followed by the bodyguard who had frisked all of us when we arrived.

"So, you're awake. Good. I have some questions. But be careful how you answer. My friend here won't be pleased if you lie." He pointed at the guy with tree trunks for arms, and I saw him coming toward me.

The massive man picked me up and dropped me like a sack of potatoes against the wall. The shove was so forceful it knocked the wind out of me again.

"First question: How do you know Akil?" Tarek thundered.

I decided to be completely open with him. What other choice did I have? "I only met him once yesterday. He was a friend of Henry's."

"What was your business with him?"

"Henry talked with Akil a few days ago and asked him about a relic. Akil said he had a lead, and they agreed to meet yesterday in London. Look, we're only interested in the relic, nothing else."

"What did you do after he gave you my details?"

Even in my current state, bruised, drugged, and probably

with a concussion, I realized this was the heart of the matter. If I said the same thing Henry did, I had the foreboding notion I'd quickly become a punching bag. So, I decided to stick with the truth to avoid any misunderstandings.

"Akil gave Henry a piece of paper with what I think was your phone number. Then he went to the restroom."

I cleared my throat, but it remained dry like sandpaper.

"We, Henry, Dea, and I, were waiting for him at the table when we heard a scream and rushed over to investigate."

The tree trunk loomed over me, blocking my view of Henry and Dea.

"Akil's body was lying on the floor in a pool of blood. Someone must have stabbed him. The police were on their way, and we didn't have time to answer any questions. So, the three of us left the pub."

Tarek's eyes remained locked on me, and his face remained an unreadable mask.

"Then, on our way to the hotel, someone tried to ram a car into us, and we barely managed to survive. The next day we boarded a plane and came here. I swear to you, it's the truth," I pleaded.

"Why did you run when you heard the police coming? Why didn't you want to answer any questions?" Tarek planted his hands on his hips and towered over me.

"Because we didn't want to be interrogated by them. None of us knew what to say. And we needed to get here as soon as possible. Akil already told us other parties were interested in buying the scroll."

"Then explain to me why the police are asking about three suspects: two men and a woman. They even have descriptions that sound a lot like you three." Tarek slammed his fist down onto the table, and in my peripheral vision, I saw Dea's eyes flutter open.

"I guess they saw us on the CCTV." I raised my shoulders.

Tarek didn't say anything. And for several seconds, his

eyes bored into mine. It felt like he was looking straight into my soul, trying to read my mind. His powerful gaze creeped me out. But a few seconds later, without a word, he left the room, leaving only tree Trunks inside with us.

Outside the door, Tarek talked to someone in what I assumed was Arabic.

The guy with the tree trunks started cracking his knuckles menacingly, then he eyed Dea, and a malicious smile crept over his face.

I felt rage bubbling up inside me. If he took one step toward her . . .

And then it hit me—an extremely intense feeling of danger, like nothing I'd ever experienced before, surrounded me.

The hair stood up on the back of my neck, and I realized with horror, the hashashins were here; more than one. There was no escape, not with my hands tied and Dea and Henry out. We were dead.

The despair must have shown on my face, and our guard's excitement grew. He probably thought I was afraid of him, or he was contemplating his plans for Dea. He opened his mouth to say something, but an inhuman scream drowned out his words.

A heavy thud followed, like a body hitting wood, and his face contorted into a concerned scowl—then, by the look in his eyes, fear. He turned around and left the room, locking the door behind him.

In my panic, I stood, wincing, and immediately started to strain against the ropes with my hands.

It was no use—they were too tight, and the more I strained, the more they cut into my skin, like burning coals. I took a deep breath and looked around.

Dea appeared to be drifting in and out of consciousness; one moment, her eyes were half-open; the next, closed, and Henry wasn't moving.

I scanned the room for anything I could use, and in my sitting position, I started moving my hands up and down, rubbing the ropes against the wall, hoping the friction might break the fibers. I kept looking around for something sharper, like a nail, to help cut through them.

Suddenly, another scream from nearby sounded, and then several loud, massive booms, like someone falling down the stairs.

"Dea, please wake up, if you can hear me, please wake up!" I shouted panicked.

Her eyes opened slowly, and I could see them focus on my face. Then, with a loud bang, the door opened, and my heart froze.

A humanoid shape wearing a black sleeveless leather hooded cardigan, loose baggy pants, a familiar knife, and dull white eyes devoid of emotion was standing in the doorway. He seemed to watch us, assessing the situation, and planning his next move.

I sprinted and kicked the table, hoping to at least clip him and make him lose his balance.

Unfortunately, I shouldn't have bothered.

The hashashin launched himself over the table with a graceful jump from a standing position. Then he landed in front of me.

I'd made a huge and quite possibly fatal mistake. If I hadn't acted, I probably would have been able to catch him by surprise. Now it was too late, and he was looking straight at me with a sneer.

The hand holding the knife moved like lightning without any warning, coming at me in a vertical slash. I tried to jump back, but I barely had time to take a step and rotate my body when the hot dark blade slashed through my T-shirt and flesh, from my shoulder to the elbow. He then quickly followed with another slash that seared through the skin of my lower-left abdomen.

I hit the wall, my arms bound behind me. I faced him with nowhere else to retreat. If I was to die, at least I could do it facing my opponent. I wasn't afraid. I've always thought my number should have been up the night of my parents' murders. Since then, I'd been living on borrowed time.

Now, I watched how his arm tensed. His grip intensified, then he lunged straight for my heart.

For some odd reason, a peaceful sensation enveloped me, and of all the things I could be thinking, I remembered a Zen story about a tea master who had to duel a samurai. The tea master had no training in using a sword, so the fight meant his death. So, the tea master and the samurai faced each other.

The tea master raised his borrowed sword, closed his eyes, and started performing the tea ceremony in his head. Later, when he opened his eyes, he was all alone. An odd feeling of calm washed over me, and I closed my eyes.

"Death smiles at us all," I whispered. "And all we can do is smile back."

A loud cracking noise made me open my eyes, and my gaze landed on a giant hole in the wall next to the door. Through it, I saw a body covered in dust. It looked like the hashashin who had tried to kill me.

Dea was standing with her right hand raised. The palm pointed at the door. My beautiful, dangerous witch had woken up, and she looked enraged, but when her gaze washed over me, her face softened.

"Are you okay?" she asked in a tight voice full of muted rage.

Everything was so surreal. One moment I was preparing to die, and the next, I found out I was going to live. It took a few seconds for my brain to catch up, then I slowly nodded at Dea, whose face was tense. I was just glad that the look wasn't for me.

"I'm alive." My feelings, a mixture of amazement and happiness, flooded my mind. "Thanks to you."

Dea nodded, then came closer and touched my bound hands. Something like sand ran over my wrists, palms, and fingers, and the ropes vanished. She then moved to help Henry, who was still unconscious.

I gently rubbed my wrists to get the blood flowing and looked over at the hashashin lying on the floor.

Somehow he wasn't dead. His body had not yet transformed into goo. I was amazed by how he withstood such an impact, but even so, he must have had some internal damage, maybe even a broken spine. I'd never had time to study their healing abilities and had no intention to start now.

"What happened?" Henry's voice sounded to my right, and he slowly rose with Dea's help.

"I think they drugged us, probably because they thought we killed Akil," I said. "They asked me some questions, but they mainly wanted to ascertain if we had killed him. I told them we didn't, but I'm not sure they believed me. Soon after, I felt them coming."

"Are there more?" Dea asked, narrowing her eyes.

"Yes, I think so. We'll have to figure out a way around them. I don't think I can fight." I was trying to bandage my arm with my T-shirt when I felt more hashashins closing in.

Footsteps pounded the floor off in the distance. Others stomped down the staircase, then the pile of rubble and dust next to the door started to vibrate.

"Guys," I whispered, "I think we have some trouble coming our way."

"I think Robert has a point. We should avoid a confrontation with them if at all possible."

It was the first time I'd heard Henry panic. All of us looked around, trying to find a way out. Unfortunately, the only obvious path was the one where the danger was coming from.

"Look here. I think there used to be a door." Henry moved his fingers over indentations in the wall. "Do you think you can create a portal to the other side?" he asked Dea.

"Not quickly, but I have a better idea." She raised her hands and planted her palms on the wall, and Henry hurried over to where I was standing.

Steps echoed down the hallway, and the hashashin buried in dust and rubble started to sit up.

A loud explosion followed, and thunderous rumbling shook the entire house. Then, a massive hole opened in the wall.

Dea had made a portal big enough even for the guy with the tree trunks to fit through easily.

On the other side, there were bushes and trees, like a garden.

"Let's go," she shouted, motioning for me and Henry to move.

Henry, still dazed, was closer, so he went through first. I glanced at the remanence of the actual door, and my blood froze.

Another hashashin had appeared in the doorway. His right arm moved, and the knife was flying end over end through the air toward Dea.

"Watch ou—" was all I managed to say.

The knife hit an invisible wall a couple of feet from Dea's face and dropped to the floor with a clang.

She kept her left hand raised, fingers spread wide. "Now would be as good of a time as any, Robert."

I ran through the hole and then turned and shouted, "We're outside."

She turned and walked through the hole, her left hand pointed toward the door where the hashashins were. I could see another one joining the group, and all three were looking at us with their creepy white eyes. When Dea emerged, they started toward us, weapons in hand, ready to kill.

"Move back," Dea shouted.

I took a few steps back, not taking my eyes from the approaching hashashins. My only hope was they would have to exit one at a time—it was my chance to keep Dea clear.

Their graceful movements caught my eye with morbid fascination.

Dea shouted, and a deafening blast, followed by an earth-shattering crash, brought me back to reality.

A part of the house collapsed over the room, hopefully killing or at least trapping the hashashins.

"Let's get out of here." Henry started walking quickly, leading the way out of the garden.

The three of us soon found ourselves stepping out into the street through a gate a few dozen yards to the left of the house's main entrance.

"We'll need a car." Henry searched up and down the street.

There was a silver BMW parked in front of us and a white Mercedes behind it. Across the street, there was a white van with tinted windows.

"Let's get this one." He touched the door handle of the BMW. A couple of seconds later, the doors unlocked them-selves, and he slid onto the driver's seat.

If I hadn't witnessed Dea collapse most of a house on those hashashins, I probably would have been more impressed.

Dea and I took the rear seat, and Henry accelerated, putting some distance between us and the hashashins. My brain must have realized the danger had passed, and my adrenaline levels went down just as the pain caused by my injuries skyrocketed.

It was a strange sensation—I was in pain, but at the same time, I could feel my energy ebbing away, the blood pouring out from my loosely bandaged wounds.

"Stop," Dea shouted. She turned toward me.

Henry slammed a foot on the brake pedal, making the pads squeal. And the momentum made me cry out in pain.

"Do you trust me?" she asked with an intense look on her face.

"With my life." I groaned, both my arm and abdomen throbbing with pain.

"Okay, this may hurt a little."

"As opposed to these?" I motioned to the open wounds.

She dipped a finger in the blood oozing from my shoulder. I wanted to laugh because I was already hurting. A lot! She then traced some strange symbols on my arm and abdomen, close to the wounds. Simultaneously, she chanted some incantation in what sounded like Latin, or something close to it.

The more symbols she traced, the more my arm and stomach burned. Hell, It was like someone had injected me with boiling water. It was spreading through my veins, burning everything in its path, and I wanted to scream, to run away from all this, but my eyes met Dea's. Then the sensation went away as fast as it had started and took with it all my pain, leaving me depleted of energy.

With my eyes closed, I had to focus on not passing out.

"We're ready, go," said Dea. After a few deep breaths, she whispered, "I'm sorry about that, Robert. I had to heal you and make sure the blood you left behind can't be used against you. I've only closed the wounds and sped up your healing process. Proper healing will take more time, but I don't think you have any internal damage, so you should be fine. But just in case, take it easy for a day or two."

I nodded, trying to catch my breath. I looked over my wounds, and it struck me, I couldn't see a drop of blood or even a cut on my skin. Even the T-shirt I used to tie up my wounded arm, which had been soaked with my crimson bodily fluid, was now dry and without a drop of blood on it.

Before I had the chance to ask her what had happened,

Henry cursed under his breath, something I hadn't heard him do before.

"What happened?" Dea asked, concern in her tone.

"I just realized we don't have the scroll anymore unless one of you has it?" He looked in the rearview mirror, but both Dea and I shook our heads. "This means the hashashins have it. We can't go back to get it. I don't think we're ready for a fight with them, assuming they survived."

"Some of them did, but you're right. I'm in no shape to fight. However, I don't think the scroll is in the house." I paused a moment, catching my breath. "Hey, what's the time?" I asked, an idea forming in my mind.

"The dashboard shows 10:34."

"Then we have to go to the airport." I peered out into the darkness.

"Why? Oh, I see. You think Zaid went to finalize his original sale?" I had to hand it to him. Henry was smart.

"Yes. If I remember correctly, we arrived before ten. The transaction didn't take too long, and it seems we weren't unconscious for more than ten or fifteen minutes. So I don't think Zaid has a huge head start. He may have left only minutes before the hashashins came."

"Good point. I think it's worth a try. Now, if you'd pay ten million to buy something, you'd probably arrive in your jet, so we'll have to go to the same terminal we were in a few hours ago. Good thing this car has GPS and a map because I don't remember this part of town well."

I let Henry pick the best route and turned toward Dea. "Thank you for saving me." I poured into it all my sincerity. "Without you, I would be—"

"Hush." She put a finger over my lips. "Without me, you wouldn't have been in this situation."

A sadness lined her voice, and a pang of guilt stabbed me in my chest.

I don't want her to be sad, not now, not ever.

I had a good idea of what she was feeling. I was all too familiar with guilt, not to recognize it. After all, I never stopped blaming myself for things I did or didn't do, and I knew if I continued pressing her on the subject, it would only make matters worse.

"Back there, what did you do to untie me? Did you use a knife?" I asked to change the subject.

"No, I transmuted the ropes into some of their basic components. It's hard to explain, as it's advanced magic. But once you've mastered the basics, you start feeling the composition of each material or type of organic matter and instinctively know what to do to break it down or change it, if you use the proper spell."

"But I thought you could only do telekinesis, or whatever you call it. Oh, is this your second power?" I asked, glad I was able to detour her train of thought.

"Something like that."

She threw a glance at Henry and then continued to speak, "That was my first power. I've had others manifest themselves since." She looked out the window. "Let's talk about it later. For now, let's focus on what we need to do."

"Okay." It felt like there was something more she wasn't telling me, but I decided to drop the issue for now.

She was right. We had other things to focus on.

"They may meet at the hangar where the buyer's plane is parked, or if they meet at the airport, it'll probably be in one of the business lounges," I said. "I don't see any other choice."

"If they don't know or trust each other, then they won't meet at the hangar," Henry chimed in. "I think we should plan for the second option, that they'll be inside the airport."

I looked at Dea to see if she wanted to add anything, but she had her eyes closed and seemed to be resting or avoid any more questions from me.

13

THE AIRPORT LIGHTS flickered in the distance. Henry drove on an access road, along a fence enclosing silhouettes of planes and hangars.

"Okay, let's go over the plan one more time," said Henry. "We'll enter the arrivals hall one at a time, with a sixty-second delay. I'll go first, followed by Dea after a minute, and then you, Robert, two minutes after me. This way, it will be more difficult for anyone to notice all three of us." He merged into the lane marked for the airport. "Robert, you'll have to use my jacket; otherwise, you'll look suspicious with your T-shirt cut like that."

Henry pulled into the Terminal 2 parking area, and even though it was almost 11:00 p.m., there were many parked cars, making it difficult to find a parking spot.

"Wait a second," said Dea before I exited the car. "I'll need to disguise you so no one will be able to recognize us afterward."

Henry handed her a tiny knife, and she made a small cut on her palm, dipped a finger in the droplets of blood, and started drawing something on my forehead. Then she muttered something, and my face suddenly got warm, and my skin prickled, especially my cheeks and under my chin.

"So, what does it do?" I put on Henry's jacket.

It didn't fit me well. I had to roll up the sleeves, and it was tight in the shoulders, but after some flexing, it felt more comfortable. I might have ripped the seams or the stitching, but hopefully not too much.

"It acts as a mask, altering your facial structure. So you won't look like, well, you. Nothing else will change. If a security camera records you, no one will be able to say for sure it was you. Anyway, it will last until you wipe it off."

I nodded, relieved to know I'd have my face back. "Shouldn't you do the same?"

"A similar charm is embedded in my necklace and Henry's earring."

"Will I be able to recognize you?"

"Yes, the spells allow us to see each other as we really are."

"That's handy. So, what do I need to do to activate it?"

"It's already active. Just look at your reflection in the car window," said Dea with a quick smile.

I did. *Incredible.* I had a fuller face with chubby cheeks and dark, arched eyebrows, my angular jaw was less pronounced, and my square chin had a bit of fat under it. The person I saw in the window kind of looked like me, maybe if I were fifty pounds heavier.

"This is remarkable." I rubbed my right cheek to make sure it was indeed my reflection. "Imagine how many people would want something like this. You can eat whatever you want and look like you're going to the gym every day, or the other way around," I said with a laugh.

"Don't forget I can see how you really look," Dea said with a smirk.

"I can't believe it," said Henry.

Dea and I both turned to stare.

"Isn't that Zaid getting out of the white Maserati?" Henry pointed to a car in the distance.

And indeed, it was Zaid, holding a briefcase and closing the door to a white car. Next to him were two bodyguards in dark suits. The same ones we'd seen earlier, still mean-looking. They appeared to be coming in our direction, probably headed for the airport entrance.

"What do we do?" I asked, stunned at this turn of events.

All our planning was for nothing. I hadn't dared dream we'd have an opportunity like this.

"Dea, try to distract them while Robert and I take them by surprise. Take care of whoever is closest to you. We'll take care of the rest. Let's not do something which can't easily be explained," Henry said, then he disappeared between the parked cars.

I moved in the opposite direction and circled back to where I could easily see and get to Dea if something happened. I hadn't seen her reflection, but if her transformation was as convincing as mine, they wouldn't have a clue who she was.

Sitting, I waited with my heart pounding in my chest. Adrenaline coursed through me, getting my body ready for a fight. I didn't see them, but I could hear their steps coming closer and closer.

"Excuse me," I heard Dea say, "would it be possible for you to help me?"

I risked a glance and saw all three men had their heads turned toward her. Out of the corner of my eye, I saw Henry moving like a snake between the cars toward Zaid, and I did the same.

I threw caution to the wind and switched to a full sprint, preparing to tackle him. Obviously, he heard something because he quickly turned his head and saw me maybe four or five feet away from him. He must have had a weapon on him; I recognized when he shifted his weight to his left leg and then rotated his body. He was preparing to draw a gun with his right hand.

With his left hand out to stop me, I decided to change my line of attack. Instead of going for a tackle, I kept my knees bent, rotated my hips, and pivoted on my feet. I pushed off my left foot, holding my arm relaxed. My whole body turned, and I released an uppercut to his chin, tightening the fist the moment I felt the impact. His body was lifted off the ground and landed a couple of feet in front of me.

Raising my right leg, I prepared to kick, but he was already out.

I must have punched him harder than I thought.

I looked around to see if either Dea or Henry needed help, but they seemed to have the situation in hand.

The other bodyguard lay on the hood of another car. The impact with his head had cracked the windshield.

Henry had Zaid lying on the ground, and he had Zaid's briefcase in hand. He opened the locks.

"Here." Henry handed it to Dea. "Check the contents."

She pulled out not one but two stainless-steel tubes, closed her eyes, and then murmured a few unintelligible words.

A couple of seconds later, she nodded to Henry, and then we all headed toward the stolen car at a brisk pace.

Henry slowly pulled out of the parking lot and made his way to the access road, heading for the freeway.

My heart raced like a freight train. Even though I wished he would hurry, I understood he didn't want to raise suspicion. No one said anything, and I sensed we were all holding our breath—or, at least, I was holding my breath on behalf of everyone else.

"I can't believe we did it," I said when we merged with the traffic on the highway. "It was sheer luck we ran into them."

Henry shrugged, but by his look in the rearview mirror, I could tell he was pleased. "Well, I assume they left later than we estimated, or we might have taken a faster route than they did. It's also possible Zaid's house was just a location he used for transactions. Maybe he had to stop by another location to retrieve the second scroll."

"Do you think anyone saw us?" I completely forgot to check my surroundings, something I had to remember for the next time.

Even though the past couple of hours had been challenging, I should have kept a cool head. *I must remember the basic things like that.*

"It's unlikely," said Henry. "But even if they did, it doesn't matter. We didn't look like ourselves, and this car isn't tied to our names. By the time Zaid and his people wake up, we'll be far away."

"Speaking of far away," I said, "where are we going?"

"I know a place where we can ditch this car and take a taxi to our hotel. We should leave tonight. I don't want us to take any chances. I'll arrange with the pilots to set a flight plan for Ireland, and from there to DC." Henry stretched an arm over the passenger's side headrest and drove one-handed.

"Why Ireland?" I asked.

"Because we can't go to London. They may hold us for questioning. And we have some friends in Ireland." He turned off the highway and continued on a poorly lit road.

"Oh, that makes sense. By the way, may I remove it now?" I asked Dea, pointing at my face.

"Yes, you may. I've already removed mine." Her face showed no changes, alluring as the first time I'd met her.

I pulled up my T-shirt and started rubbing my forehead, the sweat from the fight helping it to come off effortlessly. Seconds later, Dea's dried drops of blood disappeared from my T-shirt.

Well, that's cool. I glanced at her, but she had a container open and was now holding one of the scrolls.

To my eyes, it looked like any other papyrus scroll I'd seen in shops or movies, with one exception. When I wasn't looking straight at it, there was a light barrier floating less than an inch above it. The light wasn't coming off the scroll. It was there above it like the light source enveloped the whole parchment.

Dea had her eyes closed, her brows furrowed in concentration.

I didn't want to disturb her, so I remained quiet and studied her face. Her skin was a flawless milky white, and she had high cheekbones, which gave her an ageless beauty.

With her eyes closed, her long and curled eyelashes were prominent. Her hair was straight, black, and long enough to reach her breasts. I would have continued admiring her, but she slowly opened her eyes, turned her head, and looked at me expectantly.

Soon, a warm smile stretched across her face, and I probably felt the same way a snowflake feels when a ray of sunshine caresses it, melting without a care in the world.

I was saved from replying by Henry, who pulled over and killed the engine.

"You missed a spot." She pointed to my forehead.

"Thanks." I started scrubbing.

"Much better now," she said with a radiant smile.

The three of us got out of the car, and I looked around, wondering where we were.

Hmm. The parking lot of a mall.

At the top of a building, some illuminated letters read Stars Centre. There were a bunch of known brand names next to it, and even this close to midnight, the mall was bursting with activity. There were many people nearby who were talking and smoking. Others were either shopping or returning to their cars with huge bags of clothes.

I couldn't stop myself from asking, "Are we here for shopping?"

Henry just shook his head. No one thought my question was funny.

I followed him and Dea and headed toward a long line of white taxis. Henry approached one of the drivers, and I overheard the name of our hotel, the Marriott. After a short negotiation, he signaled for Dea and me to get in the car.

Dea and I kept quiet the whole way, leaving the conversation to Henry.

I didn't understand what they were talking about. However, the driver seemed entertained. He kept laughing and slapping the steering wheel every couple of minutes, like Henry was telling some hilarious jokes.

It was staggering how Henry could compartmentalize everything so easily. Maybe it was something that came with age.

A few minutes into our ride, Dea gently took my hand and closed her eyes. I wondered how much power she'd used to stop a knife in midair, break through a wall, partially collapse a building, heal me, change my appearance, and subdue one of the bodyguards, but she must have been tired. I knew I was exhausted. I had used whatever reserves of energy I had taking down the other bodyguard in the airport parking lot.

My mind went back to what had happened at the house.

Why were those hashashins there? Did they come for me, us, or the scrolls? And why so many?

I had no answers, just more questions, and I was too tired to develop a plausible scenario. I needed to sleep.

"I figure we can check out in thirty or forty minutes. Is it okay with everyone?" Henry asked after we got out of the taxi. Both Dea and I agreed, and we all went to our separate rooms to get ready.

Back in my room, after a quick shower, I leaned on the bed and was faced with a dilemma.

Do I keep the same jeans on or put on the ones I wore during the flight from DC to London.

I was surprised to see there wasn't a drop of blood on the ones I was wearing and realized whatever Dea had done effectively cleaned all the blood off my clothes. I had to learn that spell.

Bloodstains are incredibly stubborn to wash out.

So much happened so quickly, I hadn't even had time to unpack anything since arriving in Egypt a few hours earlier.

I looked through the hotel window with regret. When we left Washington on Tuesday morning, I'd thought I would have a chance to do some sightseeing, maybe even go to a museum or two and spend some time with Dea. Well, I did spend Tuesday night with her, with me passed out on a hotel bed.

Now a new country and a new room, still no sightseeing, and without Dea. I sighed. Nothing on this trip had turned out how I imagined it would. At least I found out one new thing.

Hashashins are everywhere. And I didn't have to join the CIA to travel the world to find out.

It would have been cool, though, if they saw what I did today, but I knew this wasn't something I could talk about. We assaulted and stole someone's possessions, after all.

This was the first time I didn't feel sorry for the victims, especially the big brute who threw me around and gave Dea those dirty looks. Honestly, I wished I'd had the opportunity to punch him in the nose at least once.

I studied my hands. A slight tremor shook them. This night had worn me out. I took a deep breath and exhaled slowly. The bed was so comfortable, and for a moment, I closed my eyes.

Panicked, I opened them immediately, unsure if only a moment had passed or an entire hour. I got up, fearing I'd fall asleep again, and I put on a T-shirt, grabbed the luggage, and headed to the front of the hotel.

The lobby was mostly empty, so I took a seat on one of the couches and turned on my phone.

The past several days had been so unbelievably busy I hadn't even had time to miss it. Besides the regular emails from our automated monitoring systems, there was nothing, so I checked if there were any new developments about what had happened in London. The video on YouTube wasn't available anymore, but other than that, nothing new.

I was glad no one had published our photos in a newspaper under a title like "Most Wanted."

Finding no other updates, I checked the local websites, at least the ones I could read. Most of them were in Arabic, but some had an English version too. I was going through the third website when I heard Henry talking, and when I looked up, I saw him chatting with the front desk attendant. He was wearing a new suit, this time a dark one, and I marveled that he'd had time to buy a new set of clothes.

Distracted by Henry's clothes, I hadn't heard or felt when someone sat on the couch next to me. It was Dea, who was searching for something in her purse. She was wearing a white blouse with a blue blazer and bright red slim jeans—a simple but elegant combination.

Apparently, everyone but me came well prepared for this trip. And I thought my backpack held more stuff than their entire luggage combined—silly me.

"Ready?" I heard a voice saying, and when I gazed up, I saw Henry towering above me.

"Ah, yes," I said, a bit startled.

"Okay, I'll have the car pick us up in five minutes. I've talked to Lydia, and she arranged for us to fly directly to Washington, DC. We won't stop in Dublin, so no sightseeing this time, I'm afraid."

I nodded without saying anything. I would have liked to

visit Dublin, but on the other hand, I was relieved I'd get home sooner and finally get some sleep.

Minutes later, Henry, Dea, and I were on our way in the same white SUV we'd arrived in. This time, I reached out for Dea's hand, and she gave me a surprised but delighted look.

She leaned her head on my shoulder. The warmth of her body spread through me, relaxing, focusing my thoughts.

The SUV arrived at the airport faster than I would have thought. Déjà vu.

Whether because I'd managed to get some rest during the drive to the airport, or because Dea was sitting next to me, or maybe she had cast a spell to make me feel less tired and cranky, but my head felt clearer.

Unfortunately, my heartbeat started picking up its pace, and all sorts of thoughts and worries ran through my head.

What if someone saw us in Egypt? What if Zaid is still at the airport and wants his scrolls back? Had he recognized us?

By now, he probably knew what had happened at his house and could assume we had all escaped, mainly because two men and a woman mugged him. Even though we didn't look the same, I wasn't even sure he remembered us. I imagined the conversation he'd had with his other buyer wasn't too amicable, and I assumed he'd promised to find us and reclaim the scrolls.

For a moment, I thought of asking if we should disguise ourselves again—a stupid idea. We wouldn't match our passport photos.

Hmm. Can Dea or Henry put a spell on the airport clerks and workers?

"Don't worry. Everything will be fine," Dea whispered in my ear.

She probably sensed I was tense, something I'm sure wasn't hard for her to do with her abilities.

"In a short while," she said, "we'll be in the air."

It turned out she was right. The security check was easy,

they didn't ask any questions, and soon we were on board the Gulfstream G550 jet we'd used the day before.

Since it was already past midnight, I settled into a comfortable chair.

In a short time, we were up in the air—the Cairo lights shining beneath us. Up here, the stars were sprinkled over the cloudless sky, revealing the beauty and immensity of the universe. My thoughts slowed down, and the day's stress and fatigue caught up with me, helping me transition to a dark, quiet, and dreamless sleep.

14

THE PLANE WAS LANDING. I had slept for more than ten hours straight.

Feeling somewhat refreshed, I glanced out the window at a cloudy sky and the droplets of rain running over the Plexiglas screen.

This time, the landing was shaky. The wind made the plane tremble and screech. Once safely on the ground, I sat up, stretched, then headed to the restroom. The aircraft taxied toward a private hangar, and once I'd answered nature's call, I decided to see if there was anything left to eat because I was ravenous.

An image of scrambled eggs and bacon popped into my mind, and my mouth immediately started watering. I walked by Dea and Henry, may have mumbled "good morning," and found a platter with some cold cuts of ham and roast beef along with slices of cheese. Next to it were croissants, other pastries, and another platter with pieces of fruit: strawberries, pineapple rings, melon balls, and bananas.

The entire time it took for the jet to taxi to the hangar, I satisfied my hunger and, in the process, finished all the croissants, half of the meat platter, and most of the other pastries and pieces of fruit.

"Feeling better now?" Dea watched me with an amused smile on her face.

Henry, who was further away, stood near the cockpit, talking with the steward.

"Yeah, sorry about that. How long have you been watching me?"

"Oh, I don't know, since you woke up, maybe?"

"Er . . . I was hungry. How was the flight? I must have been tired because I slept the whole way."

I tried to steer the conversation away from my gluttony and made a mental note to ask Dea later if my appetite had anything to do with her healing me at Zaid's house. There were a lot more things I needed to ask her, especially about London and how I'd used magic.

"It was okay, quite smooth, actually, and we slept most of the time. By the way, Lydia texted me to say she left your apartment a couple of hours ago. And Ariel is all set until you get back."

"I'm glad to hear that, thank you. By the way, what's the time? And what day is it?" With so many time zone changes, I had completely lost track of the days of the week.

"Today is Thursday, and right now, it's getting close to 7:30 in the morning," answered Dea. "So, what are your plans for today?"

Even though she had asked this question casually, she seemed interested in my answer. I didn't need any more physical rest. However, I needed to relax mentally because all the events had taxed my nerves during the past few days. There had been too many close calls, and I felt this whole trip created more questions rather than answers. I needed some time to sort them in my head. On the other hand, I wanted to see Dea, talk to her, and be with her.

"I don't know exactly. I assume I can skip work today?" I raised my eyebrows.

I wondered if I was asking permission because she was the daughter of the company's owner or because she was my girlfriend. Probably both. Probably both. In answer to my question, she smiled and nodded.

"Good. In that case, I'll buy some groceries, because I know I'll be hungry again soon. Then, I'll relax for a few hours, and maybe I can see you later? I know we've only known each other for less than a week, even if we've been through a lot, but I want to get to know more about you."

"I would love that." The light in her eyes danced like the sun's rays reflected on the ocean beside a sandy beach in the morning. Or maybe it was my imagination, and I felt the need for a vacation.

Soon, the plane came to a stop at the assigned gate, and the three of us said goodbye to the crew. Since none of us had any other luggage, we all headed toward the customs checkpoint.

Dea and Henry went first. Everything seemed to be routine, and when my turn arrived, I got the same kinds of questions and treatment. However, before the CBP officer could hand me back my passport, he received a message on his computer screen. I could see the reflection in his glasses but couldn't read what it said. Out of the corner of my eye, I saw two people in gray suits heading in my direction.

"Sir, please wait one moment," the officer said.

"Is there something wrong?" I raised my eyebrows, hoping my face showed total innocence.

He didn't get a chance to reply before the two people in gray suits were next to me.

One of the suits said, "I'm Special Agent Coleman, and this is Special Agent Muller with the FBI. Sir, please come with us."

Coleman was an older guy, somewhere between forty and

fifty years old, with short black hair and gray streaks at the temples. His skin was dark, and he had a curved, pointy nose like a hawk's beak and black, piercing eyes. Muller was a woman about two inches shorter than Coleman, close to thirty, with brown eyes and blond hair pulled into a ponytail. She reached out and took my passport from the customs officer's hand.

"Can I help you with something?" My heart pounded wildly.

"We have a few questions. Please follow us," said Agent Coleman. He motioned for me to follow him, and I noticed Agent Muller moved behind me.

I looked around to see where Dea and Henry were and saw three customs officers encircled them. Henry was talking and seemed to be explaining something, but Dea was looking my way, phone in hand.

Our eyes met, and she mouthed, *Don't worry. Don't say*—I didn't get to see anything else because we turned a corner, and Agent Coleman opened the door to a room with a table and chairs all around.

"Please have a seat." He indicated one of the chairs at the table, the one facing the door.

"Will this take long?" I sat in the chair and dropped my bag next to it.

Agent Muller moved behind me, and Agent Coleman lowered himself into the empty seat in front of me. Neither of them responded to my question.

When I had wanted to join the CIA after college, I read about interrogation tactics, and I'd even imagined capturing a hashashin and interrogating him. From what I remembered, the person who sits in front of you plays the good cop and tries to establish a rapport with you. Having someone else behind you has two objectives. One is to act as a witness, and the other is to make you uncomfortable, to put stress on you, so you'll let your guard down.

I took deep breaths to calm myself, and I could feel my heart rate returning to a healthy level.

"Would you like something to drink or eat?" Agent Coleman held my gaze.

"No, thank you." In my mind, various scenarios were taking shape.

There could be only two possibilities. They knew what happened in Cairo or what had happened in London. I hoped it was about London because there, none of us did anything wrong.

"Do you know why you're here, Mr. Connor?" Coleman's voice and demeanor appeared to be reasonable, like a father advising his son.

"I haven't the foggiest," I remembered the advice a former martial arts training partner, who was a lawyer, gave me.

He had said, 'You should never speak with the police without having a lawyer physically present. They may try to persuade you to tell them anything, or they may say they want to hear your side of the story, but in the end, they will arrest you no matter what you say. Also, if they ask if you know why you're being questioned, you don't.'

Before I gathered up my courage to ask for a lawyer, I thought about what Dea had said—don't say anything. Since she was on the phone when they took me away, I assumed she was getting us a lawyer, probably the best one out there. So I tried to stall for time and see if I could get more information from them, which was highly unlikely. They were trained interrogators, while I had only watched some TV shows.

"Is it true you were in London two days ago?" Coleman asked.

"Yes."

"And yesterday you flew to Cairo?"

"Yes."

"Can you tell us what happened in London?"

"I don't remember, and I'm actually quite tired after all the travel of the past couple of days," I said with a fake yawn.

Only two days have passed? It felt more like two weeks with all the excitement and near-death experiences.

"You don't remember what happened two days ago?" Coleman gave me a suspicious look, and I shrugged.

"Are you saying you don't remember being at the Golden Lion Pub on Tuesday evening?" Muller said from behind me, making me jump a bit.

I turned to look at her, pursed my lips, and said, "If you say so. What's this about?"

Muller folded her arms across her chest and watched me intently.

"Does the name Akil Razak means anything to you, Mr. Connor?" Coleman asked.

I turned to face Coleman. "Should it?"

"On Tuesday night around eleven at the Golden Lion Pub in London, Akil Razak was murdered. Multiple witnesses and CCTV cameras have identified you and your friends. You were seen talking to Mr. Razak, and we only want to know what you talked about and whether you saw anything," said Agent Coleman with a flat intonation.

This wasn't good. Witnesses can be mistaken, but they had us on camera. However, they should clearly see we didn't do anything wrong. We sat at a table, drank a beer, and later found him stabbed in the restroom. I could tell them Akil was a friend of Henry's, they wanted to catch up, but there was one thing nagging me—why was the FBI interested in a crime committed in a different country? I weighed the options and decided to ask them why they were so fascinated about what I did in London. It shouldn't give anything away.

"I'm curious about one thing. Why is the FBI interested in something that happened in the UK?"

For a second, Agent Coleman didn't say anything. He just

watched me—but I'm sure with his training, he could see things I wasn't aware of.

"Because Mr. Razak was financing terrorist cells, in case you didn't know," Agent Muller said from behind me. I decided not to turn my head this time and continued looking at Agent Coleman. "And we have intel some of those cells are plotting an attack on US soil," she continued.

Oh boy! What had I gotten myself into?

It was one thing to have a contact who was an art appraiser, but a totally different thing to meet with someone financing terrorist attacks. All of a sudden, everything had become much, much more complicated. If I would have worked for the CIA, now was the time when Agent Coleman would receive a phone call, and some agents would enter the room to get me out of this mess. Unfortunately, I wasn't.

Before I started to worry about avoiding answering any questions directly, the door opened, and two people entered the room. The first appeared to be in his late forties or early fifties. He had short gray hair with a hint of black at the top of his head, a circle beard, and steel-gray eyes. He was wearing an expensive-looking navy blue suit, a white shirt, and a red tie with yellow and blue stripes. Behind him was a taller, younger, lanky guy, probably in his late thirties, with black curly hair, black eyes, and a bit of stubble like he hadn't shaved in a couple of days. He was wearing a similar suit with a gray tie and was carrying a briefcase in his right hand.

"What are the charges?" the older man asked.

Agent Coleman stood and faced them. "Who are you?"

"My name is Wayne Mitchell, and I'm Mr. Connor's attorney," Mitchell came across as a no-nonsense kind of guy.

However, the moment I heard the name, I realized who he was. If I could have dug a hole and crawled into it, I would have done so. This wasn't the way I'd envisioned my first meeting with Dea's father, sitting in an interrogation room, questioned by the FBI. "What are the charges?" he asked again, politely but firmly.

"No charges *yet*," said Coleman, with an emphasis on the last word. "We're asking for some clarification regarding Mr. Connor's whereabouts on Tuesday night."

"I'm sure you are," replied Wayne. "However, my clients have all had a long flight and a couple of busy days during their business trip, and they need some rest. They will be available for questioning afterward—with a lawyer present, of course." His lips curled into a half-smile, like a lawyer who had found a flaw in an argument. "Are we done here?" Without waiting for an answer, Wayne motioned for me to stand and follow him.

"We will have to seize Mr. Connor's passport while we continue the investigation. And we will need your clients to come in to make a statement," said Agent Muller, definitely not happy with how things had changed.

"Not a problem. You can coordinate with my assistant, Maximillian," said Wayne, gesturing toward the lanky man accompanying him.

I stood, got my bag, and without another word, followed Wayne out the door, in case the FBI agents changed their minds.

"How are you holding up?" Wayne patted me on the shoulder. "Sorry, we haven't been properly introduced. I'm Wayne Mitchell, Dea's father."

"Nice to meet you, Mr. Mitchell, and sorry about the circumstances," I said with a smile, offering my hand.

He grinned and shook my hand; he had a good firm grip, and I liked it. "Please call me Wayne, and don't worry about it."

I continued moving toward what I had hoped was the exit, but soon I heard rapid footsteps, and when I turned my head, I saw Maximillian running toward us.

"I left them our details, and they said they'd contact us tomorrow," said Maximillian.

"Good, now let's get you out of here." Wayne resumed walking.

Around the corner, I saw both Dea and Henry, this time, without any people around them.

Dea gave me a questioning glance, and I smiled to let her know everything was all right. Henry was looking directly at Maximillian, and when we stopped, he moved to his side, and Dea came closer to me and grabbed my hand, probably to reassure me as much as herself.

"Max says they'll be in touch with us tomorrow." Wayne sneered. "We shall see about that, but right now, let's get to the car. We can talk more on the way." Then he gave us a meaningful look and said, "Don't discuss anything until we're outside the airport."

The moment we stepped outside, a detail of four men dressed in suits packing heat—judging by the bulges in their jackets—fell into a protective formation around us. I thought I recognized one of them from when I first visited Dea's house, but before I had time for a better look, the security detail ushered all of us to a spacious black limo.

The driver was waiting for us outside the vehicle, scanning the area, and he held the door open. Dea got in first, followed by Wayne, Henry, and Max. I was the last one in and saw our escort moving toward a black SUV waiting nearby.

The only spot left was next to Dea. We ended up sitting close to each other, and I was glad—feeling her close, sensing the heat radiating by her body, brought me a sense of comfort. Opposite of where I sat was Wayne, Max, and Henry.

"Oh, they seized Robert's passport and now plan to hold it while they continue their investigation," said Wayne. "Do you all have your passports?"

Both Dea and Henry nodded in agreement.

"Good, it means Robert was their only target. They probably thought he'd be the weakest link, and I'm sure they were afraid of a lawsuit otherwise. We'll see what we can do to get your passport back," Wayne continued, looking at me. "It's temporary. They can keep it until they finish their investigation, but I'll have to look into it. We arrived home yesterday evening"—he pointed to himself and Maximillian—"and I've only heard a few things from Lydia and Candice about the attacks and your trip, but I would like to hear your story as well."

The man had the expectant look of a lawyer cross-examining a witness. I guessed he was looking for details Candice or Lydia might have missed.

"Where should we start?" Dea asked.

"Well, I've been gone since Friday morning, so let's start from there." Wayne glanced at me.

"In a nutshell, Friday evening, I was with Mom, Lydia, Alyssa, and Henry at the club," said Dea. "I was attacked there by an invisible assassin, and Robert saved me. He calls them hashashins."

She turned to look at me for confirmation, and I nodded to let her know she said it correctly.

"Then," she continued to speak, "on Saturday, we were attacked again at the house while we were sleeping. There were two of them, and one got close enough to trip the wards we had in front of our bedroom, draining all their magic, but Robert saved us again."

Wayne gave me a curious look, probably checking to see if I was surprised by Dea mentioning wards and magic. Even though I didn't show it, I was surprised.

And here I thought it was a land mine.

I should have realized a mine wouldn't have worked like that—it would have blasted everything in its radius. But I didn't remember seeing any damage to the walls.

"Then Mom and Henry did some research and found a trace of some old scrolls linked to these attacks. Robert has fought the assassins before, so we invited him to join us. On Tuesday, we took a flight to London, where we met an old friend of Henry's, Akil Razak, at a pub. He gave us the contact details of someone in Egypt, Tarek Khalil. However, minutes later, someone murdered him, and we don't know who it was."

"Another invisible assassin?" Wayne asked.

"We don't think so. Robert can sense when they're around." Dea turned to face me.

I shook my head. "No, I don't think a hashashin did it. I would have felt it."

Dea held her father's gaze. "We then left the pub because we didn't want to wait for the police. On our way to the hotel, a van almost ran us down—intentionally—but Robert saw it first and alerted us. We managed to stop it before it ran us over, and that's when Robert's power manifested itself. He channeled it through me when I conjured a force wall."

This was something I hadn't heard before, and it got my full attention. I had no idea what had happened or what I'd done, and it felt good to get some answers finally. Also, I was glad she didn't mention I almost fainted.

"Afterward, he almost fainted but managed not to pass out until we got to the hotel."

And there it is in all it's glory . . . how I can't handle a bit of magic.

Wayne must have seen my embarrassed expression. "Don't worry, son, that's how it is the first time, or at least that's how it was with Dea."

I glanced at her, and I noticed her cheeks reddened.

"The next day, we flew to Cairo," she continued. "We met Tarek there, who drove us to the person who had the scroll. Zaid is his name. I think he has people stealing artifacts from archaeological sites, and then he sells them on the black market."

"So, he was looking to move the artifact?" He held his daughter's gaze.

"He already had a buyer, but Henry convinced him to sell it to us. After we paid him." She exhaled a long pause. "He must have drugged us when he served us tea, and it was something powerful, especially since it worked so quickly."

"So, you paid, and then he drugged you?" The muscles in his jaw pulled taut over his smooth skin. "Then what?"

"He also took back the scroll to sell it to his original buyer. Robert woke up before I did, and they interrogated him. They seemed to think we killed Akil. Then at least three hashashins attacked the house."

"Three?" His glance slid my way.

"Yes. And I woke up when one of them was about to kill Robert. I created a hole in a wall using the hashashin's body, but it didn't kill him. I'm not sure if they have some protection against force magic or not. I didn't have time to check."

Okay, note to self: Dea's magic is called force magic, and the hashashins are possibly protected against it.

Do they naturally have this protection, or is someone else helping them?

"I created another hole for us to escape, and when they started coming after us, I collapsed the ceiling on top of them. I'm not sure if that stopped them for good or not— probably not," Dea admitted, and she bit her lip in frustration.

Dea shot a glance my way, and I wondered if this form of cross-examination happened often.

"Henry got a car," she said, "and we decided to head to the airport, where Zaid was supposed to make the transaction. Fortunately, we found him getting out of his car. We took his briefcase, left him and his bodyguards unconscious, then we found two scrolls inside: the one we had bought earlier and another."

"Do you know anything about them?" His attention never left Dea.

"They must have powerful protective enchantments, because I can feel the magic contained inside. When we got them, we returned to the hotel after first abandoning the car and taking a cab. Once there, we arranged for the flight back. Soon, we were on a plane, and here we are now."

Everyone was silent, processing all the information.

Dea had summarized everything well, and I was glad she did it. I got the chance to see things from her perspective, things I'd missed, and things I wasn't even aware of. She wasn't the type of person to talk about her family and whatever plans they had, which made sense. I was still a stranger to them, or at least to most of them.

"Do you know who the other buyer was?" Wayne asked.

Dea shrugged and looked at Henry, who shook his head. He was holding Max's hand in his, and his eyes were pained, most probably by the death of his friend.

"Do you think there's a connection between Akil's murder and the car attack in London?" Wayne continued.

Good question. I hadn't considered it, but after hearing Wayne mention it, I found various possibilities coming to mind.

If there was a connection, then it meant whoever was behind the attacks might have had an interest in the artifact as well. Or maybe another witch or a coven already had the information and wanted to silence Akil so that he wouldn't tell anyone else.

The three of us being there was a coincidence he or she capitalized on. And the only other person I was aware of who knew about the scroll was the other buyer. But it didn't mean no one else knew.

"I don't think we've considered this possibility," replied Henry, after reflecting on the suggestion.

"I think Wayne is suggesting whoever killed Akil did it so he wouldn't give us information about the scroll. There is a small chance the only other person who knew about the scroll was the other buyer," I said, looking at Wayne questioningly. "And when I say knew about the scroll, I mean they *knew* it was a magical scroll."

"Very good," said Wayne with a grin. "Of course, there's a possibility other people may have the information, but let's leave that aside for the moment. What intrigues me is how the London police were able to make the connection between Akil's murder and you in such a short time. Then, in just a day, they were able to pinpoint precisely where you were and involve the FBI. I think someone might have tipped them off and influenced the investigation process to have the FBI stop you when you arrived and possibly thoroughly search your bags. By the way, what happened to the scrolls?"

My heartbeat spiked. I completely forgot Dea had them in her bag, and for sure, the border patrol checked her stuff.

"I have them in my bag." Dea touched her luggage.

I turned and looked at her, astonished. Something had been bugging me for the past couple of days. All the frustration I'd had during this entire trip came crashing down on me, and I couldn't stop myself.

"Quick question," I said in an exasperated tone. "How is it you have room in your carry-on luggage? I've seen you wear different things every day: new shoes, pants, blouses, jackets, sometimes multiple times a day, and now, you have two metal cylinders stuck in there too. No way you could fit all that in, plus, I assume you have other things, like a makeup kit and such. I don't have any space left in mine, and although mine's larger, I definitely didn't bring anything like the number of clothes you did."

"Oh," she said sheepishly. "It's enchanted. Henry's is too."

"What do you mean, enchanted?" I asked, taken aback.

"They can keep much more inside than you think is possible just by looking at them," Dea clarified. "And if someone were to check the bag without the proper incantation, they would only see an empty bag, or whatever you decided to put there," she continued, anticipating my next question.

"Nice," was all I could think of to say.

"I'm sorry, I didn't tell you sooner. I forgot, but I'll make you a promise. We can work together and make one for you if you want."

Of course, I wanted one.

And in a split-second, I imagined all sorts of uses for it. I could have my two laptops with me all the time, along with headphones, an emergency kit, tools, knives, and so much more. It would be the ultimate backpack. Not to mention another spell I needed to learn.

"Were the hashashins there for you or the scroll?" Wayne asked, stroking his beard.

His question, however, brought me back to reality so fast, I got whiplash.

Everyone fell silent, and they all turned toward me, expectantly. I guessed I was the one who had the most experience in dealing with them.

My mind started racing again, analyzing different scenarios. We had one hashashin come for us at Zaid's house, and after we escaped, two more joined. I wondered if there were any others, but even so, it meant they weren't there for us, or maybe we were a secondary objective. Otherwise, they would have dealt with us first.

I remembered the fight we had at the house. The hashashin didn't spend time making sure it killed Henry. It went up the stairs, for Dea.

"I think they were there mainly after the scroll or scrolls," I said, still thinking. "I'm not sure if they were supposed to kill everyone in the house or if we were a secondary objective for them."

"I see," said Wayne. "If your assumption is correct, then this means we have two players. One is Zaid's buyer, and the other is whoever sent the assassins."

Initially, I'd thought the hashashins conducted random attacks because I couldn't find any pattern, but since meeting Dea, I'd started wondering if someone with magical powers might be helping them. But if that was true, then a person or group was either helping or controlling them. The implications could be huge. It meant an individual was giving orders to have people killed. And it meant a person in charge ordered the murders, my mom, my dad, and my grandmother. And that *someone* would pay for it.

Massive rage built within me. My entire body went rigid, and my hands clenched into tight fists. It was the rage I'd thought left me after my grandmother had died. It was when I'd had promised myself no one else would be hurt by them —*not on my watch.*

A cold calm had replaced the rage, or at least, that's what I'd thought, but now, I realized the anger was still there, buried beneath my desire to protect everyone else from them.

My dark side had resurfaced now, more potent than ever.

Dea touched my arm. And like a breeze cooling me on a summer's day, my body relaxed, and the anger burning inside me dissipated, at least temporarily.

Turning my head, I met her concerned look. She searched my face, then looked into my eyes, as if to determine if I was all right, to understand what had happened.

I gave her a quick smile to let her know I was better now, and her touch had helped. Then I looked around at everyone else and saw they were all watching me.

Henry had a knowing look, but Wayne and Max seemed surprised by my reaction. I guessed they weren't aware of my history with the hashashins. Just then, the car slowly rolled to a stop, saving me from having to explain myself.

"Ah, I think we've arrived at your house," said Wayne.

"It's more like an apartment complex," I corrected him but realized maybe I shouldn't have. It wasn't polite. "Thank you for the ride." I grabbed my backpack, opened the door, and stepped out of the vehicle.

As I turned, I heard Dea say, "Wait a second." She got out of the car and closed the door behind her. "I can't let you go without saying thank you."

Without giving me time to react, she planted a gentle kiss with a taste of strawberry on my lips.

"Er, I have to thank you too," I said, a tad disoriented. "You've saved my life twice already."

She smiled, but it was a sad one. "I wish it hadn't been necessary, but you're important to me, and I don't want to lose you. Promise me you'll be careful." She looked at me, studying my face intently.

Nothing else came to mind, so I replied, "I promise."

"Good," she said with a more cheerful look. "Can we see each other later today?"

"Sure, if you want to. I'd like that very much."

"Perfect! You want to meet at the club around nine?"

"It's a date," I said with a grin.

"A second date," she corrected.

Then, with another quick kiss, she vanished into the car, leaving me to watch the limo drive away, followed by a black SUV.

15

Fourteen pounds of hair assaulted me, trying to trip me in the apartment.

"Hello to you too, Ariel." Crouching, I rubbed under her chin.

She didn't like it when I held her in my arms, but she loved to lie on the floor for a good, solid belly scratching. She was kind of like a dog that way.

"Did you miss me? Did you? Oh, yes, you did." I caressed her chin and around her fluffy head, and she loved it.

She followed me underfoot to the kitchen, where I checked her food and water.

"So, Lydia did her job, huh?"

Ariel had three new bowls with food and two with water.

"Looks like someone was spoiled while I was gone."

It didn't take me long to unpack. I didn't have one of those enchanted, bottomless bags yet. Once done, I took a shower, and when I checked the time after I finished, I saw it was only 10:00 a.m.

It looked like I had the whole day available until my date tonight. I briefly considered going to work, but it was the last thing I cared about right then. However, out of habit, I checked my emails to see if there was anything urgent.

There were messages from Steven and Mark and an out-of-office from Brad. He was apparently busy working with the people from Mitchell & Associates Ventures on the acquisition details. It looked like we were supposed to receive the money tomorrow.

That reminded me to go to the bank and get some cash. After being questioned by the FBI, I thought it better to have some money in my pocket, just in case they froze my account for whatever reason.

I trusted Dea's dad, but you don't mess with the FBI.

The only reason I hadn't applied for a job with them straight out of college was because I wanted to travel outside the country. Plus, they weren't as cool as the CIA. Otherwise, their core mission was exactly what I wanted to do: to protect people.

I understood the two special agents were just doing their job. But the way they did it chipped away at my admiration for them. I knew I hadn't done anything wrong besides maybe stealing the second artifact from Zaid, but he kind of deserved it after he drugged and presumably tried to kill us. However, it was better not to leave things to chance.

If what Wayne suggested was true, someone could influence the London police and possibly even the FBI. They could make my life difficult—borderline miserable, in fact.

My whole life, I'd tried to stay on the right side of the law, and for the most part, I did, if we didn't count the hashashins. I hadn't thought of them as real people, but now I wasn't so sure. It wasn't fair if the FBI or others falsely accused me of something I didn't do. But then, life wasn't equitable, no matter how much I wanted it to be.

What would be even worse was if Henry knew Akil had ties to terrorist cells. Of course, that's assuming Agent

Muller and Coleman were telling the truth. They might have been trying the old divide-and-conquer technique.

But if Henry knows, is he the only one from the coven involved. Or are there others?

I shuddered to think what a terrorist cell with access to magic could do. And I could have played this guessing game for a while, but it was a dead-end without more information. Someone once said it's a mistake to make assumptions when you don't have all the facts, and I definitely didn't want to make a mistake, not with something like this.

Instead of staying home and brooding, I went to the bank. It had stopped raining, and a few rays of sun speared through the clouds, better to walk and enjoy the fresh air.

On my way home, my stomach started to rumble again. I needed real food, not the stuff I had on the airplane. In the past few days, I'd eaten more than usual, and the travel, all the crazy events, being close to dying twice, had increased my appetite.

I knew of an excellent steak house nearby, which was highly recommended by my martial arts instructor. When I entered, the restaurant was mostly empty, and I asked the server for a table near the window. I grew up on a farm, and far as I could remember, I always liked to watch nature do its thing, unimpeded. So, I took a seat and looked outside the window. The wind rustled the tree branches, and a squirrel climbed down from a tree. She was alert, eyes darting everywhere, making sure no one saw her.

"Are you ready to order, sir?"

Startled, I gazed at the menu I was holding. "Er . . . I'll have a steak, well done, please. Does it come with fries?"

"Yes, sir," the waiter said. "Anything to drink?"

"No, just water, thank you."

With a nod, he left, and less than thirty minutes later, I had a glass of water with ice. My throat was parched. I was bemused it took them so much time to bring a glass of water. I took a sip and closed my eyes, feeling the liquid coating my throat on its way to my stomach.

Oh, so cold and refreshing.

"I thought you were dead," said a voice I knew, and it woke me up from my reverie.

"Hello, Sensei," I said.

He took the opposite seat. Andrew was a retired US Navy SEAL, and I'd started training with him after moving to DC a few years ago. He had short black hair, bushy eyebrows, black piercing eyes that had seen too many terrible things, and a rock-solid beard. Maybe a bit on the fluffy side. But I wouldn't have dared tell him, not unless I wanted to be a punching bag next time I went training.

"Hello, Robert. I haven't seen you in a while. Everything okay?"

"Yes, sir, I was just busy with work." I knew it was a lame excuse, but it was the truth.

"If you want, you always find the time."

I shrugged, too embarrassed to say anything else. But then the waiter swooped in, saving me.

The server brought a heavenly looking steak, with fries on the side, and my mouth watered instantly.

"Anything else you need, sir?"

"No, this is perfect, thanks."

With a nod, he left.

"This is one of the few places where they serve good steaks here in Washington," said Andrew. "Did I tell you about that time in Iraq when we spent a whole afternoon trying to find a place where they served steak? We found one, but when they brought it, the meat had so many spices, we couldn't even taste it."

I shook my head. It was the first time he had shared a story about his time in Iraq. His deployment was overseas, but he had never provided any specifics until today.

"Stop by the dojo, and I'll tell you all about it. By the way, did you receive that important call you were telling me about?"

It took me a few seconds to realize he was asking me about the CIA and the interview I had with them almost two years ago.

"No, sir, I didn't," I answered truthfully, hoping he didn't notice the pang of regret in my voice.

"Keep your hopes up. You never know what the future holds." He stood and offered his hand, which I shook. "I trust I'll see you soon, son. There's still much you don't know." He left, leaving me to wonder what he meant.

I hate it when people are cryptic.

The steak had a perfect combination of flavor, tenderness, and juiciness but didn't manage to distract me from Andrew's last words.

What didn't I know?

Soon I was walking back to my apartment complex, but as I approached the entrance to my building, the gentle purr of a car engine grabbed my attention.

"Mr. Connor." I stopped and turned around, conscious I had a fat envelope containing several thousand dollars in cash.

In front of me was a black SUV with the passenger window rolled down, and inside was an older gentleman with a head of hair that was mostly white with black strands, enough so I couldn't say how old he was. He had round glasses, a pointy nose, and sharp blue eyes, and he was smiling at me. It wasn't a fake smile or a happy smile. It was an *'I have the power, and I own you'* kind of smile.

"Do you have a couple of minutes for a quick chat?" The man asked politely.

The door opened, and the front passenger, somewhere around thirty, stepped out. He had one of those faces you immediately forget. He was of medium height with a medium build and was wearing jeans and a brown leather jacket. Without saying a word, he moved to hold the door and motioned for me to get in, his attention focused on my movements.

None of the men seem to be FBI agents. Otherwise, I would have seen someone flashing a badge. And they didn't scream cop either. But there was something in the way they carried themselves and how their eyes took in the surroundings that told me they were part of an organization.

They didn't appear threatening. However, this didn't mean they weren't dangerous. Though I guessed if they wanted to hurt me, they could have done it without being so polite.

"Andrew says you haven't been to his dojo in a while. He also says there's no one else there who can give him a good workout," the older gentleman said as if sensing my indecision.

This took me by surprise because it was precisely what my sensei had told me multiple times.

Knowing about Andrew's background, I decided this group was somehow connected to the government, so I shrugged and got in.

The guy with the leather jacket closed the door but remained outside. I could see him through the tinted glass, looking up and down the street.

In the driver's seat was a younger-looking man wearing sunglasses and a black suit. Based on his haircut and build, he seemed to be military.

"Very nice to meet you, Mr. Connor. I've heard so much about you," the older-looking gentleman said.

"Well, you have me at a disadvantage, then. I don't know your name." A fake smile covered my mouth.

"Oh, of course, where are my manners? You may call me Mr. White."

"Walter White, by any chance?"

"No, you watch too much television, Mr. Connor," he said with a chuckle. "I wanted to get in touch with you because I think we may be able to help each other."

This concerned me. I didn't think Mr. White needed help setting up a website or fixing some computers. And the only other thing I was good at was fighting invisible assassins, but I was sure it wasn't what he had in mind either. They didn't know about hashashins. Or did they!

"What do you have in mind?"

"Well, your skills a couple of days ago didn't go unnoticed, and you managed to impress some of my people. They convinced me we should have a chat, and they're the type of people who aren't easily impressed." He fixed me with a suspicious look. "Would you mind if I asked you how you acquired those skills? And I'm not talking about your work in IT."

I was taken aback. They were watching me.

When? How? What do they know?

I pondered what and how much I should tell him for a few seconds.

"More specifically, I'm talking about Zaid Ansari and how you managed to kill twelve of his men."

For a brief moment, I wondered what he was talking about.

Ah, he attributed the hashashins' work to me.

"Why do you think it was me?" I tried to buy some time to come up with a plausible story.

"Come, now, Mr. Connor, are you telling me Henry M. Wright, the VP of finance at Mitchell & Associates Ventures, and the daughter of Mrs. Candice Mitchell, the CEO of the company who acquired your start-up, were able to dispatch twelve trained mercenaries and terrorists?" Mr. White said, his eyebrows raised.

Until now, I'd had no idea what Henry's full name was or what he did in real life. Or maybe I should say, in his fake life posing as a normal human being. I'd already assumed Candice had a leadership position, so it wasn't a big surprise.

I started to say no but then stopped, not sure how to continue.

"Don't you think it's more plausible someone who's been training in martial arts for more than a decade, including training with former special forces instructors, is capable of doing that?" A sly smile spread across his face.

"Well, if you know, why do you ask? And who are you?" I asked, taken by surprise.

"We know a lot of things, Mr. Connor," he said, avoiding my question. "The answer to who we are depends a lot on your answers to my questions. There's no reason to lie to us. We want to know what happened, and if you tell us, who knows? We may be able to help you."

The way he avoided my questions and trying to manipulate me into making a deal with him helped me narrow down which branch of the government he might be working for. I didn't want to mess with them, and I was also glad they'd noticed me. I might have been upset they never contacted me after my interviews, even just to say I wasn't accepted, but it was all in the past.

Part of the excitement I'd felt when I first saw their inlaid sigil on the floor when I had my interviews revived in me. It looked like I had to tell them something. Otherwise, I could end up farther down south, near Guantanamo, or worse.

However, I was part of the coven now, and from what I'd seen, it came with some perks—a good lawyer, private jet, a lot of money, magic, and so on. The problem was if I disappeared now, I didn't think anyone would be able to find me. I was pretty sure these guys knew how to erase someone from the face of the earth. Plus, they'd hinted they already knew something and only wanted me to confirm what they knew.

Could this be a test?

Of course, if I mentioned hashashins or witches, I was sure they would think I was crazy, or at least wouldn't believe me—or, who knows, maybe they would, and this could end up being worse.

"Okay, if you want to know what happened, here it is from my point of view. There may be other parts of the story I'm not aware of."

"Please continue, Mr. Connor."

"We arrived at Zaid's house, intending to buy an old artifact. The meeting went as planned, but once Henry paid them the money, they drugged us."

"With what?"

"Don't know. I'm not sure what they had in mind or what happened afterward, but I must have woken up earlier than they expected. They were dragging us by the legs, and it looked like we were somewhere in a basement. I saw the guy dragging Henry had a knife in his belt at the back. When the guy holding me let go, I jumped up and got hold of it. My intention was only to threaten them and force them to let us go. However, he and the other two guys jumped me. We struggled, but as you said, I'd had more training than they did.

"Next, I woke Henry and Dea up, and we started looking for an exit. We had started climbing the stairs when we heard voices coming, so we had to hide. Two more people came, and after they passed by us, we jumped them. I took one and Henry and Dea the other, but in the end, it only took me a few seconds to dispatch them."

I drew in a deep breath, filling my lungs, trying to ascertain the old guy's reaction to my story. But he had a poker face that even the most seasoned card player would kill for.

"Upstairs, the three of us found a room where they were storing what looked like grenades and explosives. I don't know a thing about explosives, so I took some grenades. We

183

were looking for the exit when someone found us and shouted something. I took care of him and told Henry and Dea to run down the stairs, and I followed them. I heard several people coming after us, so we went into the room we'd just left, and when I thought they were close, I threw the grenades."

Still stoned-face, the old guy looked on. I guess I paused too long because he motioned for me to continue.

"The explosion collapsed one of the walls and blocked us in, so I used the remaining grenades to punch a hole through one of the exterior walls. Once we were out on the street, we found a car and drove away." I finished, hoping it made sense, and he wouldn't ask me too many questions, poking at the holes in my story.

"I see," said Mr. Wright with a thoughtful expression. "And what did you do afterward?"

This one was tricky. If I was followed by his organization, Mr. White knew we didn't go to the hotel. So, I decided to tell the truth, or something very close to it since he was hell-bent on watching me like a hawk.

"We went after Zaid. He mentioned during the negotiations that he had another buyer waiting for him at the airport. It was a long shot, but it paid off."

"How so?"

"When we arrived, we saw him along with two of his bodyguards. Working together, the three of us took them by surprise and retrieved what he stole from us, then we ditched the car next to a mall and took a cab to the hotel. Soon after, we were on the plane and on our way to the States. That's kind of it, in a nutshell," I said with shrug.

I told the story how I hoped it would make Mr. White think Henry had hired me as a bodyguard.

"Thank you, it's close enough to what my people told me," he said with a smile.

"Speaking of which, since I answered your question, it's time for you to answer mine. Who are you and your people?" I asked, trying to steer the conversation away from me and what had happened yesterday.

For several moments, he didn't say anything. He kept studying me. But just when I thought he wasn't going to respond to my question, he cleared his throat.

"We're part of an organization responsible for making sure this country is safe. While the agency I work for is tasked with working overseas, my unit is the only one allowed to focus on domestic security. We're a small group of highly specialized people and are always on the lookout for exceptional individuals," he finished, giving me a meaningful look.

"Are you saying what I think you're saying?" I asked, sure he was referring to the same three-letter agency or TLA for short, I'd applied to a few years ago.

"Indeed," Mr. White said, smiling. "Sorry, it took us almost two years to get back to you. But we think your abilities could be useful to us. My men followed the car you left in from Zaid's residence, and they arrived in time to see your group in action at the Cairo Airport. Even though they kept their distance, they recognized you based on your stature and your training."

"So, all that time in the dojo paid off then just like Andrew said."

"You see, some of the people there had the same instructor you did. They were impressed with how quickly and stealthily you moved. Also, from what I understand, your IT skills, or more specifically, your security skills, are good, so you'll have the opportunity to use everything you know if you decide to join us. Of course, due to the unique nature of our work, you will get to know and work on things you otherwise would never have access to."

"Can I think about it?" I asked, not wanting to say yes before I had the chance to talk with Dea. I was hoping this would not impact my ties to the coven, especially since they bought my company.

"This offer expires the moment you step out of the car," Mr. White said, his tone serious. "But if you're worried about money, don't be. You also needn't worry about your current job. I believe your company will soon have a new contract with the DoD, and they will need services from time to time. Nothing will change in that respect. You would still be with your current employer. Finally, if you're worried about the FBI, put your mind at ease. They won't bother you anymore." He reached inside his suit and pulled out an envelope. "This is your passport."

It was checkmate. With this last gesture, Mr. White had shown how much power and influence his unit wielded. I didn't see another option, and honestly, I didn't think I wanted another one. This was something I'd wanted to do since I finished college.

Who doesn't want to be a secret agent or spy?

On the other hand, I had committed to the coven, but Candice never mentioned anything about not doing something on the side. She only said I couldn't get out of the coven or join another one.

What will Candice think if I work for the government? How will Dea react when she finds out?

I had to make sure it wouldn't conflict with my duties toward the coven. Plus, there was an upside to this as well. If the government ever found out about magic, it was easier to work for them than to be hunted by them—better an ally than an enemy.

"I accept," I said with a nod.

"I'm glad to hear that. Expect to hear from us in the next couple of days. Until then, if you need anything, you can call this number."

He handed me a business card. It had a circle with a blue background on the upper left corner. In the center of the circle, there was a white shield with a red compass rose and an eagle's head on top.

The card had only a phone number, no name, and above it were the words Central Intelligence Agency.

He motioned to the man waiting outside to open the door. It was my cue to leave, so I exited the vehicle, holding the business card in my right hand and not entirely believing what had just happened.

I was alone in front of the door to my apartment block with five thousand dollars in cash in the inner vest pocket of my jacket and a business card with the potential to twist my life even further, but hopefully in a lawful way.

When and how did my life become so complicated?

Less than a week ago, I was just an IT guy who hunted invisible assassins from time to time. I mean, invisible to everyone else but me.

Now I was a mage who had joined a coven, though it felt more like I'd joined the mob or some secret society, which was kind of true, I supposed. If that wasn't enough, the FBI questioned me, the CIA offered me a job, and it wasn't even lunchtime.

My mind was running in circles, and I kept blaming karma.

Clearly, I needed to focus on something else, something to help put all this on the back burner and let my subconscious handle it. So, I went to the gym.

After hours of working out, I decided to stop. I had no idea how I had so much energy. I should have been more tired, but I wasn't. My reflexes seemed faster, and punching the bag didn't hurt, which was odd because I wasn't wearing gloves. But it was getting dark, and I didn't want to be late again for my date with Dea.

Back at my place, I took a shower and planned to grab a

bite, but I had nothing interesting or appealing in the fridge, so I decided to have a protein shake. I downed it and left, looking forward to quiet hours of talking and enjoying food and drinks with Dea.

16

A SHORT DRIVE got me in the vicinity of the club. For a Thursday evening, it was crowded, cars and people everywhere. I found a parking spot farther away than I liked, but nothing could do about it. I arrived at the club's front door less than five minutes before 9:00 p.m., but at least I wasn't late.

"She's waiting for you on the second floor," said the doorman.

I nodded. "Thanks." Moving past him, I headed up the stairs to the same place we'd met last time.

As I made my way toward the familiar booth, instead of the black, darker-than-night hair I was expecting, I saw a woman with waves of long brown hair cascading down her back. Her skin was a caramel color, bronzed by the sun and radiating a soft glow. I looked around me to see if I'd possibly mistaken the table, but no one else occupied this part of the club.

I approached her slowly, a bit befuddled.

She raised her head, and when I caught a glimpse of her face, I was stunned to see how much she resembled Dea: the same high cheekbones, the same air of elegance.

The woman had large, dark eyes with a yellowish copper tint and hues of green, hazel, and brown. Her skin was perfectly tanned, and her lips were a rich plum-rose shade that complimented her face.

"Hello, Robert," she said with a warm smile. "Please, have a seat. Sorry I started without you." She lifted a glass of what seemed to be white wine.

"Hello, Diana," I said with a smile. I took the seat opposite her.

She arched an eyebrow and then nodded. Her expression changed from a warm smile to a wide grin, and a gleam appeared in her eyes. "Not a problem. Sorry for being late," I continued.

"Oh, not at all. Don't you know, a mage is never late?" She kept the same expression, which now seemed more like a challenge.

Okay, challenge accepted.

"A mage arrives precisely when he means to," I said with a grin.

"Excellent."

She then laughed a good-hearted laugh, which showed her white teeth.

"Smart, funny, and charming—what a combination. It's not easy to find someone like you these days." Without warning, she dropped the pleasantries, and her eyes became fierce. "So, I hear you're interested in dating my sister."

She focused a piercing gaze on me. Her smile was gone now, replaced by a stony expression. It seemed her entire face had changed, becoming darker, more menacing.

"Yes." I didn't feel like giving her any further details.

What happened here? We'd started a polite conversation, but now it seemed like I had upset her somehow.

"Why?" The weight of her tone carried force, and I had a flashback from my previous encounter with those two FBI agents in the interrogation room.

"Because I've liked her from the moment I laid eyes on her," I said without thinking.

For a few seconds, we stared at each other without saying a word.

"If you ever hurt her in any way, you'll wish you were never born," she growled.

With a quick wave of her hand, the wine glass disappeared, which freaked the hell out of me.

Before I had a chance to reply, I felt Dea approaching. I turned my head at the moment she walked up the stairs.

Dea saw me and waved. She was gorgeous. It was like I hadn't seen the real her before this moment. She wore a sophisticated black dress that rose a tad above the knees and had a cascading ruffle at her left side.

When she approached our table, I could see she was wearing a circular pendant made of either silver or white gold and black diamonds.

"There you are. I thought I saw you downstairs," she exclaimed. Then she turned to look at Diana, an annoyed expression on her face.

I stood to offer her a seat next to me.

"No need," Diana said with a sigh.

This snapped me out of my trance, and I moved my gaze to her.

She smiled a mischievous smile at me. "I have to go. It was nice to meet you, Robert. We'll be in touch later—much later," she said and strode off.

Dea and I sat facing each other across the table.

"Don't believe anything she says. She tends to overreact sometimes," Dea said in an apologetic tone.

"So, I shouldn't trust her when she says how nice and charming I am?" I asked, trying to change the tone of the conversation.

"Definitely not," she said with a laugh. "So, we finally have some time for ourselves. How are you? I'm sorry about the trip. I should have known better."

"Don't worry about it. I'm always glad when I can be with you, and it's even better if I can help with something."

"Oh, you helped me a lot. Without you, I wouldn't have seen the car in time, and most probably, that's where our trip would have ended."

"I'm glad it didn't." Then I paused, unsure how I should approach the more delicate subject regarding Henry and the coven.

"What is it? You can tell me anything." She had a concerned look on her face. She must have sensed my indecision.

"Okay." I took a deep breath. "Look, please don't be upset by my question, but it's not even my idea. You see, the thing is, during my questioning, the FBI suggested Akil was working for a terrorist group, and I, well, I was wondering if Henry or the coven knew about that."

She gave me a pensive look, and we both sat in silence. I could feel how she was considering my question and trying to determine if it was indeed a possibility.

"No. Neither the coven nor Henry knew about Akil working with terrorists. Henry and Akil hadn't seen each other in more than fifteen years," she explained, a determined look on her face.

"That's good." I let out a breath. Then, taking another deep breath, I said, "I was also approached by another organization, the CIA." I was careful to say the last part in a whisper. "I interviewed with them when I finished college. Apparently, they saw part of the action in Egypt—they were watching Zaid's place—and they think I saved us from being kidnapped. Now they want to hire me, or more specifically, call on me from time to time when they need my help. I won't have to leave my current job." My heart was thumping in my chest, and I was anxious to hear what she had to say.

Dea looked at me for what felt like a long time, one finger tapping on the table. "What kind of work do they need you to do?" she asked, her eyes narrowing.

"I don't know yet. The person I talked to said they like my fighting skills. They already knew about my IT skills, so probably a bit of both," I said with a shrug.

"I see. Is this something you would like to do?"

This surprised me. I hadn't expected her to ask for my opinion. I guessed she wanted to make sure I didn't feel coerced into joining something I didn't want.

"Yes." My ego must have wanted this to be more my choice rather than me asking her if she would allow it. But on the other hand, I was or would be a member of a coven of witches and mages. And I had to abide by their rules.

"Thanks for telling me. I'll let Mother know, but I don't think it will be a problem. While we have contacts inside the government, we don't have anyone in the CIA yet." After a short pause, she continued. "There is one thing I want you to do, though."

"Sure, anything," I said, glad my revelation went better than I'd expected.

"I want you to promise me something. You'll be careful not to expose us. And that includes you," she said, her eyes boring into mine.

"I'll be careful. I have no intention of telling anyone about, you know, magic."

"This is as much for your protection as ours," she clarified.

I stared into her eyes with an expression I hoped was solemn, imagining I could convey my sincerity through eye contact. I knew if the government found out about their existence, or I should say our existence, our lives would become extremely complicated.

"Now, have you had a chance to look over the scrolls?" I asked with interest, trying to change the subject.

"Since we arrived home, Mother and Henry have been reviewing them, although they've kept the scrolls away from everyone else. I'm not sure why. They're written in an ancient Egyptian language. I think it's called Ptolemaic Demotic, or at least that's what Henry said. All I can say is I think they contain some extremely potent spells."

"Why do you think so?"

"I had a look at them on the plane. First, somebody wrote the spells on the papyrus, which has a magically protective shield to resist the effects of time. Even now, the text is easy to read and hasn't faded. Trust me when I tell you, it requires a tremendous amount of skill and power to protect an item for hundreds, never mind thousands of years."

"And point number two?"

"Second, even though I don't understand the language, I feel there's some kind of pattern indicating a powerful incantation or charm."

"A charm to do what?"

"We don't know yet. Henry is researching some sources he thinks might help him translate the scrolls. The language, used more than two thousand years ago, offers some difficulty in translating. However, based on what he's found so far, he thinks the letters are scrambled, protected by a cipher script." She pursed her lips.

"Really? Cool. If you want, I can help with that. I've always liked puzzles and cryptograms. I mean, I do the NSA crypto challenges almost every week. I even wrote a program in Python that has a dictionary of the most common English words."

"How does it work?"

"I apply it to the encrypted text. The program matches the words based on their size and then substitutes letters until it finds something meaningful."

She propped her chin up in the palm of her right hand and smiled at me.

"Oh, sorry. I'm boring you, right?"

"No, not at all. I enjoy listening to you talk. I have one question, though."

"Sure, what is it?" I was delighted she was able to follow.

"What's Python? Is it some kind of snake program or sneaky program?" she said with an impish grin.

"Uh, no. Python is a language you can use to tell the computer to do something. Basically, you can use it to automate different tasks."

"Makes sense, I think. Please tell me more."

"Oh, okay. Well, there isn't much more to say. I mean, I have to do some manual work afterward, but the program takes care of most of it. I think we can do something similar with the scrolls."

"What do you mean?" She arched her eyebrows.

"Well, I'll need to come up with a dictionary for the demo. What was the name of the language?"

"Demotic."

"Ah yes. Demotic. So, I'll have to create a dictionary with the most common words, probably between three and five characters long. We'll then copy the text from the scrolls to a file and run various permutations until we find something that sounds coherent. Once we have that, we'll run a basic translation."

"You make it sound so easy."

"Well, it's not difficult, not compared to what you've done."

"Ah, it was nothing." She waved a hand. "Just a bit of magic."

"A bit of magic, you say. Well, it's definitely more than I thought I'd ever see. It's something I imagined when I was reading fantasy books."

"What you told me you can do with your Python sounds like magic to me, too." Her eyes sparkled.

"Pffft. That? Anyone can do it."

"I don't know how to do it, and Henry doesn't know how to do it either. Actually, besides you, I don't think I know anyone else who can do that. It seems you know more people who can do magic than I know who can use Python."

"Touché." I raised a hand. "Okay, a small change of subject. Do you remember when we were at my place last week, and you told me about some of the history surrounding witches, at least over the past thousand years or so?"

"Yes?" She gave me a questioning look.

"I was curious if you know anything about the period before that. For example, how were things like when witches used these scrolls? How did it all start? Are there any legends?"

"Ah yes. Let me think for a second." For a few moments, she appeared lost in thought. "Okay, so it goes like this. We think at some point in time, when Homo sapiens evolved, the evolution process went a step further in some cases. Those people were the ones who became the shamans—the healers, fortune-tellers, and spirit guides of groups and tribes of people. We call them the Ancients. For example, they healed the sick or helped when there was a drought. Later, when people learned more about medicine and physicians appeared, their role became more of a religious one."

"Like spirit guides."

She nodded in response then continued, "Then, when civilization evolved, the world needed less and less help, so we faded into the background. Of course, it wasn't a simple process. Some of the witches and mages were good and tried to help people. Others were evil and tried to use people to gain power. From that perspective, we're the same as everyone else. Remember what Henry said about magic, and how it's tied to our DNA? The need for power is also built into our DNA. We need to either have more power or be around someone who has an abundance of it."

She went quiet for a few seconds, studying my face. I felt she was arguing with herself about something.

"You know you can tell me anything," I said quietly.

She took a deep breath, then several seconds later, let it all out. "That's the reason I suspect you're attracted to me." She stopped and looked straight into my eyes like she was staring into my soul. And who knew, maybe she was. I remembered I'd read somewhere the eyes were actually a window into one's soul. I wanted to laugh. I was supposed to doubt her, not the other way around. I knew my feelings. They were unwavering.

"It's not true. I'm attracted to you because I like you, and I want to be close to you." A cold realization swept over me. "Wait. You're saying I'm only attracted to you because you have power, right?"

She nodded.

"Then why are you attracted to me? I don't have—"

"But you do, Robert. You have a lot of power—more than you know. I feel it in you. And I think you feel it in me too, even though you probably don't realize it. But there's another thing. Usually, witches and mages are only attracted to each other at this level when their powers are comple-mentary, and this doesn't happen often. In fact, it's quite rare. While witches and mages may have partners, like Mother and Father or Henry and Max, it's a mutual commitment. This is more than that."

"What do you mean, complementary? Like black and white?"

"No, not opposite. Complementary means we're a good match." Her face lit up with a sly look. "It means we enhance each other's abilities. When we're together, we're more powerful. And it's not simply the sum of our powers. I can't explain it very well because I only know what I've read in books."

"Oh, that's cool." Immediately, I realized my words

sounded lame. "So that I understand this correctly, you're saying the only reason we're attracted to each other is that we have these complementary powers that make us more powerful? Does it make us destined to be together?" I asked, but I also suggested the thought, even though I knew I shouldn't have used such a big word like destiny.

It pissed me off a tad that she didn't believe I liked her for who she was. But if I was honest with myself, deep down, a fear was lurking *inside me.*

What if I don't have the free will I always thought I did?

"Well, it probably affects you more than me, but yes."

"Why do you think it impacts me more than you?" I asked bemused.

"Because there are some spells you can use to defend against any kind of compulsion. This means that what you're thinking and all the decisions you make are yours, and no one else can interfere."

"I see. Would it be possible for you to cast such a spell on me? This way, we can be sure of our feelings, or should I say, you can be sure of my feelings. I already know how I feel."

"That's a nice thought. Unfortunately, the effect is more powerful when you cast a spell on yourself, compared to when someone else does it."

"Oh, I see," I said, a bit crestfallen.

"If you want, I can teach you," she said, trying to cheer me up. "Actually, that's one of the two reasons I wanted to meet with you today—to discuss your training."

Images of Hogwarts started floating in my mind. But before I could fantasize more about me in robes and using wands, I stopped because I wanted to hear the other reason, worried it might come with a high price—and I wasn't thinking about money.

"And the other reason?" I asked cautiously.

"Well, I'm hoping we can spend time together after all that's happened."

Happy wasn't a strong enough word to describe how I felt. However, among the joy, there was a shade of uncertainty. I'd seen Dea in action, using her magic, and it wasn't something to be taken lightly. I was definitely on board with learning magic, but I needed some time to reflect on how I felt about it. And how my life would change, because I was sure right then I was at a crossroads. For the moment, I decided to focus more on her second reason, spending time with her.

"I had the same thought. What do you say we order something to eat? I'm starving."

"May I take your order?" I heard from my left. I looked up to see Lydia wearing an outfit similar to the one she had on the first time I saw her: a black top with a floral print and black wide-leg pants.

"Wow, you are fast," I said with sincere admiration. "Do you serve steak here?"

"I'm sure we can come up with something."

Perfect. May I have two with fries, please?"

"Someone's hungry today," Lydia raised an eyebrow.

"I'll have the usual," Dea said, a smile on her face. I guessed our banter amused her.

"Okay. Two steaks and one mushroom ravioli coming up," Lydia said, and then she faded out of sight.

"Show-off," muttered Dea.

"Wow, that's amazing."

"Yeah. She likes to do it when there's no one else around."

"How does she do that?"

"It's her primary innate ability. She is, well, fast."

"Hey, how come she's a waitress here? If I remember correctly—during our first meeting, Alyssa was doing the same? Or at least for our table."

"Oh, they're not waitresses," Dea said with a laugh. "Mostly they keep an eye on me. Last Saturday, Alyssa was here because she was curious about how our date would go."

I could see a blush forming on her cheeks. "She doesn't usually read my mind or anyone else's in the coven, but during our date, she was focusing enough on surface feelings to know whether the date went well or not. She told me later that she couldn't get anything from either one of us for several minutes—no thoughts or feelings—and it scared her. When she came to our table, she said we both looked like we were in a trance. After a few minutes, she started getting glimpses, but she said she didn't understand what was happening and was afraid, so she decided to try to wake us up."

As I listened, I was stunned for a moment. I somehow knew what Dea had felt and experienced during our "connection," but I forgot Alyssa could read minds because I hadn't seen her using her power. It made me glad I didn't hide anything from Dea or anyone else in the coven.

"Now, with Lydia, it's different. She mostly likes to find out the latest gossip. If you haven't noticed, she likes to flirt, and sometimes it leads to her spending the night. She doesn't like to get entangled in relationships, and when she leaves, she casts a forgetfulness spell. When they wake up, her companions don't remember what happened," she said with a grimace.

I felt uncomfortable. It didn't seem fair to make someone forget something like that, and Dea must have read the expression on my face well enough.

"They don't completely forget what happened. That requires a lot of power, control, and precision. And it's also dangerous. This is something mild. They just forget what she looks like. The spell muddies their memories a bit," she clarified. "She will look familiar, but they won't know why."

"How do you learn to cast spells in general?" I tried to change the subject. I didn't want to start an argument. Honestly, mind reading and mind manipulation were kind of sensitive matters for me.

Not being able to remember the first eleven years of your life can do that to a person.

I knew exactly how it felt not to remember something, and I wouldn't wish it on anyone. Asking myself if I've seen or done this before and being asked by other people about things I did when I was younger was challenging, to say the least. Especially when they found out about my "condition."

The looks they gave me expressed more than their words. The doctors said it was highly unusual, but not unheard of, in such traumatic cases for the subject, aka me, to develop amnesia. They also said it usually resolved over time.

Yeah, well, I was still waiting. But what if it wasn't amnesia? *Did someone cast a spell on me to erase my memories? Will I ever know?*

"Everything relies on incantations, which help focus your mind on the desired objective. A long time ago, we found that using incantations is the easiest way to cast a spell," said Dea, waking me up from my self-pity.

"Is it possible to cast a spell without an incantation?" I asked.

"Yes, it is, but requires a focus object. You're probably familiar with some of these objects, like a wand or a staff enchanted for a specific purpose. However, you can use anything you want. The main thing is to have a conduit for your power."

"Wow, wait a second. What do you mean by 'enchanted,' and why haven't I seen you or anyone else using wands?" I said, thinking maybe all the fantasy books I'd read weren't so wrong after all.

"Well, 'enchanted' means the item has undergone a ritual that allows it to channel energy. During the ceremony, it's cleansed of any residual energy, and then we apply some runes to strengthen the core and allow energy to channel through it."

I tried to wrap my head around the concept, but visions

of kids flying on brooms and playing magical games filled my mind.

"Think of it as an electric cord," she said. "You want to make sure it's safe to use and works as expected. Usually, a focus item is needed when you channel enormous amounts of power, but this hasn't been done for ages."

"What do you mean? From what I've seen in the past week, you, your mom, Lydia, and everyone else in the coven have these marvelous superpowers. To me, you seem to be able to do anything."

"You asked me earlier about our legends from a time long since past when the ancients wrote the scrolls. We think they created the scrolls to make sure some important spells wouldn't get lost. There is an old legend about a fight with Outlanders—we assume a fight between rival covens—that had access to unlighted magic."

"What's that?"

"Probably means dark magic. Anyway, something happened during the war. The legend doesn't go into specifics. But many years after, the scrolls were created to preserve several important spells from being lost to time. So, you see, the powers we have now are nothing compared to those wielded long ago."

Her words stumped me. I couldn't imagine anyone with powers more substantial than what I'd already witnessed.

"Think about how much energy you would need to make it rain in the desert. Or to teleport to a distant location. That's why, in ancient times, both witches and mages used things like wands and staffs. It helped them channel vast quantities of energy." She paused for a moment as if allowing me time to catch up. "Imagine if someone had to divide a sea to allow people to pass through unharmed."

It took me a couple of seconds to realize what she had said. "Are you saying what I think you're saying?"

"And he used a staff to do it," she said, her gaze fixed on me.

"But that's, I mean, how can that be? How come no one knows about this? The Bible is probably the most researched book in the world, and you're telling me no one thought Moses might be a mage? And how is it he had so much power? Aren't mages supposed to be less powerful than witches?"

"Yes, they are less powerful now, but thousands of years ago, things were different when it came to spells and raw magical power. Back then, there was no differentiation in terms of power."

"What do you mean?"

"Everyone was more or less equal. What a single witch or a mage could do in ancient times was orders of magnitude above what an entire coven can do today. Then something happened. We're not sure what, but most of the witches and mages had their powers diminished, or maybe locked," she said with a shrug. "The only witch who still had access to that amount of power was the high priestess. To answer your other question, doesn't the Bible describe a world where beings have different kinds of powers? Where people can do magic?"

"No, they didn't do magic. God did those things."

"Who do you think wrote the Bible? In its current format, the book was negotiated by the Council of Nicaea just before the Dark Ages began. Henry has some suspicions that plans were set in motion long before that happened, based on his research of the Dead Sea Scrolls. Don't you think it might have been easier and also served their purposes to attribute all the 'miracles' to one supreme being instead of saying witches and mages were responsible for them?"

"But why?"

"What do you think someone who has power wants? More power. All the people who attended the council had privileged positions. They were all bishops and cardinals, and all of them had a certain number of followers. Do you think they wanted to give up that influence?"

"Probably not."

"They came up with such a good story that for almost two thousand years, their influence grew. And they became one of the most powerful organizations on the planet. They were also responsible for the witch-hunts. Don't you find that a bit odd?"

"You're saying they planned the entire course of history? How could they? It was done over centuries."

"Exactly. Imagine if someone behind the council wanted to destroy most magic users or kill all witches systematically. What mages and witches did, how they evolved to a higher power. Well, no one can meet during this lifetime. The only way you can reach it is if you listen and do what they say. You have to be obedient and endure every hardship. They came up with a truly ingenious way to control people."

"It's worked for thousands of years," I said more to myself than Dea. "Yes. And once they had that level of control, they started to systematically search for and kill witches. They did it for centuries until only a few covens remained—definitely not enough to pose a major threat. And nowadays, almost everyone thinks magic doesn't exist."

It was a lot to take in. But having grown up with things I couldn't easily explain, I understood her line of thought. But, like many others, I'd dismissed all the miracles I read about.

Who influenced the minds of the era? How did they change people's opinions and effectively lead them to ignore the truth? To whom were the covens a threat? Whoever or whatever organization was behind this must have been insanely powerful.

"A threat to whom? The church?" I asked to see if Dea had more information.

"That, Robert, we still don't know. Of course, this is all a theory, and it may be completely wrong." Her gaze told me she didn't think she was wrong, not for a minute.

"Hey, guys, sorry to interrupt your talk, but your food's here," said Lydia.

I looked up to see a huge plate filled with steak and fries coming toward me. Instantly, my mouth began to water, and everything else became background noise.

Sometime later, with only a few fries left on the plate, I glanced around to see what was going on. Dea had cleaned her plate and was studying me with an amused smile.

"Welcome back."

"Sorry, I guess I was hungry," I said sheepishly.

"Yeah, maybe a bit," she said, then giggled.

I pointed at the empty plate with my fork. "The food here is great. This is probably the best steak I've ever had."

"Maybe . . ."

"How was your ravioli?" I asked, hoping to change the subject to something other than myself.

"Delicious. But probably not as good as your steak."

Okay, that didn't work. Let's try something else.

"About what you said earlier—"

"Don't worry about it. They are suppositions. Everything happened more than two thousand years ago. It doesn't really matter. Let's talk about something else, okay?"

I actually had a lot more questions, but I decided to drop the subject for now. It was probably better this way. Later, I would have time to put my thoughts in order and go through what she said in greater detail. I wasn't a religious person, and what she said didn't shake me to the core. However, it wasn't something to be taken lightly.

Of course, I had the whole notion of God well established in my head thanks to my grandfather, but I wasn't the kind of person who went to church every Sunday. Even so, there had been times when things were tough, and I had prayed for them to get better, especially after my grandmother's murder. So, facing a revelation like this wasn't something I could easily digest.

With a deep breath, I set my worries aside to deal with another time, and for the next few hours, which felt more like a few minutes, we talked about her life.

I was interested in her and how she learned magic, how she spent her free time, what spells she'd cast recently, and all sorts of other things a woman—or rather, a witch—did. I wasn't too surprised to find out she hadn't had too much free time. She started training and learning about magic when she was young. Before her powers manifested themselves, her mother explained magic to her: how it worked, what you can do with it, and, most important, what you can't do.

There was one cardinal rule, one I agreed with wholeheartedly, not to use magic to harm regular humans. I had a suspicion this rule appeared mostly after the witch trials, but I didn't press her for details.

Besides magic stuff, she had to learn about math, geometry, and trigonometry. She needed them to draw runes and magical symbols and to know how to combine them. This formed the foundation for her astronomical studies.

Apparently, the gravitational effects of the stars, planets, and moons were significant for some spells. She didn't provide any specific examples, but she said some spells could only be cast when there was an eclipse or when certain planets were aligned. Otherwise, the energy needed to power them up would be astronomical.

Honestly, a lot of it went over my head. I barely remembered the math I'd studied in high school and college. At work, when I needed to calculate something, I wrote a program to do it for me.

Luckily, at some point, she changed the topic. We talked about the books we'd read, movies, and general mundane things, and she did look enthralled when I explained or described typical stuff I did at work, school, or back at the farm with my grandfather.

A couple of times, I tried to discuss what had happened during the past three days, but she always found ways to divert my questions.

"It's getting close to midnight, and I have to go," she said, but her eyes were saying something else.

"Already? Sorry, I didn't realize how time flew."

"Don't worry. It's just that we have some guests tomorrow, and we have to prepare."

"Oh, no problem. Can I ask who?"

"Some members from a coven in Mexico. The coven leader is an old acquaintance of my mom's. They are here to talk to Mother, but Diana and I have to be there too."

"Got it. I guess we won't see each other tomorrow?"

"Oh, we can see each other," she said quickly. "We have to do it earlier. Is that okay?"

"Sure, it's fine with me."

We both got up and headed toward the exit. The club remained packed with people even at this hour, and it took us a few minutes to squeeze through.

A limo was waiting for us in front of the curb. The back window rolled down. Inside, I could see Alyssa waving and smiling at me.

I waved back. "Hey, Alyssa! How are you?"

"I'm good. Do you need a ride?"

"Yes, he does," I heard Dea say, and she grabbed my arm and pulled me inside next to her. "Where did you park?"

"Just three blocks that way." I pointed in what I hoped was the right direction.

A few moments later, the limo stopped. I thanked the ladies for the ride and prepared to get out. I felt Dea's palm gently caressing my cheek. I turned my head toward her, and her face was inches from mine.

Her breath was warm and smelled like strawberries. Mine

was probably minty from the chewing gum I'd had while we were making our way through the crowd at the club. We both closed our eyes, and our lips met. Hers felt soft, and I soon realized we were both hungry, but not for food.

A few moments later, I think we both decided we shouldn't start something we couldn't continue right then, so we slowly returned to reality. When I opened my eyes, I could see Dea doing the same. I was breathing hard like I'd been running, and it suddenly felt like a hot summer's day instead of a chilly night at the end of spring. She seemed to be in the same boat I was in, which brought a grin to my mouth.

"See you tomorrow," I said but didn't move a muscle. I looked into her eyes.

"Yes, see you tomorrow," she said, her gaze locked with mine.

Dea and I stayed lost into each other's souls.

Alyssa cleared her throat. "Dea, we have to get going," said Alyssa.

"Oh, sorry," I said, not meaning it. "I didn't mean to . . ."

"Don't be. I'm not," said Dea with a seductive smile.

"Okay, then. I'm not," I said and gave her what I hoped to be a devilish look. "Call me or message me tomorrow when you wake up, and we can decide then what we want to do."

"Okay, talk to you tomorrow. Call me after ten." She brushed her fingers over mine.

I exited the car, happy with the outcome, and the limousine was soon heading away.

The drive home seemed to take a fraction of a second. My mind was busy running through the night's events. Soon after I got into my apartment, I received a message from Lydia.

Dea told me you could help with the translation. Henry asked me to give you his notes (see attach). Kisses from Dea!

Attached were several image files with Henry's notes and the text from both scrolls.

Like all other nerds, a surge of energy ran through me when faced with a puzzle. I opened up my laptop and started coding a script to decrypt the enigmatic content.

THE PHONE VIBRATED on the nightstand not long after my lids closed.

Slowly, I opened an eye. The morning sun filtered into the bedroom.

"Not now." A grunt passed my lips.

The phone kept buzzing. The LED screen identified the caller. It was my grandfather. This woke me instantly.

He didn't usually call—he waited for me to do it.

"Good morning, Grandpa," I said in a hoarse voice.

"Were you asleep, boy? Didn't I teach you better?"

"Yes, you did teach me better, and you still do." I could hear the smile in his voice.

"It's Friday. Isn't it a work day for you?"

"I have the day off since I put in some long hours this week."

"Anyway, the reason I wanted to talk to you is I had an FBI agent stop by, asking questions about you."

My heart started beating faster. From what Mr. White had said, the FBI shouldn't have been a problem anymore. And for some reason, I trusted him, at least on this matter.

I thought back to the two agents who questioned me. I

wasn't sure if they had played good cop, bad cop, but I hadn't gotten a good vibe from Agent Muller.

"Did you get a name?" I asked, but I thought I already knew the answer.

"Yes, one second. She left me a card." A solid clunk let me know he had put the phone down, probably on the kitchen table. After a few seconds, he picked it up.

"It's Special Agent Sarah Muller."

"Yes, I know her. We met yesterday. What did she want?"

"As I said, she was asking about you, nothing too specific. It feels like she was fishing for information. My question is, why is the FBI knocking at my door at eight in the morning asking about you? Are you in any kind of trouble?" His voice warmed up and trembled.

"Well, it's kind of a long story, but I don't think so. Can I stop by today? I can tell you all about it." I knew he would say yes. Then I had a great idea. "Do you mind if I bring someone?"

"Of course not. You know I'm always happy to see you. Actually, you should visit more often. I can barely remember the last time you were here."

"That was a few weeks ago." I tried to visit him at least twice a month. I always invited him to come over, but he refused, saying he couldn't leave his chickens. He had only visited once since I moved here for college. Back then, I lived in a small, cramped studio where I could hear everything my neighbors did—and I mean everything.

In the beginning, it was funny, but it soon became annoying. I couldn't wait to finish college, get a job, and move out.

"Oh, was it? It feels longer. So, who are you going to bring?"

Now, how could I best describe Dea? The most beautiful witch I'd ever seen? The most incredible woman I'd ever met?

Hmm. It was a tough choice, and he probably wouldn't believe me anyway.

On the other hand, I didn't want to call her just a girl I'd met—it was too banal.

"My girlfriend," I said simply.

"Oh, she must be a hell of a woman if she managed to get your attention." I could feel the unspoken question in his voice. He was aware of what I was struggling with. He knew I wouldn't expose just anyone to the danger rooted in my life, especially someone who might not be able to handle it and defend herself against it.

"You have no idea."

"Well, in that case, I can't wait to meet her."

"Great. I'll ask her, and we'll probably be there around lunchtime."

"That'll work. I'll make sure there'll be something on the table. No one who visits me will ever complain about not having something to eat," he said, more to himself than to me.

"Thank you, Grandpa. See you soon."

"See you, Rob." He always called me Rob, unless I'd done something wrong, in which case it was Robert.

"Bye," I said, waiting for him to have the last word.

"Bye-bye," he said and hung up.

The clock displayed 8:37 in the morning. It took me less than ten minutes to freshen up and make sure Ariel was all set for the morning.

At my stomach's request, I headed over to the fridge to prepare something. A feeling of dread washed over me.

My fridge was empty. I'd forgotten to go to the grocery store yesterday.

It took me a couple of seconds to debate what I should do. Make another protein shake or buy some real food.

My stomach growled loudly. It was clearly in favor of the latter option. I picked a T-shirt from my closet and went to get the pair of black jeans I'd left lying on the couch in the living room last night. I started putting them on, but my eyes fell on a piece of paper sticking out of one of the back pockets. Thinking it was probably a receipt of some sort, I pulled it out and unfolded it. Instead, there was a note written on it.

Saturday, 9:00 a.m., 2430 E St. NW, South Gate.

—W

After the initial surprise, my brain resumed thinking, and it took a couple of seconds to make the connection and realize who wrote it. But how had it landed in my pocket? I only had these pants on yesterday evening.

If someone had been in my apartment while I was sleeping, they would have left the note in a more visible place. Considering all this, I had a pretty good idea when it had happened. I thought I was a vigilant person, especially when it concerned the people I cared about and me.

I was slightly miffed. I didn't feel it when it pushed into my pocket. Even though the club was packed, I definitely should have felt something.

On the other hand, I was dealing with professionals. I was both disappointed and a little happy about it. Disappointed in my skills at detecting whether I was under surveillance, which were evidently sorely lacking, but glad I had something new to learn.

When I Googled the address, I wasn't surprised to recognize the CIA's old headquarters. However, I wondered why it wasn't the new one, on the other side of the Potomac River.

My stomach, however, wasn't too interested in my findings. Another growl reverberated in my otherwise quiet apartment. I even saw Ariel open one eye at the top of her cat tree. Then she changed her position, her back toward me. Message received.

In five minutes, I was out the door. It was a good thing there was a store close by.

Fifteen minutes later, I returned with three full bags, plus another bag from Dunkin' Donuts, which was next to the market.

Three ham, egg, and cheese English muffin breakfast sandwiches plus two double chocolate donuts later, I felt ready to tackle the most ambitious thing I'd had to do this week—and probably the one that scared me the most.

What's the best way to invite a witch to lunch?

I wondered if she would think it was too early. Basically, it was like asking her to visit my parents, as my grandpa was the only relative I had left. On the other hand, I'd already met her mom and dad, even though the circumstances were a bit unusual, considering her dad had to get me out of an interrogation room.

At 10:01 in the morning, I decided I couldn't wait any longer and texted her: *Good morning. Are you awake?*

A few seconds later, I got a reply: *Yes. I was preparing to write you a message. Can I call you?*

As I started typing, my phone rang, and Dea's name appeared on the screen.

"Morning. I hope I didn't wake you up with my message."

"Good morning to you too. No, you didn't. I woke up a few minutes ago," she said in a raspy voice.

"Good." I took a deep breath to gather my courage to ask her. I'd only known Dea for a short time, but deep inside I felt she should meet my grandpa, the only living member of my family. "I wanted to ask you if you have any plans for today."

"Not really, why?" she asked, and I could sense my question had piqued her curiosity.

"Well, you see, I was talking to my grandpa this morning, and I kind of said we'd go to see him today. Of course, if you don't want to or can't make it, that's fine. I can always resched—"

"I'd love to," she said, sounding surprised and excited. "What should I wear? Should we bring him something? Of

214

course, we should," she answered herself without waiting for a reply. "What does he like?"

"Wow, that's great. I appreciate it. But there's no need to bring him anything. He'll be happy to have us there. About what to wear, well, it's a farm, so don't expect much. Wear some comfortable clothes," I said, pleasantly surprised by how enthusiastic she sounded.

"Okay," she agreed, but her tone didn't sound like an agreement. "What time should we be there?"

"Well, I was thinking of picking you up by noon so that we can be in Laytonsville by one o'clock."

"Oh, that's in two hours. I hope I have enough time. Can't wait to see you. By the way, what's your grandfather's name?"

"It's Thomson, but everyone calls him Tom."

"Great. Bye," she said, "Lydia. Alyssa . . ." The line went silent.

A smile stretched across my face. I could only imagine what kind of hurry she must be in. It usually took me way less than two hours to get dressed to meet someone, but then, I wasn't a witch.

At noon, I pulled up in front of her house. The front door opened, and Dea stepped outside and walked toward the car. She was wearing a rust-colored top with a crisscross cutout design on the shoulders and a flattering V-cut front that made room for the same pendant she'd been wearing yesterday.

She had paired the blouse with a floral-stamped leather belt, classic denim jeans, knee-length brown leather boots, and a black handbag. Her dark, silky hair was straight with curled ends gently tossing from side to side.

I didn't know why, but each time I saw her, it was like seeing her for the first time. My heart started pumping, and I got butterflies in my stomach. Briefly, I wondered what I'd done to deserve a girl like her, or more appropriately, a woman like her. And a smart one too. Not to mention beautiful and extremely powerful.

Utterly forgetting my manners, I quickly jumped out of the car and raced around to the door on the other side to open it.

She smiled, then repaid me for my effort with a peck on the cheek.

"I'm thrilled you could come with me."

"Thank you for inviting me," she said with an enchanting smile. "So, tell me everything about life on a farm."

As we drove off, I started telling her about my childhood and teen years at the farm, before college. I described the house, which was one of the rare Colonial-style houses made of bricks in the area.

On the ground floor, there was a central stair hall with a living room on the left, a dining room on the right, and the kitchen on the far side. Upstairs, there were three bedrooms, but my grandpa had converted one into a study for me to keep my books and do my homework.

It also had a magnificent view of the entire farm. As a kid, I had often got lost in thought there while watching Benji, my dog—who'd, unfortunately, died while I was in college. That dog loved running around the farm, scaring the chickens or the squirrels in our apple orchard.

I also explained to her about daily life on the farm, which usually started early in the morning and finished after sunset, whether it was a weekday or the weekend.

It's a good life, a simple life.

She listened avidly, asking me questions when she needed me to clarify what things meant or describe what something looked like.

Soon, I turned into a familiar driveway. The front door opened, and my grandpa, wearing jeans, a white shirt with blue stripes, and a baseball cap, stepped outside. He was pushing seventy, but he looked twenty years younger.

I stopped the car in front of the house, and both Dea and I got out. I guessed she didn't want to wait for me to come and open the door for her.

"Good to see you, Rob," my grandpa said. He turned his gaze to Dea. "And who is this charming lady of yours?"

"She's Dea, my girlfriend," I said, bursting with pride.

I could see Dea beaming and holding a hand out, which my grandpa took and kissed.

"It's lovely to meet you, Mr. Thomson. I'm Dea Mitchell."

"The pleasure is all mine, and please, call me Tom. Why don't you two come inside? It's going to start raining soon."

Earlier this morning, there had been scattered clouds, and now the sky was getting darker. Gray clouds were pressing against each other, trying to block the last rays of sunshine that managed to get through.

The wind swirled dirt in the air. A storm was coming.

"After you." I motioned for Dea to go first and then followed her. My grandpa, being the last one in, closed the door.

I smelled the mouthwatering aroma coming from the kitchen. "Something smells delicious!"

"I hope you're hungry. I've made enough stew to feed an army."

"I'm starving," I said, and shot a look at Dea.

She smiled at me. "It does smell good."

"Have a seat while I set the table."

"Nonsense. We can do it," Dea offered. "You've done enough already, Tom. I'm sure Robert knows where everything is in the kitchen."

I could see he was pleasantly surprised to hear Dea say this.

"Very well, kids. I'll go rest these old bones and stay out of your way," he said and went to the living room.

Soon, I heard the television's familiar sound, and I knew he was searching for the sports channel.

"This way." I led Dea to the kitchen. Like the rest of the house, everything looked modern and brand-new. A year after I moved to DC, I'd earned enough money to completely remodel the place, including the kitchen and the appliances.

"The plates should be here, Dea. I'll get the bread, the silverware, and the stew." On the stove, there was a big black pot. I knew exactly what was in there—my grandpa's favorite stew, an old family recipe.

It took the two of us a few minutes to set the table. Dea even added a vase with flowers. *We didn't have any around the house.*

"Grandpa, it's ready," I called out to my grandpa, who made his way to the dining room.

"Oh, I can see Dea has a magic touch," he said and took a seat.

My heart rate spiked. Alarmed, I glanced at Dea. She was stone-still, with a smile frozen on her face.

Look how much better everything is."

"You're right. It does." I took a deep breath, and I saw Dea relax as well. Then I took a seat on my grandpa's left with Dea next to me.

"Please, go ahead," said my grandpa, gesturing for Dea to serve herself.

Dea nodded and ladled out enough stew to fill half of her plate. She then looked at my grandpa, who frowned, but it quickly transformed into a smirk.

She added more, then rechecked his expression. This time, he had a satisfied grin on his face.

Dea then passed me the ladle, and my plate was soon full to the brim. The same went for my grandpa.

"What are you waiting for? Dig in." He waved his spoon at us.

The three of us laughed and started eating. The stew was delicious. The beef was so tender it melted in my mouth. It was infused with a lovely flavor from being slowly cooked in the oven. I knew because he had shared the secret of how he prepared it with me. I must have inherited my love of cooking from him.

"Which wine did you use this time?" I asked, knowing full well which one he liked.

"Burgundy," he said with a smile, realizing the reason I asked was to make conversation.

"This is scrumptious. I taste so many flavors. What ingredients did you use?" Dea scooped another bite and brought it to her red lips.

I took a quick look at her plate and decided she'd made good progress.

"Oh, it's an old family recipe. I first add bacon to a pot, then I season the beef with salt, pepper, and a bit of flour. When the oil is hot, I brown the beef. In a second pot, I add wine and mushrooms and let it cook longer. While the mushrooms simmer, I add olive oil, carrots, onions, and garlic. I leave it a couple of minutes, and then I add tomato paste and some paprika. I stir all that, and then I add everything to the pot where I have the bacon and the beef. The last step is to add potatoes, beef broth, dried thyme, salt, and pepper. I leave it in the oven for an hour and a half, and this is the result. Let me know if you want the recipe, or you can bring Rob here more often."

"I think I will," Dea said with a grin. "Bring *Rob* more often, that is."

"Good answer," my grandpa said, a smug smile on his face.

Usually, one round was enough, but this time the stew was so good, I actually had another full plate. Soon, all the dishes were wiped clean, and everyone was resting after a full meal.

"Such a delightful meal," said Dea with a look of satisfaction on her face.

"I'm glad you liked it. I know Rob did. He almost finished

the entire pot by himself. His visits are one of the few times I have the opportunity to cook something for someone other than myself. Honestly, I'm a bit rusty. Rob here told me this morning you'd be stopping by, so I didn't have a chance to prepare anything for dessert."

"Oh, no need to worry. I brought you something I hope you'll like. We can all enjoy it for dessert."

Dea opened her bag and took out a wooden box with intricate carvings. She stood and walked over to my grandpa.

"This is for you." She handed it to him. "It's an assortment of teas from all over the world."

"Thank you, dear. You shouldn't have," he said, and I saw his eyes welling up with tears of happiness. No one had given him a present, not like this, in a long time. Mine didn't count.

"If you want, you can open it," Dea said, looking at him.

A warm and grateful feeling spread through me.

Inside the box was the familiar sight of a wide variety of packets of different colors, similar to those I saw last weekend.

"Rob and I will take care of the dishes and prepare the tea."

"It's so thoughtful of you," said my grandpa, and with a bit of effort, he stood.

His back was causing him problems again. He was in otherwise perfect health, but a few years ago, he started complaining about back pain whenever he was sitting too much in one place.

"I'll wait for you in the living room." He then ambled along to the adjacent room.

I stacked the dishes and took them, along with the stew pot, to the kitchen. Dea followed me with the empty bread basket and the tea box. In the kitchen, she filled the kettle with water, and soon I heard it boiling. I directed her to where my grandpa kept the cups, and by the time I was done washing the dishes, I saw three steaming mugs of hot tea.

"Does your grandfather like the tea sweet or not?"

"Not—but I like it sweet," I said with a grin.

She handed me one of the mugs, and I poured the equivalent of two teaspoons of sugar into it. She took the other two cups, and we went to the living room.

It wasn't a big room—it was what I'd call cozy. There was an L-shaped gray couch with blue cushions. I thought it blended nicely with the dark hardwood floors.

A small coffee table sat in front of the sofa. Across from it, there was a big-screen television I'd bought for him after the renovation. Beside the couch was an armchair, my grandpa's favorite place to rest. He always sat there.

"Here you go, Tom." Dea handed him his cup, and then we both took a seat on the couch.

"This is very good. I don't think I've ever had tea as good as this," he said after taking a sip. "Maybe similar, but definitely not the same," he continued several moments later, smacking his lips.

"I'm glad you like it," Dea said with a knowing smile.

After a few moments of silence, he asked the question I'd been expecting ever since we arrived.

"So, what's the story with the FBI agents?"

I looked at Dea, who seemed puzzled. Then I remembered I forgot to tell her about the conversation I'd had with my grandpa this morning.

"Sorry, I forgot to tell you that my grandpa got a visit from one of the FBI agents who questioned me the other day." I turned toward my grandfather. "It's a long story, and it may take a while."

"I have some time left in me," he said, narrowing his eyes.

"Okay, here goes nothing," I said under my breath.

I told him almost everything. I only skipped the part when I woke up at the hospital and when Dea had told me about herself, magic, and her coven.

"After we landed and were going through customs, we all

221

got stopped by the police, and a couple of agents took me into an interrogation room and asked me a bunch of questions about Akil's death. Luckily, Dea's father is a lawyer, and he was at the airport, so he convinced the agents they had no case and got me out. They're investigating us for a crime we didn't commit."

The whole time, he listened intently to the explanation, which was more than an hour. My grandfather didn't say a thing and sipped his tea. I did most of the talking, but Dea filled in the details I forgot.

"I see," my grandpa said after a minute or two of silence. "I think there might be something you forgot to tell me." He gazed straight at me. He was giving me a look I'd rarely seen from him, a stern look. "You forgot to mention Dea is a witch."

My jaw literally dropped, and a glance at Dea told me she was surprised too. Her face froze again, this time without a smile.

"I, uh, how do you . . ." I mumbled.

"I think this tea is bringing some long-buried memories to the surface of my mind. I don't know why, but right now, it feels like a curtain has lifted, and memories are coming back to me. Memories I never knew I had—first, her pendant and the bracelet you're wearing. I've seen similar symbols before," he said, glancing at the bracelet Dea gave me.

I'd gotten so used to it. I forgot I had it on.

"Second, when you arrived, I saw a black SUV parked on the other side of the road. First, I thought she was just a rich woman with her own security. But now, I think there are two possible explanations for those two things."

Dea and I remained silent.

"Either she's a rich woman with interest in the occult, or she's a witch, and those are bodyguards assigned by her coven, sworn to protect her. And I know it isn't the FBI because the car is too expensive for their budget," he said with a chuckle.

I glanced at Dea, and she nodded.

"But what really convinced me was the vase with the flowers." He must have read my confused look. "I planted some seeds last week in a plastic pot. Usually, it takes weeks before I see anything. I don't have any other flowers in the house or even around the house, and I didn't see you bring any either. Now that I look back, your reaction earlier when I mentioned magic gave you away, dear," my grandpa explained, gazing at Dea. "I don't know what made me choose to mention it, probably my subconscious was trying to tell me something, but now it's starting to make sense. I can feel there are more memories up here"—he pointed at his head—"somewhere, but I can't seem to recall them. And if I'm not mistaken, the tea you gave me has restorative properties, probably from a spell."

I saw her eyes widen, but she soon regained her composure.

"Yes. It was the only packet I had time to cast a spell on this morning. I wanted to give you a gift. I know how much you mean to Robert, and I know he cares about you. It's also a gift for him, something to boost your health and delay aging."

I didn't know if I should be annoyed she didn't tell me or happy she wanted to help my grandfather. And what a fantastic gift.

"With the flowers, I used a simple spell to accelerate their growth. I cast it on half the seeds you planted. I didn't think anyone would realize what I did. If you don't mind me asking, you say you recognize the symbols on my pendant and Robert's bracelet. How?"

He held up a hand to ask for time and then remained silent for several minutes. His eyes focused on something we couldn't see, possibly, something from his past.

"Well, dear, I think my mom, your great-grandmother, Robert," he said, looking at me, "was also a witch."

Just when I thought there could be no more surprises, I got hit with this one.

"This part I remember now, clearly. When I was young, she showed me some of her books and told me about witches, mages, and witchcraft. Since I had no powers, I mostly thought they were stories and nothing more. Sadly, she died in a tragic accident, along with her entire coven. Or so I thought, until now."

"And the tea brought all of this to the surface?" I glanced between my grandfather and Dea.

"Yes. I should have realized there was a connection, Rob, when you first told me about the man who killed your mother—my daughter—and your father. I can see how it may not have been an accident. She could well have been murdered by the same group of people, the hashashins."

Hearing the word slip out from between his lips, hashashins, really grabbed my attention, and from the looks of things, it garnered Dea's full focus, as well.

"Please, continue." Dea took a sip of her tea. "Tell us about your mother."

"Well, I was young when my mother died, and my father raised me as best he could. But he didn't know what my mother was. I think, after a few years, I stopped believing too, and when Rob arrived here to stay with me and his grandmother, I must have forgotten about it because until now, I've never even thought about it. Not even when that thing came here, into our house, and murdered my wife."

My grandfather let out a ragged breath, then took a few seconds as if to compose his thoughts.

"It's like something had blocked my mind," he continued. "Though when you killed it, and I saw it melting into a pile of dung on the floor, I did realize there was much more to the world than I knew. Something kept me from seeing the truth and remembering there was magic in this world."

"Possibly a spell," said Dea, barely above a whisper.

"Nevertheless, from then on, I tried to support you even more to become the best warrior you can be," he said to me. "Now that I'm starting to remember these things, I know I made the right decision."

For a few moments, he had a look of deep concentration, which neither Dea nor I dared to interrupt.

"My mind is still cloudy when I try to remember you when you were little before you moved here. However, I know one thing for certain. To see those hashashins, you must have the gift. So tell me something, Robert, have your powers manifested themselves yet?"

For several seconds I was speechless and didn't know what to say. It was like I only knew half of my grandfather, a simple man concerned mostly about life on the farm. The other half was a completely different man.

"Yes," said Dea. "Apparently, his powers were dormant, but less than a week ago, they came to life. Henry gave him a tea and cast a revealing spell. It was supposed to bring forth any latent powers, but briefly."

"I see," said Grandpa.

"However, it seems it was a catalyst, and now his powers are developing. Also, when we kissed for the first time"—a light, rosy blush covered her cheeks—"there was a power transfer between us. It felt like we both achieved some kind of balance. Later in the week, he used his power to fend off a car attack. We weren't injured because Robert saw the danger, and then we both channeled a force wall to stop it, after which we were able to hide in a safe place. He's also becoming stronger and faster than a normal human."

I saw my grandfather nod and mutter, "The way he eats." I had indeed been eating much more than usual, but hadn't had time to consider why.

"An increased metabolism happens to all witches and mages when their powers start manifesting themselves. However, it usually only lasts for a few days. For some reason, his transformation seems to be taking longer. Either it's slower, or he's gaining more power." She fixed me with her gaze. "Time will tell."

The three of us fell silent. My head was spinning with all the new information dumped on me. I was jumping from one train of thought to the other. If I had to describe this in computer terms, it felt like a buffer overflow or information overload.

"Good. Now that we're all on the same page," said my grandpa, "who do you think this buyer is? By the looks of it, he's the one who tried to kill you in London to get rid of the competition."

Dea and I looked at each other, and then we each shook our head.

"We don't know yet," said Dea. "My mom's working on tracing the phone calls Zaid made this week, but it'll take time."

"She can do that?" I asked, amazed that such spells were possible.

"Yes. She hired private investigators and other people to, well, investigate," she said, looking at me with a smile. "We'll find out eventually."

The rest of the conversation centered on last week's events: the FBI's involvement, what Dea's father could do to deter any legal actions, and so on.

By five in the afternoon, after we both promised to visit more often and my grandpa finally agreed, in principle, to make a trip to DC, we were on our way to the nation's capital. This time, I immediately spotted the car following us.

I dropped Dea off at her home, with more than enough time to get ready for the meeting with the coven from Mexico, which was supposed to happen around midnight.

She assumed it would last until close to dawn, and we agreed to talk tomorrow afternoon.

Once I got home, I made sure Ariel got her dinner, and then I crashed on the couch. I opened my phone to check for new messages. It felt so good to be away from work the past week. It was my first vacation in, well, forever. In terms of how the holidays went, I hoped I could do better.

Struggling to avoid getting killed is not my idea of relaxation.

Three messages were waiting for me on WhatsApp.

Steven: *Guys, Yuugen tomorrow at 7 p.m.? I'm meeting the girl from last week, and she said she has a sister :D Who's interested?*

Mark: *I'll wait for Robert to answer first. Otherwise, it won't be fair, us being in the same office while he's working remotely.*

Steven: *Okay, I'll let her know one of my colleagues is interested, but I won't say the name :P*

Even though I wanted to keep a piece of my semi-normal life away from everything else, I realized it might not be possible. Too much had happened. I was a mage and had joined a coven, or would at some point. I had also joined, in a way, the CIA. And ultimately, I was an IT guy with some fighting skills. If I tried to keep everything separate, I would go crazy, attempting to remember all the lies. I thought about Mark Twain's quote, *"If you tell the truth, you don't have to remember anything."* And he was right. Instead of keeping everything separate, I should go with the flow and let my different worlds merge together.

I took a deep breath and texted them back.

Robert: *Thanks for the invite. Mark, no need to worry about me. I actually have a date :) What time should we meet tomorrow?*

I didn't think Dea would mind a triple date with my colleagues, especially at her club. I decided to leave all other thoughts aside for the moment and focus on tomorrow morning. It had the potential of being a life-changing day.

My life wasn't boring, especially not this week when I'd

had quite a few life-changing and life-ending moments, but this was a big deal.

I wasn't confident about wanting to be part of the CIA. It wasn't because I was afraid of danger. It was because I would have to keep secrets from both Dea and my grandpa.

At some point, I knew my double or triple lives would collide. To make sure it wasn't disastrous, I had to merge them, one step at a time.

One thing I knew for sure, my semi-regular life as an IT guy was about to end.

SATURDAY MORNING, at 8:50, I parked in front of the old CIA headquarters on Twenty-third Street.

Engine off, I took a deep breath to calm myself. A glance in the rearview mirror showed a dark gray Ford Taurus pulling in behind me. No other car was in sight.

A man in his thirties with a vaguely familiar face and wearing dark pants and a brown jacket stepped out of the car and approached me.

"Mr. Connor, my name is Paul Davis. I'm to escort you to our office. Please come with me."

"Nice to meet you. Lead the way." I locked my car. Given where we were, it would probably be safe even if left unlocked.

Instead of going to the gate, we crossed the street and headed toward the side entrance of a large gray building.

"After you." He opened the door and motioned for me to go in first.

It looked like a regular government building, similar to those I've been in when assigned to various DoD contracts to take care of IT systems.

Paul Davis opened a door that led to a stairwell, and we both started climbing the stairs.

"I thought it was the other building, the one across the street," I said, trying to engage him in conversation.

"The CIA has a close relationship with the State Department. Several small active groups like ours, affiliated with the CIA, use the offices here. This way, we can maintain plausible deniability in case anyone gets caught. That's why, officially, we aren't employed by them." He stopped on the third floor and opened the door to a hallway with offices.

Everything was closed, and no sounds came from within any of them. I guessed there weren't too many people working during the weekend.

"And what happens if someone gets caught?" I asked.

He stopped in front of a metal door protected by a badge and a biometric fingerprint reader. The reader signaled green, and an audible click sounded.

"If we get caught, presidents resign, Mr. Connor." Paul stepped inside.

"You mean like the actual US President?" I asked, not sure if he had made a joke.

However, my curiosity got sidetracked when I stepped in behind him. There were lots and lots of screens. And in the middle of the room, an enormous monitor displayed a map of Washington, DC.

This is way better than NASA.

To a nerd like me, this was what paradise looked like.

"Welcome, Robert," I heard someone say, and I turned my head. Mr. White emerged from what looked like a conference room, based on what I could see through the glass walls.

Three people, two men and one woman followed him.

Mr. White approached and shook my hand. He had a good grip, which I liked. I've encountered people with weak grips, and they usually have something to hide.

"Let me introduce you to the other team members," said Mr. White. "This is Jack 'MacGyver' Anderson."

Jack looked to be in his mid-thirties, with brown eyes and brown hair in a military-style haircut.

"He's our main driver, mechanic, repairman—you name it. If it doesn't need fixing, he'll break it, or is it the other way around?" Mr. White grinned.

Jack returned the grin, then gave me a nod.

"This is Samantha Walker." He pointed to the woman, a blonde, tall—almost my height—with dark eyebrows, hazel eyes, and thin lips.

Samantha was cute in an effortless way, and it wasn't easy to determine her age. She could be anywhere from twenty-five to thirty-five.

"She's our expert in languages and surveillance." Mr. White waved me on.

I met her gaze, and she gave me a brief smile. She appeared fragile and vulnerable, but because she was part of this group and this institution, I assumed it was all a facade.

I smiled back.

"Over here," Mr. White pointed to an athletic-looking black guy, "is Christopher Browder. A former Green Beret, he's our weapons specialist, our one-man army, and, most importantly, our backup when things go wrong."

I expected a smile or a polite nod, but he ignored me, looking somewhere past me.

"Last but not least, you've met Paul Davis. He is the team's appropriator. Also, if you ever forget the keys to your apartment, give him a call." He patted Paul on the back. "They've all been on this team for more than three years, so they can help you and answer any questions you may have. Questions about logistics go to me. Feel free to ask questions, but don't expect anyone to have all the answers."

Reason: the team is not new.

He then moved to my left, grabbed my shoulder with his right hand, and turned me to face the team.

"Robert is the newest member of our team. He'll be our close-quarter combat specialist and IT wizard. When I say close-quarter combat, I mean using nonlethal techniques to take down opponents," he said, glancing at Christopher.

It seemed the last phrase mostly addressed Christopher, and I inferred some history took place there between them. I had an inkling I shouldn't ask Christopher about it directly, or at least, not now.

As if sensing something was up, Christopher asked me, "Anything you want to say?"

The man was watching and waiting for me to say something. Actually, they were all looking at me expectantly.

Excellent. No pressure. Just what I need for my first day.

I was terrible at public speaking, and I didn't have anything prepared. "Hello, everyone, nice to meet you." This probably wasn't the best first impression I could make. "I'm glad to be part of the team, and I'm looking forward to working with you." I finished with a nod.

Mr. White retook the floor. "Now that we all know each other, I think the best way to get a measure of someone is through a trial by fire. We have a mission today. Would you be interested in joining us?" I guessed he wouldn't have called me in today if not needed. It was considerate of him to allow me to choose, even though I couldn't refuse it, not unless I wanted to blow my only chance of joining them.

"That's why I'm here," I said with a smile.

"Good. Just a reminder—your top-secret clearance"—I had it since Brad's company had contracts with the DoD—"applies to all you hear and do with us. Now, if you would all join me in the conference room, I'll brief you on our mission." He headed toward the glassed-in room. Once everyone had a seat, he started the briefing.

"We got a tip from CNO that a Chinese delegation has arrived in DC for a meeting with one of our defense contractors, DynCorp, for a potential sale. Two of the Chinese nationals are members of the TMSS, their intelligence agency. The backstory is they want to obtain some highly classified information and bribed one of the DynCorp senior sysadmins, Daniel Schulte. The meeting will happen at noon today at the hotel where they're staying. Our priority is to make sure the information doesn't reach foreign hands. Any questions?"

"Why not let the police or the FBI handle this?" Samantha asked.

"Excellent question. If we let them handle it, there will be an investigation. They will then ask questions during the investigation regarding how the information was obtained. CNO doesn't want to tip their hand and reveal they're embedded in the DynCorp networks."

"What is CNO?" I asked. It wasn't an acronym I was familiar with.

"Sorry for not explaining earlier. CNO stands for Computer Network Operations, but basically, it's the former TAO, if you've heard of them."

The acronym was familiar to me. Basically, TAO members were the NSA's hackers. They infiltrated networks and systems for exfiltrating data and keeping tabs on the bad guys. Or at least that's what I remembered from a YouTube clip I had watched a couple of years ago.

I nodded, letting him know I knew about TAO, or Tailored Access Operations.

"What you may not know is we work closely with them, specifically the ATO, the Access Technologies Operations, branch, to help them in their surveillance efforts. And sometimes they'll give us a tip when they 'hear' something we can act upon. We have a similar deal with our IT guys, but they mostly operate overseas. Unfortunately, they don't have the same intel the NSA does when it comes to domestic intelligence. Any other questions?"

"What's the plan?" Christopher asked.

"Plan A is to replace the USB with a different one. CNO was able to see what data Schulte copied onto the USB stick, and they've created similar documents with fake data and a back door." Then, from his inner vest pocket, he pulled out a transparent case containing what appeared to be two small USB sticks. "They're similar to the one containing the real data. Plan B is we make this look like a robbery. It's not pretty and may raise suspicions, but we don't have any other choice. Under no circumstances are you to use lethal force, do you understand?" he said with a stern expression.

Everyone in the room, including me, nodded. I was sitting opposite Christopher, so I was able to see the annoyed look he gave me. He definitely didn't like me.

The problem was I couldn't fathom why.

Mr. White continued with the briefing, "Okay, both Team A and B will get a USB stick. If there are no more questions, we'll go over—"

"Sorry, I'm the new guy here," I said, "but wouldn't it be easier to arrest or rob Daniel before he gets to the hotel?"

"Easier, yes. The thing here is we want to see where the money is coming from. That way, we can connect more dots and see if the account they pay from connects to payments made to other US citizens," said Mr. White in a fatherly voice, like a parent explaining something evident to his child. "Okay, now let's go over the details. We don't have much time left."

Next, we went into operational details. By the end of the briefing, we had a primary plan and a backup. Plan A would be handled by Paul and Samantha, who would try to get close to our two Chinese targets. But if the plan failed, my team, or rather, the team I was part of, would handle Plan B.

Christopher insisted a couple of times they shouldn't

involve me, and I should be kept in reserve to see how things work. But in the end, he was overruled by Mr. White.

It meant Jack, Christopher, and I would bash some heads —hopefully not each other's.

Once the meeting was over, I approached Jack, who was sitting next to me.

"Hey, quick question, Jack. Do you know what the deal is with Christopher? He doesn't seem to like me."

"Don't worry about him. Give him some time." Then he continued in a whisper. "We had an issue in Saudi Arabia, and he used lethal force when we were trying to capture a journalist. This triggered a major international incident, and our team was close to being disbanded. Luckily, we didn't leave any evidence around, so no one pinned it on us. But there was a lot of pressure on Mr. White to get someone who isn't so trigger-happy. Now, I'm not saying Christopher is. However, his experience in the Green Berets taught him to kill or be killed, and that's tough to get over."

Feeling a bit better, it wasn't something I said or did. I followed Jack and everyone else out of the room to get dressed. For Paul and Samantha, this meant putting on suits. They would be seen in public and by cameras. For the rest of us, it meant a combination of black tactical clothing and footwear. The plan was to go through the back entrance where the kitchen deliveries were received. There was only one camera. And a broken one at that.

Our clothing consisted of black cargo pants, black hoodies, gloves, and ski masks. Under our hoodies, all three of us had covert bulletproof vests and earpieces to receive instructions.

"Hey," I leaned over close to Jack. "Why are we using black clothing in the middle of the day?"

"No one would think we are professionals." Jack grabbed a pair of gloves.

"As most of you well know, in case you're caught, sit tight.

We'll resolve the situation through back channels. Now, Mr. Connor," said Mr. White, looking straight at me, "as this is your first op, if you get caught, the same applies to you, plus one more thing. Don't even think of coming back."

His voice didn't leave any room for doubt. If I didn't pass this test, I was out.

It kind of dampened my mood. Even though I understood why he said it, but it didn't make me feel any better. Ultimately, though, it meant I had to do my best to pass this test and finish the mission without getting caught.

Both groups left for the hotel in two different vehicles. The other team took a black GMC Yukon and were supposed to park across from the hotel. No time wasted in waiting for the valet if they needed to exit rapidly.

My team and Mr. White climbed inside a minivan. On the outside, it looked like a regular white delivery van. Inside, it was anything but ordinary. It had a dark gray bench on the right side, and on the left, a table with two large screens on it. Both the bench and the table were bolted to the floor.

Under the table, I could see two racks with a lot of blinking lights coming from computers, switches, a printer, and something like a police scanner. The ride to the destination felt like it took a few minutes, and I spent most of the time looking in fascination at all the equipment and imagining how many things a person, let alone a team, could do from this van.

Jack parked the van on a side street, where we had a good view of the hotel's back entrance. Our vehicle had cameras mounted in various places, enough to display a 360-degree view on the two large monitors. And of course, you could zoom in and out if needed.

We still had forty-five minutes before the meeting was supposed to occur, so we had plenty of time to study the terrain, so to speak. We again looked over the blueprints Mr. White provided, and Christopher walked us through the best route to intercept our targets once they left the hotel lobby. He was good at this kind of stuff, and I could definitely tell he had a lot of tactical experience

As he started explaining the best ways to avoid bumping into other people, I couldn't help myself. The question was heating my tongue.

Wouldn't it be easier if we flash some badges?" The second the words became airborne, I wished I could recall them like a bad email.

Christopher stopped, looked at me, and, with a condescending smile, said, "Who do you think we are, the FBI? We'll be in and out without anyone else noticing a thing until it's too late." He continued with the instructions and planning.

There were cameras inside the hotel along the hallways, but outside, none of the cameras covered the back entrance. This was good. Otherwise, the sight of three masked men running into a hotel would attract a lot of attention.

At T-minus fifteen, based on what I heard from Mr. White through my earpiece, Team A exited the car and left for the hotel's main entrance. Unlike us, they didn't have any bulletproof vests, but they had earpieces and microphones to listen and talk if there was a need. Unfortunately, we had no visual on them. There was no easy way to get the van from the main entrance to the back if Plan A didn't work. We wanted to reach the two targets while they were on the ground floor without letting them get to their hotel rooms. Otherwise, things would have been more complicated.

The hotel elevators were in a reasonably secluded area close to a stairwell. We planned to reach them when they were waiting for the elevators, so we could grab our targets, push them inside the staircase, then block the door.

All three of us had telescoping batons to make sure they quickly complied. I asked if we should focus on the person Schulte handed the thumb drive to, but everyone else said we couldn't take the risk the USB drive might have changed hands.

Therefore, we waited to see what Paul and Samantha could accomplish. A small part of me hoped they didn't find an opportunity so that I could be part of the action.

They reported they'd identified the two Chinese agents, and they headed toward a location where they could keep them insight.

Ten minutes passed, and no contact with Schulte.

I must have been checking the time on the monitors every few seconds because Jack put an arm on my shoulder.

"Relax, buddy," said Jack. "Try to relax."

I nodded, but I couldn't say I was relaxed. It was baffling how anyone could relax in a situation like this—it was nerve-wracking.

At 11:57, there was still no word about Schulte, but when I turned to ask Jack what we would do if he didn't show up, my earpiece offered a bit of static.

"He's here," said Mr. White, his voice came through crisp and loud over the audio device.

I thought my adrenaline level must be low or something. I had no energy left, and my hands were clammy. I couldn't believe this was happening. Now I wanted Paul and Samantha to succeed. I didn't think I would be able to take even a single step. But then I remembered all I had done the past week and what I'd found out about myself and the world around me. I had been through worse situations than this. All I was doing was sitting in a van. This was easy.

A smile started stretching across my face, and I realized I must have gone into my world for a moment.

"In that case, Team A, abort your mission and try to distract them when they reach the elevators," said Mr. White. "Team B will take over from there."

What happened? What did I miss?

Jack started the van and headed toward the hotel's back entrance. A hand grabbed my shoulder and shook me a bit.

"Focus," said Christopher. "Follow Jack's lead. Don't forget who our main targets are, and don't get sidetracked with their bodyguards. Either Paul and Sam will take care of them, or I will."

A grin spread across his face. And it wasn't a pleasant one. No. It was terrifying. Precisely what I needed.

I took a deep breath and let the energy rushing in. It was as if a dam broke and all the water was pouring in, unrestrained. I felt the excitement, the thrill of the hunt, but this time, my head was clear, and my thoughts focused. It was action time.

Jack stopped the van, and we all put our ski masks on and got out. Christopher, Jack, and I headed toward the entrance door, and Mr. White took the wheel, waiting for us with the engine running.

A random thought crossed my mind—*I hope we have enough gas*, but everything changed when I stepped inside.

My senses grew sharper, and my ears transformed into something like radar, trying to detect even the tiniest noise.

People shouted in the distance, or maybe they were just talking loudly, but they weren't coming toward us. Either we were lucky or had made an effective plan. We soon reached a door with a big G painted on it.

I assumed it meant we were on the ground floor, next to the elevators.

Christopher raised his fist.

It was a good thing that Andrew, a former Navy SEAL instructor, had taught me the standardized hand signals for close-range engagement operations.

I immediately recognized the sign and instantly froze.

Through the door, I heard people talking but couldn't understand what they were saying.

Christopher held up four fingers, meaning we had four

targets on the other side. With a wave, he signaled for us to follow and immediately opened the door.

Two people in suits blocked Paul and Samantha from getting to the two people behind them, the Chinese agents, the targets.

Christopher was the first to reach one of the agents and punched him hard in the face. I thought he would continue to the second target for a second, but he looked around and then changed direction toward the bodyguards. I didn't want to lose sight of my mark, so I kept my eyes focused ahead of me.

Jack went straight for the second target, so I grabbed the guy Christopher had just punched and quickly dragged him by the leg into the stairway. Still dazed, and I didn't think he understood what was happening. It bought me time to survey the situation.

Team A wasn't a combat team. Both Paul and Samantha were on the floor, trying to catch their breath, probably from being punched or kicked by the two guards, who now had their hands full with Christopher. He seemed to be managing well. His technique was sound.

Jack had tackled the second target to the floor. And by the looks of it, he needed some help because the second Chinese agent was on top of him.

So, I punched the dazed agent next to me, then hurried over to help Jack. One easy way to control an attacker from behind, especially if he's on top of someone, is to put your fingers into his nostrils and pull up.

This was precisely what I did. In an instant, he no longer had his hands on Jack's throat but instead on my arm, trying to free himself from my grip.

I was expecting something like this, so I dug the fingers of my other hand into his eyes under his eyebrows and pulled him toward me while quickly moving my body backward. Of course, this was much more painful, so he immediately tried and succeeded in turning around, effectively escaping from my grasp.

Unfortunately for him, I had both hands free.

He was still off-balance and bent forward. From here, I had multiple options, but what immediately came to mind was an old technique called *ganseki nage*, which was an arm hook used to throw the opponent.

So I hooked my right arm under his armpit, moved my right leg in front of him, and twisted my body, effectively sending him flying through the door into the stairwell, where there were no cameras. I quickly looked and saw Jack standing up, massaging his throat.

We ran to the door, good timing too because the guy I threw stood, leaning on the wall.

When he saw us, he tried to run. But I leaped on top of him, knocking him into the wall. I followed up with a succession of quick punches to the kidney, liver, and temple. He collapsed to the floor.

"Check his pockets," said Jack.

I went through his trouser pockets first and found them empty. So I turned him and checked the inner pocket of his suit jacket.

Jackpot. He had the USB stick. When I turned to let Jack know we had what we came for, I saw Jack's body flying toward me. He landed on top of me. And we fell together in a heap, both of us groaning from the impact.

I managed to get my head out of the way, but his body pinned me to the floor.

The second guy, the one who had been unconscious, stood up, supporting himself with a hand on the wall. He put his right hand inside his jacket, where I could see a shoulder holster.

Quickly, I pushed Jack off me. Then, as fast as I could, I got to my feet. I kept my eyes glued to the guy drawing his weapon, but despite my best effort, I was not fast enough.

In the time it took me to push Jack aside, stand up, and take a step forward, the Chinese agent had his gun on me. Then a loud bang tore through the room, and a body collapsed to the floor.

Luckily it wasn't me, and I had Christopher to thank. He came running through the door at the last moment and slammed the agent into the wall. The impact was so violent the guy immediately lost consciousness, or worse. I didn't see any blood splattered on the wall. So, he was probably out for a while.

"Thanks," I said. I realized I was clutching the USB drive in my right hand and held it up. "I have it." Christopher pulled something from his pocket and tossed it to me. Once I caught it with my left hand, I realized it was the fake USB drive.

"Plant the fake one and get his watch and wallet," said Christopher and disappeared, only to return a moment later with a laptop case.

"Let's go—people are coming," he said and started running.

Jack and I followed him, and in less than thirty seconds, we were outside where the van was waiting for us. Soon, all three of us were safely inside and closed the door. Mr. White drove away.

"We did it," I shouted, but the ski mask muffled the sound. "We did it!" I exclaimed again after I took it off.

"Hold your horses," said Christopher in a much more reserved tone, but I could see the beginning of a smile on his face. "Let's wait until we're clear before we give ourselves a pat on the back." Then, in a businesslike tone, he stretched out his hand and said, "The drive, please."

"Oh, sorry. I forgot." I checked my pockets to find it. For a brief second, I thought about making a joke and say I didn't know if I had it, but something told me no one would laugh. I handed him the drive.

"Thanks." He put it in his pocket.

The rest of the way, the others and I assessed our injuries and applied bandages where needed. Mostly it was just scrapes and bruises. Although Christopher must have taken a few punches, they didn't seem to bother him much.

I guess he's used to much worse.

When he changed his shirt, I saw a few serious-looking scars on his torso. I shuddered when I imagined how he got them, probably torture.

Instead of going directly back, we first stopped at a parking lot where we exchanged the van for a sedan of a make and model similar to what Paul was driving this morning.

As we entered the office, we found Paul and Samantha waiting for us. Samantha had a big red welt on her left cheek, and Paul's eye was purple and swollen.

"I'm glad we're all in one piece," said Mr. White. "Briefing room in five minutes." He started toward what seemed to be a private office I hadn't noticed before.

"How are you feeling?" Jack placed a hand on my shoulder. "Thanks for the help back there. You have some nice moves. What was that? Some sort of aikido?"

"Yeah, I did some aikido a while back," I said with a smile.

The technique I used was from a different martial art called ninjutsu, but aikido had something similar, so it was technically correct. Plus, each time I mentioned ninjutsu, people started thinking about guys in black pajamas.

I almost snorted. It wasn't much different from what I'd worn earlier.

"By the way, do you lift weights or something? The way you pushed me off was impressive—I know I have a few extra pounds," said Jack.

I hadn't considered it before—I hadn't had time to—but he did look like he was pushing two hundred pounds, or possibly a bit more, even though most of it seemed muscle.

"Yeah. I go to the gym often, almost every day," I said, not mentioning I didn't usually lift weights.

"That's cool. I wish I had the time, but this and, well, other things . . ." he said, without completing his thought. Our discussion stopped there.

Mr. White came out of his office and gestured for everyone to follow him into the conference room.

The next hour the group and I spent recounting the mission's events, with everyone describing what had happened from his or her point of view. The whole time, Mr. White took notes and asked clarifying questions. This helped paint a clear picture of everything that had happened, especially for me, and I assumed for the others too.

As a group, we only knew what had happened from our perspective. Once everyone had finished, a silence spread around the table. I was happy I didn't get shot and was thrilled to have managed to help the team achieve the objective. At the same time, I felt kind of sorry for Samantha and, to a lesser degree, Paul. They took some heavy punches.

"Given that no plan survives its first contact with the enemy, it looks like the only thing we have to worry about are the cameras near the elevators," said Mr. White once he finished going through his notes.

"That's not a problem. They were above the elevator entrance, so we were never within their field of view," Paul said, pointing at himself and Samantha. "And the guys had their masks on, so . . ." He nodded toward our side of the table.

"Perfect. This makes our life much easier," said Mr. White with a smile.

Then I realized something. Besides the cameras, they also had two bodyguards who could identify people, especially if the police brought in a sketch artist or showed them pictures from one of the other cameras.

"What about the bodyguards? They saw your faces," I said to Paul.

"They were probably hired by a local company, judging by the way they talked to us," said Samantha, as if that cleared everything up.

"So? Can't they describe you?" I insisted, turning to face Samantha.

"Mr. Connor, most of the local security firms here in DC have some connection with the Department of Defense," said Mr. White. "At this moment, I have people looking to see which company the two targets used. Soon the bodyguards will receive a call from their boss, who'll tell them to keep their mouths shut. They know better than to say too much when questioned by the police. At least not immediately after an incident like this. Plus, Sam and Paul did nothing wrong."

"What about Daniel Schulte? He may have seen you guys." I looked over at Paul and Samantha. "He may give information to the Chinese if they suspect foul play."

"Oh, Daniel Schulte will be too busy to identify anyone or give anything. An hour ago, the FBI received an anonymous tip the DoD contractor Schulte is working for has an insider threat. The tip also mentions there was an internal breach of their computer systems, resulting in stolen data.

Right now, he's a person of interest, having access to the stolen data."

"Won't the Chinese suspect us then?"

"No more than they suspect us now. In the data provided to the FBI, nothing was tying Schulte to the two Chinese agents. But once the FBI starts digging, we'll see."

"Sorry for asking so many questions," I said, a bit put out that my big revelations were things they'd already considered.

"Not at all, Mr. Connor. I want to ask you to keep doing that, all of you. We're all just humans, after all, and therefore prone to make mistakes. Now, I want to congratulate all of you on a job well done. Know I'm proud of you, but most importantly, your country is proud of you. Thank you again and—dismissed." Mr. White said in a powerful and intense voice.

His charismatic praise left me feeling elated and energetic. By the look in everyone's eyes, I could tell they felt the same.

As he exited the conference room, he turned, looked at me, and said, "Robert, before you leave today, please stop by my office. I have something to talk to you about."

"Sure," I replied, wondering why we couldn't do it now.

Jack shouted, "Party time," answering my unspoken question.

Their idea of a party consisted of beers, soda, and pizza.

I spent the next ten or twenty minutes listening to the "guys" telling all sorts of war stories. They asked me a few questions, and I happily answered them, but I mostly wanted to hear more of what they had to share. Anyway, most of the things I'd done I couldn't share with them, so I may have appeared dull.

Even Christopher was in a much better mood and didn't seem irritated by me. I guessed we both knew he'd saved me from being shot, which was something I gave him credit for during the debriefing.

Once I finished six slices of pizza, I wished the guys a good weekend and went to see Mr. White.

"Shut the door and have a seat," he said.

He had a medium-sized office, big enough to fit a couch, two chairs for visitors, and a desk with what looked like a comfortable chair for him. There was also a US flag standing on one side. However, I didn't see any personal photos or awards. There wasn't anything to indicate who he was. I'd asked the other members of the team if they knew his full name or even if White was his real last name, but they said they didn't know.

"I was impressed with you today. Good job. I've asked you here before you leave to clarify some logistics. This was a test, and you passed with flying colors. As I said during our first meeting, the DoD will reach out to your company, and the contract will require your skills from time to time. Besides the amount covered by the contract, you'll get a bonus after each mission. We usually know a few days in advance when our missions will be, but always be prepared, just in case there is an emergency. Most of the time, our missions will be here in the United States. The Special Operations Group handles covert operations on foreign soil. However, there have been cases when they ask us to participate in joint missions. If that happens, you don't need to worry about papers and visas. We will provide you with everything you need. Any questions?"

I hadn't expected anything like this. To say the least, his words stunned me.

"Thank you, sir. No, I don't have any questions," I mumbled.

"Okay. And don't worry, we take good care of our people," he said with a smile. "A few more things." He opened a drawer, pulled out a phone and a business card, and handed me the phone. "First, keep this phone with you at all times in case we need to contact you." He then gave me the business card with nothing but a phone number on it. "This is in case you have an emergency and need to reach us. Once we finalize the contract with your company, you will receive an access card for this building. Second, I hope I don't need to remind you everything we're doing here is about national security. You can't disclose anything you've seen and done. Everything stays inside the team. Is that understood?"

"Yes, sir," I said, shouting.

"Finally, you need to resume training with Andrew. We need you to be in top shape for each job."

Nothing he asked seemed too difficult, even though I was

a bit embarrassed to return to the dojo after skipping several months of training. Of course, I had a good excuse: I didn't have time, being busy at work and now other things.

"And tell him I said hi," said Mr. White with a sly smile, probably to let me know he would be watching. "Good day, Mr. Connor, and congratulations again on a job well done." He stood and extended his right hand.

"Thank you, sir." I shook his hand. Then, with a polite nod, I left.

WHEN I GOT BACK to the car, it felt like an entire day had passed. I needed to relax. I was too hyped up. Thoughts swirled through my head, making it difficult to do or think anything.

I implemented the same methods I used during meditation, an essential part of my martial arts training. With my eyes closed, I took deep breaths, letting the air enter my nose and guiding it through my body.

During my training, I had learned and noticed in my daily life that taking deep breaths led to better overall health, a calmer nervous system, balanced emotions, clearer perceptions, improved focus, and more energy. Deep breathing could change a person's mental and physical state in an instant. It had for me back in the van.

Imagining myself alone on a beach and facing the sea, I left my eyes closed. The warmth of the sun's rays slowly comforted me. The ocean breeze bustled through my hair and pushed my thoughts aside, leaving me focused on the sounds made by the waves pounding on the shore. If my mind wandered, I gently brought it back.

Time passed. It could have been a couple of minutes,

could have been longer. The ocean was now a lake. There was no breeze, and the waves were barely lapping the shore. I synchronized my breathing with the sound of my imaginary waves, and slowly it calmed down. I became more relaxed, and I opened my eyes.

The light was so bright I had to blink to grow accustomed to it.

'Hello, Robert, I've been waiting for you,' said a voice from, actually, I had no idea where the sound was coming from. It seemed to be coming from everywhere and nowhere. I looked around, but I saw nothing, just emptiness, and light.

'Where am I?'

'Where do you think you are?' replied a voice I didn't recognize.

I had no idea where I was. Had I been drugged and kidnapped, or was I on a table with doctors leaning over me?

'No one kidnapped you. And you can leave whenever you want,' I heard the voice say. It sounded truthful, but it still sent chills down my spine.

The voice knew what I was thinking, which meant it knew I knew it knew what I was thinking.

Oh, damn. This is complicated.

'Who are you?' I asked, wondering if I might actually be talking to—

'I'm not,' said the voice in a pleasant tone. The answer relaxed me a bit but also creeped me out. 'At least, not the way you imagine it.'

For sure, I knew he was able to read my thoughts—at least some of them. And I wondered what would happen if I tried to clear my thoughts and focus on one thing. So, I concentrated on *shijosho* or the three rings of a bell, which denotes the start of the meditation in the Zen temples in Japan.

What do you mean?' I asked with a frown.

'I'm not an old man with a white beard sitting on a golden throne. I'm more of a prophet. What I preach, men listen to.'

'Oh, like the ones in the Bible?' I asked quickly, this being my only reference book on prophets.

I'd done a lot of research, but few of the things I'd investigated related to the Bible.

'Not exactly, although I've met some of them.'

'Have you?' I asked, surprised.

'Yes. A few even studied with me, like Jesus, for example.'

'What are you talking about? Jesus wasn't a prophet.'

'He was a great person and smart. He went on to spread a lot of my teachings. But no, he was like us. Same as other prophets I've met and guided. Why do you think both Jesus and Muhammad preached similar things?'

'I may not be a religious person, but I think the Bible and the Qu'ran are quite different.' It was disconcerting.

Before last week, I would have ruled out this as a dream. But with all the witchy things I'd found out, I had to wonder what sorcery this was.

'Because my teachings have been altered by people over the years to fit their desires. The instructions are simple. We're all connected to this earth, to ourselves, to everyone else—to the entire universe. When you hurt someone, you're only hurting yourself. When you are kind to others, you are kind to yourself. I want to help people. I want to stop you from making a big mistake. You seem to have reached a stage where we can communicate like this. It makes things so much easier.'

I was stunned. Of course, I didn't believe a thing the voice was saying. Not sure why, probably my subconscious. But I had the feeling something was off. I willed this conversation to end, but I was also curious to see where it would go.

'And what do you want to talk about?'

'You.'

'What about me?'

'I want us to work together instead of against each other.'

'I don't think I've worked against you,' I said, a bit perplexed.

'Oh, but you have, and you do. You call them hashashins.'"

My blood ran cold.

'Why are you fighting them?'

It took me a few moments to answer. I had to move past my first answer, which would have been an angry one, and provide a more rational one.

'Because they've attacked me, and they kill innocent people,' I said, taken aback.

'That's from your perspective. You were never the real target, Robert. What would you say if I told you some of the people you saved will commit acts of great evil in the future? What would you say if I tell you that what you call hashashins are actually here to keep a balance?'

His words left me speechless. I had never considered this point of view. I never felt the need. The hashashins were evil and had to be stopped. Or did they? 'How do you know that?'

'I know many things, Robert. One of them is that the witch you saved has the potential to bring devastation, chaos, and great suffering to the world. Is this what you want?'

I refused to believe Dea was such a person. Of course, I saw Dea using her power in anger, but she did it to protect me and others. She wasn't the kind of person who would bring devastation, unless . . . No, I didn't, couldn't believe she would do such a thing.

But then why did this voice, whatever this was, feel the need to tell me these things?

'But how do you know all these things? Can you see into the future?'

'I can see many paths,' he replied in a patient tone.

'Assuming you're right, and I'm not saying you are, how do you know which one is the right one? How do you know your way is the best?' I asked, now feeling a bit resentful.

'Because I know where my way leads.'

'What if your way isn't the only way? What if there's another way?' I tried to find a flaw in the voice's logic.

I knew one thing for sure. Life was like a chessboard, and there was no one sure way to achieve something. Each move one made created new ramifications. One could achieve a goal through many paths.

For a few seconds, everything was quiet, and I wondered if he had left, leaving me alone with my thoughts.

'My way is the easiest. Other methods are more . . . much more complicated and challenging to see.

'But what if I can prevent the destruction and chaos you're talking about?'

Again, a few moments of silence.

'The only thing we can control is ourselves. We cannot truly control others.'

'You're saying there's nothing I can do to prevent whatever destruction you're talking about, and I should let the hashashins continue to kill people?' I asked, completely baffled.

'You should let them achieve their purpose, the reason they were created for.'

I knew what purpose they had. To kill. I knew myself, and I couldn't let it happen. Not on my watch.

'Did you create them?' I shouted, wondering if it was only in the recesses of my mind. A cold rage built inside me.

'Yes, they are my creation. I live through them. I see through them. And, Robert, I die through them.'

'So, you're not an immortal being?' My rage grew with every second that passed.

'No one is truly immortal. Even the infinite universe will have an end. But one can live for a long time, and one can see many things, things that have come to pass and things that will be. Trust me when I say this, you should not fight me—you should join me. Together, we can make sure the world will continue for a while longer.'

'And if I don't join you,' I forced myself not to shout, 'what exactly will happen?'

'A great war is coming. Powers which have not been summoned for millennia will be unleashed, and devastation and destruction will reign everywhere. You think you have time, but you are gravely mistaken. You do not. You must decide soon. Join me,' the voice said with a tone of finality that echoed in my mind.

Even though I didn't want to, I took some time to consider what the voice said. If everything I heard it say was correct, then there was only one choice I could make. But that was a big *if*.

'If what you say is true, then I don't really have a choice, do I?' I said with a bitter tone. 'There's only one problem. You made my decision for me a long time ago.' My voice was barely a whisper, and I still didn't know if this conversation was only in my head. The rage inside me came to a boiling point, filling every cell of my being, then I screamed, 'The night you killed my parents!'

I focused on *hozensho*, the single ring of a bell that ends a meditation.

All I could see was the light around me dimming, and I felt a sensation like being on a roller coaster enveloping me. My stomach dropped, and I was plummeting to the ground.

The last thing I heard was, 'You think they were your parents? How interesting.'

My eyes flew open, and my head bumped against the steering wheel. I jerked myself upright and looked around. I was still in my car across from the DoD office building.

I checked the clock, and it seemed only a couple of minutes had passed.

What happened? Was it real, or was it a dream? Should call Dea and tell her about my—I didn't even know what to call it. *Dream? Conversation? Premonition?*

In the end, I decided I should first get home and let all

this sink in. I was planning to see Dea later. I hoped she would have more answers.

The drive home was uneventful, and I arrived a few minutes before three in the afternoon.

My apartment must have had good *feng shui* because my internal turmoil ceased the moment I stepped in. I was finally able to put my thoughts in order. Feeling better and much calmer now, I decided to have a quick shower and then give Dea a call, hoping she was awake.

At the fourth ring, she picked up and said, " Hello," in a sleepy voice.

"Sorry. I didn't know you were sleeping. I'll call later," I said, secretly hoping she wouldn't agree.

"No, it's fine. I was waking up anyway."

"That's good, but if you want, I can call you later, once you're fully awake. I wanted to ask you something, but it's not important."

"I'm fully awake, Robert. What do you want to ask me?" she said, now clearly curious.

"Well, it's a lot to say over the phone. It's better if we can meet later, but basically, I want to ask if you or someone you know can contact a person remotely and talk to them," I asked, hoping she would get my meaning.

I didn't want to say the word *witch* over the phone, just in case. I was quite sure her first thought wouldn't be about a telephone or the internet.

For a few seconds, there was no reply. A thought even crossed my mind. Had she fallen asleep?

"Someone contacted you?" Her voice contained a solemn ring to it, and she slowly enunciating each word.

"I think so. I mean, I'm not sure."

"Can you come over, please?" she asked in a polite tone, but for some reason, it felt more like a command.

"Ah, yes, sure."

"Okay. Talk to you later, then," Dea said and hung up.

Without knowing what to think, I got dressed, pocketed my keys from the kitchen counter, and went to my car.

I'd already been to her house multiple times this week. So, the drive went by automatically, and without much focus on my part. Shortly after four, I was in front of her mansion. The gates started moving without waiting for me to buzz the intercom, and I stopped in front of the house.

The door opened, and I saw Dea standing there, studying me. She was wearing red fleece pants, a white tank top, and pink slippers. It looked adorable on her.

She motioned for me to come in and closed the door behind me.

"How are you feeling?" she asked but continued without waiting for an answer. "Please tell me everything that happened."

I followed her into the living room, and we both took a seat on the couch, which was much more comfortable than I expected.

During my drive, I'd had time to think about what I should tell her. Mostly, I debated whether I should mention that my mental conversation or hallucination included a warning about her. If I did, she would probably be upset, especially if it was a hallucination reflecting my thoughts about her.

But what if it isn't my imagination?

There were so many things I didn't know about magic. In the end, I decided to risk it and tell her everything, including what I thought I heard at the end about my parents. She listened carefully without saying a word.

"Do you think it was a dream, a premonition, or something else?" I asked once I finished telling the story.

"It was an astral projection directly into your mind," she said, studying me. "When someone has a link to you, they can use it to establish a connection from mind to mind."

"What do you mean by a link to me'?"

"Either a spell using something you own or a blood link."

"A blood link? Like a relative?"

"Not exactly, even though that will work, especially between a parent and a child, or siblings. The other possibility is through an exchange of blood."

"But I haven't exchanged blood with anyone," I said, a little scared.

"Well, you kind of did," she said, "when you saved me last week. You were cut, and when you removed the knife, our blood got mixed."

"So, this means you can contact me using a mind link?"

"In theory, I could, but to be able to talk to someone through a link like that requires a great deal of power and focus. The farther away you are, the more power is needed. Now, there's a possibility whoever was behind it was able to read your surface thoughts. Alyssa can do something similar. She is more precise because she can actually read them, but she has to be nearby. I don't think whoever did this was close to you."

"Why do you say that?"

"Otherwise, the conversation would most likely have been face-to-face," she said thoughtfully. "No, I think whoever contacted you was far away. Not even an entire coven can summon the power for such a spell. In fact . . ."

She looked lost in thought. I couldn't judge what she meant. I had no reference frame, but if she said it required a great deal of power, I believed her.

"Do you know why I couldn't tell if it was a male or female?" I'd tried after the conversation to remember if the voice was male or female, but I couldn't figure it out.

"Oh, yes. When we communicate directly from mind to mind, there's no such concept. You don't know who the other person is unless they want you to know. However, there are some risks. This method allows access to an individual's true self, to his or her thoughts and feelings. This also allows the planting of thoughts where there were none." Before I could fully comprehend the magnitude of what she had said and what might have happened to me if she, he, or it planted thoughts inside my head, she continued. "However, the process of putting thoughts into someone's head is difficult and can damage the mind. I think what you did, narrowing your focus on the bell, might have helped to prevent it. Also, a cleansing spell should remove any foreign thoughts."

"Should?"

"Well, all the things I'm telling you are things my coven and I learned from old books. We don't usually do them. The incantations required to implant thoughts over an astral projection have been lost for a long time. That's why what happened to you is disconcerting."

A thought occurred to me.

"Can a spell-like this have been written on a scroll similar to the ones we got in Egypt? What if someone found other scrolls?"

"It's a possibility. From what you say, the voice mentioned it had wanted to speak with you for a long time. And it also said he or she is creating those hashashins you've been fighting for the past decade. Everything points to the fact that whoever is behind this has had access to potent spells long before today. I don't think we can wait any longer—we have to start your training now." She stood and motioned for me to follow her.

"You mean, right now?" I asked, taken by surprise, and I hurried after her. Then I remembered the other thing I wanted to talk to her about. When we reached the stairs, I said, "Actually, there's something else I want to ask you, but I think we'll have to cancel."

"Have to cancel what?" she asked, climbing the stairs.

"Um, my work colleagues are planning a triple date at your club tonight, and I agreed we'd go, hoping you wouldn't mind. But I don't think we'll be able to make it, so I think I should cancel—"

She quickly turned around—a mischievous glint in her eyes. "We'll have plenty of time. When is this date?"

"It's at seven tonight, and right now, it's almost six. Unless my training only lasts a few minutes, I don't think we'll have enough time. But I can call and let them know we won't be able to make it." To be honest, I was glad to be starting my training at last.

"Don't worry about it. We'll have plenty of time. Now let's go into my room."

Usually, when a woman tells you this, it probably means something else, and while I confess, I'd had thoughts of hearing those words during the past week, the image I had in my mind was quite different from the reality of what was happening now.

Her room was not what I had expected. I anticipated some witchy things, maybe a cauldron or a broom, or even a pentagram on the floor. Instead, it was a standard room with light green paint on the walls, a queen-size bed, and two white nightstands to frame it. The only thing out of place was what seemed to be an antique armoire against one wall.

"If you're wondering what this is, it's a mirror." She opened the armoire to reveal a full-length mirror with a solid wooden frame with a black finish. "Except this one's no normal mirror."

"What is it, then?"

"That's where we'll train," she said with a wink.

"Ah, say again? Train with a mirror?"

"Not with a mirror—in a mirror."

"In a mirror?" I asked dumbfounded. "Really? How does it work?"

"This mirror allows us to step into a different dimension that mirrors, pardon the pun, our own. When we step into the mirror, we'll step into whatever the mirror reflects, which right now is this room. Once we're inside, we'll be out of normal time. Therefore, the time we spend there won't count in real life. For example, let's say we spend an hour there. Once we get back, it'll be like we never left."

"That's amazing. You mean we can spend days, weeks, or even years there, and when we get back, we won't have aged a day? What about food and water?"

"You won't feel the need for food or water, but there is a catch. Your time there is powered by your energy. The more time you spend there, the more energy you lose. It's a constant drain. You must never, ever fall asleep in there," she said in an ominous tone.

"Why not?"

"Because if you don't wake up in time and the mirror drains all your energy, you'll end up a wraith."

"I'm sorry I must have missed that class. A what?"

"A ghostlike image of yourself that will remain trapped in the mirror forever. Trust me on this. Don't ever fall asleep in there. However, we'll both be in there, so the drain won't be so bad. Even by myself, I can easily spend one or two hours in there without any issues. Now, follow what I'm doing."

She raised her right hand, and with her index finger, touched the mirror. A second later, I did the same.

"*Speculum speculum onerariis Nobis in Mundo tuum,*" she whispered in Latin and then turned toward me, smiling.

I don't know how, but everything surrounding me seemed to become reversed in the blink of an eye. Instead of my right hand extended and touching the mirror, it was my left. I looked around me, and everything in the room appeared reversed.

"One other thing about this place. It's a mirror image of the outside world. So, whatever we do here won't have any impact on the real world. However, we have to be careful about the mirror. If something happens to it, we'll be trapped, so try to avoid that area if you can," she said, pointing to where the mirror was.

"But what if something happens to the mirror in real life? What if there's an earthquake or something?"

"We're out of normal time, so nothing will happen there as long as we're here."

"So, whatever happens here stays here, just like in Vegas," I said with a grin. I don't think she got the meaning of my attempt at humor. She continued without even the hint of a smile.

"Okay, let's start your training. I hope you brought a notebook because your phone will be useless here."

Naturally, I didn't. I wasn't aware I would be starting my magical training, so I shook my head.

"Don't worry." She smiled. "You can take notes afterward."

"Thanks." She seemed to be a bossy teacher, but I didn't mind.

"The first thing is to visualize your inner power. It's the 'well' where your magic is stored. Everyone sees it differently. For some, it's a white globe or a cube. Others visualize a cauldron. They all have one thing in common. A vessel where energy can accumulate."

"And what happens if it overflows?"

"It doesn't overflow." She chuckled at my naïveté. "You can never accumulate more magic than your well allows. You can use items to store magic, but they won't be part of you. One other thing. If you use all the magic within you, you die."

This sounded like something I should avoid.

"And how can I visualize my magic well?" I was starting to get excited about this training.

"That's what I'm going to teach you. Now close your eyes, let your mind flow free for a second, then look inside yourself and focus on these words *power come forth*."

I did what she said, but no matter how much I focused, nothing happened.

"It's not working," I said after a while, frustrated.

"The first time is always difficult. Witches train for years before we are allowed to make this attempt, but you're a natural. I've seen you in action. Remember what you felt when your power manifested itself in London. Focus on it. Hold that feeling and try again."

For a few seconds, I looked into her eyes to calm my thoughts, and then I slowly closed my eyes and welcomed the darkness behind my lids. My mind no longer wandered. I gave it a direction by focusing on the small area of my brain, which held the memory of what had happened earlier this week. I remembered the cold fury, the rage I couldn't do anything to stop the van from crushing Dea. Then I remembered the words "not her."

Something started to happen inside me. I could feel it. A pressure was building just below my navel. It was like there was nothing, and all of a sudden, there was something tangible there. But it wasn't something physical. It felt more like a flow of water, ready to burst open.

So, I focused on the meaning of the words "power come forth" and willed it, whatever was gathered inside me, to manifest itself.

My feet were touching the sand, and there was water up to my ankles. Everything was hidden by a milky mist, gently floating around me. I held my hand inches from my face, but I couldn't see it. I crouched and touched the water. It wasn't too cold, and it felt refreshing and energizing. I cupped my hands and took a small sip. It tasted sweet, like ambrosia filling my mouth. I instantly realized this was precisely what I had been looking for—my power. I opened my eyes.

"I did it! I did it!" I shouted triumphantly.

A warm smile appeared on Dea's lips, and her eyes sparkled. "I knew you could do it," she said proudly. "What did you see?"

"I was somewhere with my feet in the water, and all

around me, there was a mist. I took a sip from the water and instantly knew it was my power. That's when I opened my eyes."

Excitement filled me to the core, but I could see a frown forming on her face. Her reaction wasn't what I expected.

"Isn't that what's supposed to happen?" I asked, afraid I did something wrong.

"No. Yes. I'm not sure," she said, looking confused. "We should be able to easily visualize our powers so that we'll always know how much we have available. You seem to have some kind of block or veil over your well, and I'm not sure why."

"But I thought . . ."

Confusion etched my mind because now I doubted myself.

Did I do it right or wrong?

"Anyway, let's worry about this later. Today, we'll start with two basic spells," she said, enthusiastic again. "One is to protect against magical attacks, and the other is a cleansing spell to eliminate any residual foreign magic. Many of the rituals we perform have a circle as their base. Often, we use a circle to create a sacred space and form a magical protection ring against outside interference. It provides a peace of mind to perform whatever spells you want inside it."

"Quick question. How do I draw the circle? On the floor or on a piece of paper? Can I use a pen?"

"Ah, yes. Usually, a protection circle is made of salt infused with your blood, power, and will. It's one of the most powerful ways of doing it besides using certain metals. But today, we're going to use chalk."

Dea handed me a piece of white chalk she produced from a pocket in her pants.

"Let's see your drawing skills." A grin formed on her face, and she pointed at the wooden floor.

Unfortunately, my circle had a bit more of an oval shape.

"That won't do. It has to be a circle. Otherwise, the energy won't circulate properly. Try again."

I must have drawn half a dozen circles until she was satisfied.

"Okay, now, let's step inside." She beckoned for me to follow.

Once we were in, she placed a finger on the ring of chalk and said, *"Protego."*

I felt a sudden change of pressure, and my ears popped. "What just happened?"

"I closed the circle," she explained, drawing an imaginary circle with her finger. "Now it's your turn." She smudged a bit of the circle line, and again, the pressure changed.

Using the chalk, I fixed what she had erased, and then, mimicking her gesture, I pointed my finger to the line I had just drawn.

"Protago," I said.

Nothing happened, and I glanced at her, confused. She looked back and smiled.

"Two things. One, you have to touch the circle when you say it. Second, it's *protego*, not *protago*, and you need to accentuate the *O* at the end. Try again."

After a few more tries, I finally felt the change in pressure, and when I looked at Dea, she seemed pleased.

"Well done. Now let's move on to some incantations. The first one is for protection. Repeat after me, *Si malum vult habitant in loco hoc, prohibere et tueri.* Basically, it means the circle is your home, and nothing can get inside. Now let's hear it."

"Wait a second. Can you please repeat the incantation? A bit more slowly?"

Half an hour later, once I had the incantation memorized along with the proper intonation, I decided to try it.

"So, how will I know if it works?"

"Great question. Let me get out of the circle." She stepped out and turned to face me.

"I didn't feel my ears pop. Does it mean the circle is still intact?"

"Yes. If you don't destroy the line, the circle will remain intact. Now let's hear the incantation. And don't forget to touch the floor inside the circle."

I took a deep breath, closed my eyes, pressed my right index finger to the hardwood floor, and said in a clear voice, *"Si malum vult habitant in loco hoc, prohibere et tueri."*

I felt something like a small electrical current at the tip of my finger and opened my eyes to look at Dea. She was smiling and nodding.

"I think it worked. Let's give it a try." She raised her right palm, and then sparks appeared inches from my face.

"Hey, I wasn't ready. What if it didn't work?" I exclaimed, thrilled and scared at the same time. I hadn't expected her actually to try something against me.

"Don't be a baby." An impish grin covered her beautiful face. "We both know the incantation worked. You have to learn to trust yourself. Otherwise, the spells won't be as powerful as they should, and they might not even work at all. Now, let's look at the second incantation." She stepped inside the circle.

"Why can you step in and out without affecting the circle?"

"Right now, it's been raised to stop magical attacks. We haven't raised a circle to stop physical intrusions."

"We can do that?"

"Yes, but it's much more complicated. We did something similar last Saturday when those hashashins attacked us here. That's why they couldn't get through to us. However, it took both my mom and me to do it. But there were a few more spells woven into it. Now, even a basic circle to protect against physical attacks is difficult to raise on your own.

Okay, now let's look at the second incantation. Repeat after me, *Et cingor fulgentibus orbi auri praesidio solatium purgationis.*"

I did everything she said numerous times until she decided I was ready to try. She sat next to me, took my left hand in hers, and nodded for me to start.

I did the same thing I had done last time. I closed my eyes, lifted my right hand, so the palm faced my forehead, and, in a confident voice, repeated the words she'd taught me.

As I uttered the last word, "*purgationis*," my palm heated up, causing something akin to a burning sensation. Then, all of a sudden, the heat moved away from my palm, enveloping my forehead and then my entire head. It felt like I was in the desert, and the sun was beating down on me.

Slowly, the heat started moving to my chest, arms, belly, pelvis, legs, and feet, and then it gradually dissipated into the ground. I slowly opened my eyes and looked at Dea, who was beaming with joy.

"That was astonishing, Robert." She kissed me.

I was a little surprised, but my body reacted before my mind had time to register what was happening. I pulled her closer and started kissing her hungrily.

Instead of exploring each other's mouth and lips, it was more like we were both controlled by one of the most fundamental instincts, our minds consumed by lust.

A small part of me started to feel tired and drained, but I ignored it and then forgot about it. We began to breathe more deeply and in sync. I gently pushed her down, shoulders touching the floor. I kissed her mouth, lips, neck, earlobes, and neck again.

"Robert," I heard her say in a hoarse voice, but I ignored her, my mind full of lust, my body getting more and more tired. "Robert, we—" she tried to say, but our mouths met again. I could feel her hands trying to get my T-shirt off.

So, I stopped for a second to help her, but then she opened her eyes, and our gazes met. I could feel the heat burning in those emerald eyes, and I knew she could feel mine as well. However, at the same time, we both felt something else, an enormous drain of energy that shocked us both out of our drunken lust.

"We have to go." Dea tried to get up, a frightened look on her face, and I quickly helped her to her feet. "Put your hand on the mirror—fast!"

As instructed, I placed my palm against the surface.

The moment I did it, I heard her whisper, *"Speculum onerariis Nobis in Mundo tuum,"* and everything reversed back to normal.

I still felt tired, but the constant drain I noticed earlier had disappeared.

"What happened there?" I said, panting.

"I'm not sure," Dea said, a bit out of breath. "I've never felt anything like this. Let's not do that again until I can figure out what happened," she said with an apologetic smile, and I saw her cheeks redden.

"I agree. We won't do *it* in there."

She gave me a big grin and a wink. "We'll see. Until then, didn't you say we have a triple date planned?"

"Oh, yes. I completely forgot about that, but I think it's too late now." In truth, I wasn't feeling too bad about it.

"Actually, if you check your watch, you'll see we have plenty of time. Now, do you mind turning around so I can dress?" An alluring smile played on her lips.

I wanted to sneak a peek, but I didn't. I opened my phone to check my email and read some messages on WhatsApp from Steven and Mark, confirming the time and place. My eyes fell on the icon of my news app, and the whole morning came crashing back into my reality. During the past few hours, I had completely forgotten how my day began. With a hand trembling both from fear and excitement, I pressed on the icon and started scrolling through the headlines. Nothing. I then checked other sections, but there was still nothing. I felt Dea behind me, her hand on my shoulder.

"Everything all right? You seem tense," she said, a concerned look on her face.

"Oh, it's nothing," I said and turned to look at her, "I was—"

Whatever I was about to say died on my lips. Seeing her in a skin-tight shiny black leather skirt and a semi-transparent white blouse showing quite a bit of cleavage made all the lust I'd felt a few moments ago erupt again.

My heart raced faster, my face grew warmer, and my eyes, trapped right in front of me, staring at her chest.

"Ahem. My eyes are up here." She lifted my chin until I was gazing at her smiling face.

"Oh, right, sorry," I said, not meaning it.

Now I noticed she had makeup on and curls in her hair, which I didn't remember seeing before.

"You look wonderful," I said lamely, then recalled the days when we were in London and Cairo and how she'd managed to have a completely new look in minutes. "How do you get ready so fast? Do you use the mirror?"

I inclined my head toward the armoire. Of course, using a mirror had a completely different meaning now.

"Ha-ha. No," she replied with a smile. "A girl has to have some secrets, right?" Then she gave me a quick peck on the lips. "Let's go. You don't want us to be late, do you?"

20

THE SUV, her detail, tailed my car the moment I pulled out of the mansion's private drive. Spotting the men brought a wave of pure happiness to wash over me because I knew they followed in tight formation this time. I even almost asked if she wanted to have them drive us around but realized she might prefer to be with me, away from everyone else. I assumed having someone escort you everywhere could get tiring.

I eased into the club's parking lot, scanning the area for a parking space.

"Stop at the front door and ask for the valet service." Dea ran a hand through the ends of her hair, smoothing them.

"Is this a service the club usually provides?" I didn't recall seeing valets prior, but then again, I never looked for one.

"No. It's a service only for the club owners and their close friends." She winked at me.

I guessed parking wouldn't be an issue from now on.

Dea and I were the first to arrive, even though it was fifteen minutes 'til seven. Once inside, a hostess led both of us to one of the VIP booths.

"A member of the waitstaff will take your order shortly."
The hostess smiled.

"Thanks," I said. "Oh, wait. I'm expecting some friends."

"When they arrive, I'll personally show them to your table, Mr. Connor," she said. Then with a nod, she walked back to the hostess desk downstairs.

"What can I get for you?" The server's voice rode a tad higher than the soundwave of the music.

"A virgin Cuba libre." I got settled at the table.

"One Coke coming up." The server smiled. Either she had received a similar order in the past, or she was sharp. "The usual, ma'am?"

"Yes." Dea frowned at me for a second, but I could see the wheels spinning in her mind, then a grin stretched across her beautiful lips.

"Hey, isn't Lydia doing a shift today so she can keep an eye on you? I didn't see her at the house. Actually, I haven't seen anyone else."

"No, they left on some urgent business at the office." Her smile was gone, and her look darkened.

"Oh, okay, I thought they were still sleeping after the party last night."

The server delivered our drinks. Neither of us said anything, and I took a long sip from my Coke.

"The meeting didn't end well," Dea said in a subdued voice. "That's why everyone is at the office."

"What do you mean?"

"They, the Reyes Coven, want to take over the East Coast."

"What? How?"

The details aren't significant, but they already control all the covens in South and Central America and the south-western part of the US," she said with a tight voice. "They're looking to control the entire continent."

"Can they do that?"

"We're not sure. Remember the first night I came to your place, and I told you what I was?" I nodded. "I briefly mentioned a war erupted between the covens in Europe, and after that, we had the Dark Ages."

"Sure, I remember."

"Well, to prevent another conflict from happening . . ." she took a drink then continued, "the twelve most powerful covens established a set of rules every witch and mage must follow."

"Such as?"

"Some of the most important rules are not to tell regular people about our existence and not to fight among ourselves. We're so few in number. In the end, each of the twelve covens moved to different countries where they had to maintain peace among the magical community. And remember, there are beings other than witches who don't necessarily respect our rules."

"More supernaturals?"

The mere suggestion of other supernatural beings made my brain work overtime, scrubbing every movie I'd ever seen. Demons, werewolves, and other fae, the possibilities were endless.

"For centuries, this worked well enough, but the past several decades, the Reyes Coven, the one we met with earlier today, started to take over smaller covens. Most of us prefer not to live among regular humans. Only recently, we found out that entire covens have disappeared from the face of the earth."

"And your coven suspects foul-play?"

"Maybe," she took a drink of her wine. "Something similar happened in the Middle East after the First World War. Many of the covens there were destroyed, including Henry's first coven, which was one of the original twelve. Right now, out of the twelve, only seven are left standing."

I was stunned and immediately remembered what the voice had said to me earlier about a war coming.

Could this be it? Will someone attack Dea's coven—my coven? Should I ask Dea to teach me more spells so I can fight?

Everyone else had decades of experience casting spells and dealing with magic, not mere hours like I did. For a second, I got the crazy idea of involving my new acquaintances. Even if they believed me, they wouldn't necessarily devote resources to something like this.

The CIA had a lot of resources, but the coven had money and magic to help us convince whoever needed convincing, one way or another. But first, I needed more information.

"How did it happen? Were they taken by surprise?"

"We're not sure. From the snippets we've heard from those who survived, the covens were caught unprepared. A few escaped. But only because they weren't there at the time. Whatever or whoever attacked the coven homestead killed everyone else."

"Is it difficult to attack a coven? I assume they can defend themselves."

"Yes, we can, but we need time. Witches or mages are much more effective when they have time to prepare instead of being forced to do something on the spot. That way, you can set up defensive wards, imbue items with spells that will trigger at your command, cast force domes—"

"Force domes? What are those?"

"They're protective shields that surround a person, object, or structure. They're designed to stop physical attacks."

"Ah, like what you did in London when the car came at us, and then in Cairo when you stopped that knife?"

"Like what we both did in London," she said with a smile. "You also provided the power necessary to raise the force wall. But yes, it's similar, except a dome is designed to protect from attacks coming from all angles, and it requires a lot more power."

I sat back, Coke in hand, and got comfortable.

"After the meeting with the Reyes Coven, we conjured a force dome to protect the house, except this one is slightly different. It will stop any kind of attack, whether physical or magical. It's similar to the wards we deployed when the hashashin came to our house, except we've modified the spell not to react, just to withstand."

"But I didn't see anything earlier. And I had no problem getting into your house."

"You're already known to be welcome in the house. So, the spell won't have any effect on you. It is an invisible barrier that stops anyone who doesn't have an invitation. If you're not allowed, you'll find yourself going somewhere else, without knowing exactly why. Right now, besides the coven members—which includes you—our security guards, and a few others, no one can get past the front gates uninvited. It will stay that way until either we remove the spell, or there isn't enough power to maintain it."

"And how do you power it? I assume it's not something you can plug in, like into a wall socket?"

"No, you definitely can't," Dea said with a laugh. "But we do use a Source, which is something like a magical battery. Every day, we store some of our power in the Source. We've had it in our coven for hundreds of years, since my great-grandmother created it, and I don't think we've used more than a couple of times. We're not worried the power will be depleted anytime soon. Right now, we have the most well-protected coven house on the entire continent—not that anyone would be foolish enough to attack us."

"Why? Because of the protections you have?" I asked, happy to see how confident she was.

"Remember what I told you about the seven covens? Well, we're the most powerful of them all. With that shield up, nothing will get through—not even if all the other covens attack at the same time."

"Who are the seven remaining covens?"

"Well, the Reyes Coven is one of them. Initially, they controlled only Central America, but now they want more. Then there's the Sokolov Coven in Russia, which is based in Moscow but controls all the smaller Russian covens. And it has a lot of ties in Eastern Europe."

"Interesting." Somehow, I wasn't surprised by this news. It seemed logical a coven would call Russia home.

"In China, there's the Ying Coven. It's located in Hebei Province, north of the Yellow River. And they control most of the covens in East Asia. India doesn't have a coven, but they have several powerful witches who, for the most part, are under the control of the Ying Coven. Only one coven remains in the Middle East, the Dhanyal Coven. They're located near Islamabad in Pakistan."

"That leaves three, your coven, and who else?"

"The last two powerful covens are the Lupei Coven, based in Romania in the Carpathian Mountains, and the O'Toole Coven in Ireland. They live in Bray, a lovely small town near Dublin. Siobhan, who's in charge of the O'Toole Coven, is a close friend of my mother. And she's one of the people I mentioned who are welcome in our house. There are other covens on the other continents, but they're smaller and lack significant power, which is why they're not counted among the seven."

"So, why is the Reyes clan allowed to destroy other covens?"

"We think they have an understanding with a few smaller covens and one or two of the six, the ones who don't have an interest here."

"Do you know which ones they are?"

"No, but we have our suspicions. Most probably, it's the Sokolov and Dhanyal Covens," she said bitterly, "even though

I don't know why those two would work together. Mother says our friendship with the Irish coven is quite unique, and none of the other covens trust each other. They see everyone else as a potential enemy trying to undermind their power."

"Do you think the Reyes clan will attack you, I mean, us?"

"I don't think they will, at least not directly, even though I would prefer it if they do," she said with a malicious smile.

"Why?"

"Even though they have more territory and more witches and mages than we do, we are more powerful than they are. However, they will most certainly attack us financially first, and this is why everyone went to the office."

"To prepare for that possibility?"

She nodded, then took a deep breath.

"There is another thing I haven't told you."

"Which is?"

"For a while now, our influence, and I mean the coven's influence, is diminishing because someone is actively working to make sure we don't have the same influence we used to."

"What do you mean?"

"Once, a long time ago, my coven was involved in the ruling process. Kings and queens highly regarded our advice. Then things started changing. And right now, we have to closely guard whatever influence and allies we have in the governments."

"Why?"

"A lot of them either disappeared or were found dead, and the only thing we managed to find out was a name."

"And it is . . . ?"

"*Efreeti*. We don't know what it means, but we know it's an old name given to death spirits and demons. That's why I was sure my mother would be happy to support you joining the CIA. We need allies, and they can help us find out who's behind this."

I wanted to ask more questions, but I heard voices, and when I looked up, I saw Steven and Mark alongside two blondes, the sisters I'd learned about, coming our way.

For the rest of the evening, Dea and I made the bare minimum of polite conversation to maintain an average couple's appearance on a regular date. I don't think we succeeded, but at least the guys were too used to my quirkiness to give it much thought.

The table mostly listened to Brenda and Nicki talk about television shows, music, clothes, and other things that completely flew over my head. I was too distracted by what I'd found out earlier, and both Steven and Mark seemed distracted by Dea.

Later in the conversation, I realized the two girls were interested in the money the guys and I had received following the acquisition completed on Friday, which I'd forgotten about.

Several hours later, after checking her phone, Dea announced she had to leave. Based on the smiles and looks the two sisters exchanged, they were pleased to see her go. And I assumed they perceived her as a threat to their new boyfriends.

If Dea noticed, she didn't show it. I had the feeling she didn't care what anyone else at the table thought about her—except for me.

We said our goodbyes and headed toward the exit. On our way out, she opened her purse to check her phone. It was the first time I saw her doing it, totally different from Brenda and Nicki—it felt like they checked their phones every few seconds.

"Do you have to go?" I asked, hoping she wanted to go somewhere else less crowded and more private.

"Unfortunately, I do. I need to get to the office as soon as possible," she said with an apologetic smile.

"Okay, we can take my car." I fished through my pockets for my keys.

She smiled. "No need, a car is already waiting outside, and I think you left your keys with the valet."

As we exited the club, lo and behold, the same black SUV was waiting outside, and next to it, there were two security guys I'd previously seen at the house. We said our goodbyes and had a long kiss, which finished sooner than I liked, but that—I hoped—promised more to come.

Moments later, my car appeared, and the same valet who had parked it earlier got out and held the door open for me to get in.

I thanked him and handed him a twenty-dollar bill, but he smiled and politely refused it. I wondered whether he declined it because of instructions he was given or because I didn't tip him enough.

It didn't take long to get home, and I exited the car and headed toward the elevators to go to my apartment. Thoughts of what Dea and I talked about turned over in my mind, especially the information regarding the warring covens.

Something like a truck crashed into my right shoulder. A sharp pain electrified my shoulder, and I thought I heard a snap.

My body flew into one of the support pillars of the parking structure. The back of my head must have hit the concrete because an intense pain gripped my skull, and everything became blurred.

The sounds faded. I felt like everything was still, and I was spinning with my head underwater. It took me a few seconds to recover, and when I raised my gaze, I saw two gleaming red eyes staring at me from the shadows. They were the eyes of a predator.

There was motion in the darkness, and in front of me stepped a very tall and ashen-looking man. His hair was white, but there were only a few strands left. He was almost bald and had large ears, pale and sickly-looking skin like he was anemic, and thin white lips. The red of his irises swirled like flames of fire, giving off a hypnotic effect.

"Where 're the scrolls?" he said in a heavy Scottish accent.

"What scrolls?" I asked, trying to get up. Sharp, stabbing pain in the ribs on my left side, pinned me down.

"The ones ye took from Cairo," he said in a poisonous sweet voice.

"I have no—" I started saying through my clenched teeth.

"Don't play games with me, lad. I recognize yer scent. Ye were in London along with the witch and her mage," he said menacingly.

"Look, I really don't—" I started saying but froze.

He became a blur, and suddenly his fiery red eyes were less than an inch from my face. I was horrified, like when you wake up and see a giant black spider on the white pillowcase next to you, with its hairy legs almost touching your face.

Not sure exactly what the trigger was—probably my brain recognizing the futility of a fight against him—but a memory from long ago flooded my mind . . .

"What other techniques do I need to learn to be like those SEAL guys you've trained?" I asked Andrew.

"Son, it's not only about the techniques." When he saw my disappointment, he continued. "Let me give you an example. Let's say there's a huge guy who's an excellent fighter who wants to steal a piece of bread from you, but he knows he's doing something wrong. Then imagine there's a woman who thinks you've done something terrible to her baby. Which of those two would you be more afraid of?"

It took me less than a second to answer, "The woman, of course."

"And why is that?" Andrew asked me, obviously pleased.

"Because the woman won't stop. She'll attack relentlessly."

"Exactly. That's the difference between anyone from this dojo

or any other dojo and one of the SEALs. Each fight they're in, it's to the death."

As the memory flashed through my mind, I decided to try a technique I'd never used before, mainly because I'd never felt so desperate. I focused on my increased speed and strength, and my right hand shot up in a blur toward the attacker's face, trying to gouge his eyes out with my index and middle fingers.

It would have been impossible for any human to dodge such a thrust with such a short distance between us. But the moment I moved, I realized I was right—my speed had greatly improved, and my blow was definitely too fast for any human to block.

Unfortunately, he wasn't human, and he batted my fingers away in a blur. A second later, the pain struck, and to my dismay, I realized he had broken my fingers.

"Some people need motivation. Ye know whit the best motivation is, laddie?" he asked in a mocking tone but didn't wait for an answer. Something cold grabbed my leg above the ankle. It felt like my leg was caught in a vise, slowly crushing my veins, muscles, and bones.

My vision blurred. Darkness was creeping around the corners, and tears rolled down my face.

I screamed with everything I had until there was no more air left in my lungs. At some point, he stopped because the pain receded, but only by a fraction, enough to let me gather my thoughts.

"Oh, whit a sweet sound," he said, licking his lips. "So, where 're the scrolls?"

"I don't know. The coven has them." I was barely able to speak, fearful I would start screaming again.

"See? It wasn't too difficult, was it?" He snickered gleefully. "Do ye know where they keep 'em? Have they managed to translate 'em? And don't think ye can lie to me, lad, I can feel yer pulse. And I can smell the blood in yer veins."

"I don't know," I screamed, hoping he wouldn't notice my lie.

"Whit did I say? Why 're ye trying to deceive me? All this could have ended quickly for ye. But now it will be much more painful. Let's start with a taste, shall we?"

I saw two huge fangs elongate and protrude from his mouth. Their points were sharp, like ice picks. A vicious smile stretched across his inhuman face and scared me to the bones. However, it also enraged me.

Maybe it had to do with everything that had happened the past week, perhaps it was the desperation before death, or it was a mixture of both, but I could feel the arm with Dea's bracelet on it starting to rise and pressure building inside me. Then, all of a sudden, a wave of heat started traveling through my body. It began in my stomach, ran up my torso, down my left arm, and then pushed through my open palm like a torrent of water from a large fire hose.

The vampire, or whatever it was, went tumbling through the air and into the wall.

Vampires can fly.

I felt a strange sensation enveloping me—strange at that moment, at least.

It was a feeling of pride and satisfaction. I was overjoyed to finally be able to cast a spell entirely on my own without any help and without even being shown how.

Unfortunately, dizziness and terrible nausea replaced the joyful feelings, and I started taking shallow breaths to force myself to remain conscious and alert, but I found it challenging to do so.

My left side felt like a hot iron was poking between my ribs. And each time I took a breath, a deep pain in my chest made it hard to draw a full breath.

"And I thought this job wouldn't be interesting. Is that all ye got? Pitiful." He slowly picked himself up off the ground. "Ye don't smell like a mage, not exactly," he said, giving me the once-over. "It doesn't matter, anyway; now besides yer blood, I'll take yer power."

In a blur, he was next to me, his gleaming eyes focused on my throat, and something like saliva started dripping from his fangs, much like a rabid dog.

I tried to kick him in the knee with my uninjured leg, but the kick didn't have enough power.

He stomped on my foot, crushing my bones, and I howled in pain. I would have screamed for longer, but I didn't have enough air left in my lungs. Next, a powerful kick landed on my stomach, and for a second, I was afraid it went all the way through me, into the concrete pillar behind my shattered back.

The impact seemed to puncture something, possibly my lungs or some other internal organs. When I tried to breathe, a sharp pain stabbed through me, and I made a wheezing sound, then pink foam started dripping from my mouth, landing on my hands.

I was amazed at how part of my brain could be so detached with all the pain and suffering. This week had been the most dangerous in my life, and quite possibly, the most successful until now.

Our actions in Egypt had given a blow, hopefully, a crippling one, to whoever was behind the hashashins. Never in my life had I felt so many of them before in one place, and I was sure they were there for the scrolls. I had narrowly avoided death two and a half times.

The first two times, Dea saved me from the hashashins, who tried to stab me to death, and I only counted the time earlier today, when I almost got shot, as half because I had a bulletproof vest on. But there was no one here to save me this time, and I doubted even a bulletproof vest would have made any difference in this case. I couldn't get up. I couldn't breathe. I had internal damage to some of my organs. I was sure of it. And I had broken ribs, possibly a whole lot of other things I didn't know about, as well.

Then I saw the gleaming blade of the knife he must have pulled from his black robes, and when I looked closely, I realized it was a familiar knife. The blade was short, curved, and made of something dark like obsidian. I knew the hilt appeared to be made of wood with different inscriptions on it, and it had a large red ruby at the end. If anyone else but me and the hashashins touched the knife, they should get a cold burn. However, this guy didn't seem to have any issues.

"Ye've seen one of these up close and lived," he said, narrowing his eyes. "How interesting. I've never heard of anyone escaping a *waerloga* before."

It was all he had to say. And I felt the exact moment he decided to attack. Something screamed inside me to move, but I couldn't.

I closed my eyes, waiting, hoping for a quick death to escape this nightmare and the pain. I didn't wear a crucifix, and even though I am not a religious person, I started to pray, hoping from the bottom of my heart and soul, this creature wouldn't go after Dea.

Quickly, the familiar feeling of losing consciousness returned.

But then I heard a whoosh and felt a breeze of air blow over my face, followed by a thump.

"Impossible!" I heard from farther away, and for the first time, I recognized fear in the vampire's voice.

I was too tired and in too much pain to even open my eyes. I was barely able to manage to keep it together without passing out.

A few moments later, in a barely audible whisper, "My apologies, Cat Sidhe, I wasn't aware this was yer territory," the vampire said in an apologetic voice. "Until we meet again, mage. Next time, there won't be anyone to save ye." His voice was full of malice now.

A familiar purr hummed in my ear. And a fraction of a second later, a ball of fur was sitting next to me.

I'd read somewhere that cats were supposed to have healing powers, but I was sure all my injuries were way beyond Ariel's ability, even if she had one. I tried to move, but it was the worst idea I'd ever had.

Claws of fire gripped my chest, constricting it, and I could barely breathe. The pain reached levels I'd never thought possible, and I felt myself slipping into darkness, and this time, there was no coming back.

At the same time, I heard a hiss next to me and felt the fur ball backing farther into me, like she was afraid of something.

But of what? The vampire or a hashashin?

Then something soft touched my forehead.

"Don't worry, my son," someone whispered, "everything will be all right. Help is coming." With those words, a warm sensation started spreading through me, dulling the pain.

After the pain receded somewhat, with an almost super-human effort, I opened my eyes. But there was no one there, just my cat cuddled close against me and looking at me with what seemed like concerned eyes.

I closed my lids and took a deep breath, surprised to see it wasn't painful anymore. A thought nagged at me, letting me know the moment before death, there is no more pain, and your deepest desire will resurface. It could have been moments, or it might have been hours, and I felt my grasp on reality was slipping away. My mind slid slowly into the ether, and if the situation weren't so dire, it would have been funny. This week I had fallen unconscious several times, and rarely in a bed.

"Robert, can you hear me?" I heard a familiar voice.

I started to nod, but when I tried to move my head, it felt like I would lose consciousness. I tried to say yes, but only something like a grunt came out.

Apparently, it was enough because I felt myself lifted to something akin to a feather bed.

A hand touched my cheek, and moist lips, with a hint of strawberry, brushed against mine, then the same familiar voice, which I now recognized, spoke.

"Rest now," whispered Dea. "I'll be here if you need me, and when you're better, we have to talk. I need your help. They attacked my family."

Just before I landed in the darkness, a thought came to mind.

If it weren't for Dea, I'd wish the past week had never happened. So, I could go back to my old life and leave all this behind me.

My mind, thoughts, and body sank into deep black waters.

Above me, a milky white mist dissipated to reveal an ocean of fantastic proportions. The water flowed over me, pulling me into its depths.

The sky took on various shades of orange—a color of hope—and the sun rose on another day, a day that promised to be better than the one before.

DC COVEN SERIES

FUTURE WORKS

An inexplicable attraction draws an IT guy with a secret to a witch marked for death by invisible assassins.

A globe-trotting adventure, secret organizations, magical relics, and a long-forgotten evil all lurk in the darkness, waiting to be unleashed in the DC Coven Series.

Robert Connor knows not all things are as they seem. He has long since known supernaturals walk the earth, threatening to break the balance between good and evil. And now, a war is coming. The fate of an alliance between the most powerful covens on earth threatens to rip Robert's world apart, and he's the only one who can save humanity from annihilation.

Will he have the power and strength to achieve his mission, or will his true nature stand in the way?

Stay tuned, for there's more to come . . .

ABOUT THE AUTHOR

Andrei Saygo is an avid reader, dreamer, and father. In his other life, he gets to do some fantastic things in cybersecurity.

He thought about writing a book for a long time. His work in cybersecurity flew him all over the world, offering him the opportunity to meet people from different cultures, and it helped him gain some wonderful experiences in the process. But it wasn't until after his daughter was born when he finally sat down to type something out.

During the few quiet moments, late at night, the screen sat there, inviting Andrei to share a thought or two. That's how all books start, with an author staring at a blank screen, ready to share a dream with others.

"Inside the pages of this book, readers will find my dream," says Andrei, *"I hope you will enjoy it."*

Printed in Great Britain
by Amazon

30754570R00165